LAYNE CLOSURE AHEAD

Alliances are broken and hearts stolen.

BROKEN ALLIANCES SERIES
BOOK 2

SADIE WINCHESTER

Dad, you would have been so proud.
You should still be here to see that all my dreams have
come true:
I got the Jeep. I became a mom. I wrote the book.

Fuck cancer.

OFFICIAL PLAYLIST

Alkaline - Sleep Token

Bad Things - I Prevail

Battling My Demons - Jeris Johnson, BOI WHAT

Hostage - No Resolve

It Had to Be You (Dark Version) - Tommee Profitt, Tiffany Ashton

Joke's On You - Charlotte Lawrence

Judgment Day - Five Finger Death Punch

Kryptonite (Reloaded) - Jeris Johnson

Leave A Light On - Papa Roach

Let the Sparks Fly - Thousand Foot Krutch

Porn Star Dancing - My Darkest Days, Chad Kroeger, Zak Wylde

Ready or Not (I'm Coming) - OOMPH!

Saviour II - Black Veil Brides

Sugar - Sleep Token

Top O' the Mornin' to Ya - House of Pain

Welcome to the Chaos - Fame on Fire, Ice Nine Kills

The official playlist can be found on Spotify.

(Tap "Search" in the Spotify app, tap the camera icon, scan and go!)

If you or a loved one are struggling with substance or prescription drug abuse and/or mental health, please call the SAMHSA (Substance Abuse & Mental Health Services Administration) national hotline 1-800-662-HELP (4357), text 988, or visit their website (samhsa.gov) to find a treatment center near you.

You matter.

Please visit SadieWinchester.com or email SadieWinchesterAuthor@gmail.com with any questions regarding content/trigger warnings.

PROLOGUE

Four months have passed

Had it really been four months since the funeral took place? Layne couldn't be sure, as everything had blurred together ever since. Since then, her life had taken a series of zig-zag turns, leaving her with whiplash. Instead of trying to juggle balls like a circus performer, she was juggling politics, sticks of dynamite, and her will to keep waking up to see another day.

Yet, here she fucking was again. Her annual self-sabotage party at McGregor's Pub had inevitably rolled around on the anniversary of her mother's death. Now, she just referred to it as the most cursed day of her life. It was the same damn day that Joey motherfucking De Luca had encountered and ultimately destroyed two O'Reilly women, only years apart.

She slung back another shot of whiskey, no longer feeling the burn down her throat as her intoxication numbed the pain.

With concerned eyes, the owner of the pub stood

behind the bar watching the worst unraveling he had seen of Layne yet on this day over the years. "Layne," Sean gently tried to interject himself into the world of pain she was wallowing in. "Maybe it's time to call it a night."

Her eyes didn't even look up at him, the emerald hues remained staring blankly at the empty shot glass cradled in her hand.

"It's a pleasure to meet you, Layney."

The memory of *his* voice twisted the knife of betrayal a little deeper into her damaged heart. Her face winced briefly before the rage reared its ugly head. She forcefully pitched the glass at the wall as she screamed out. "Yeah, I bet it fuckin' was, motherfucker!"

Between her sudden outburst at seemingly no one in particular and the glass shattering against the wall, it elicited a flinch from Sean as he raised his arms to shield himself from any flying shards.

Layne got out of her seat, stumbling to find her drunken feet underneath her. The second she noticed Sean opening his mouth to speak, she tossed her hands up wildly. "I'm fuckin' leaving! Christ! You happy?! Because nobody else is!"

The smart man that Sean was promptly shut his mouth, standing there in silence. The remainder of the occupants inside the bar also had a hushed quiet come over them as eyes settled on the angry little Irish girl.

Thanks to copious amounts of booze, her body felt like it was floating as she left McGregor's. Once she made it outside, she began walking without a care for whichever direction she was heading while her mind wandered.

The same day she had kicked Joey out of her life ten months ago, she had an even bigger emotional bomb dropped on her. A cruel chain of events followed, each one popped off and struck her back down anytime she tried to get back up on her feet.

Her father, Scott O'Reilly, the kingpin of the family's criminal empire, had been taking business trips up to Boston quite frequently. As the head of the organization who had built things from the ground up, it wasn't out of the norm for him to travel across state lines on occasion, but this had been different.

During her investigation into the Project 227 rumors to assist Joey during that time, Layne found herself digging for answers as to what had captured her father's interest a few states away. When she got her answers, they hadn't been what she had pictured in her wildest nightmares.

It turned out that when her gut instincts were screaming at her that something wasn't right, she needed to listen. Through the use of her technologically inclined associates, she illegally obtained medical documentation from the top cancer center in Boston. At the top of those documents was her dad's name. Right underneath it? *Diagnosis: Stage IV Kidney Cancer.* The news had struck harder than a freight train squishing an empty beer can.

He had hidden his diagnosis from everyone, including both his children. Despite that, Liam was supposed to be the one eventually taking over the family business, and he hadn't even been told. When Layne brought the evidence to light, Liam refused to believe it. It wasn't until she had dropped the papers into her dad's lap that Scott O'Reilly finally revealed the full extent of his illness.

What a sick and twisted game fate was playing. Her dad's right-hand man, Mickey Flannigan, had betrayed them all, and then her dad ended up following him to the grave nearly six months later.

Sure, this business always had a high risk of death, but dying of a cancer that spread through your bones and left a path of destruction behind while it metastasized? Orthopedic surgeries to attempt to strengthen joints and damaged bones did little to stem the tide. At the end of the day? No one ever anticipated this gruesome end to the head of the O'Reilly family.

Outwardly, Liam had taken their dad's premature passing the hardest. Currently, with his mental state on the fringe, he was handling his new role as the new head honcho as well as Layne had expected. He wasn't handling it at all. Some days, he was all in on taking leadership, and other days, he was trying to issue everyone around him a death sentence. Then, there were weeks when he would abandon all responsibilities for a lick of his dick and a handle of booze.

As for Layne? She had been trying to pick up all the pieces falling around her, except those of her own. Buried in the deepest, darkest sea inside of her were all her unwanted emotions. If Layne had been capable of being honest with herself, she was holding herself together with a prayer and Elmer's glue.

Dealing with Liam as the official figurehead of the organization made for a political shitshow while attempting to clean up his messes. Often, she found herself pussy-footing around issues, coordinating cleanups to the side, and trying to plant ideas in Liam's head to think of as his own. Lord knew that if she tried to insert her opinion on anything business-wise, he would shut her out entirely. It was thoroughly exhausting.

Before all of this transpired, she had an anger problem. But now? Layne was permanently pissed off. She questioned everything she had ever done in this family, even after she said her goodbyes to the one parent she had left while he lay on his deathbed.

She should have been involved more. She should have asked more questions. She should have considered trying to play her role the way her dad had wanted her to. She shouldn't have had to suffer another loss in her life. She shouldn't have had to take on the weight of this world while the threat of the next loomed over them.

There was no fairness or logic to any of it. Her mother was gone. Mick was gone. Her father was gone. Liam was on a suicide mission and looking to bring everyone down with him. Joey was out of her life…

…or so she thought.

CHAPTER ONE

She had been in her silver Beamer sitting at a traffic light in midtown just a few blocks away from Times Square when Diego from the Brass Mirror called her in complete dismay.

He had been running the club on behalf of the O'Reilly family for the past seven years. For the most part, he knew his place, how to handle the elite clientele, and how to resolve any disruptions to the services rendered there.

So, when there was panic laced in his voice and his words stuttering, she was quick to believe him when he told her that shit was hitting the fan at the exclusive VIP underground gambling club. Also, a good indication was the sound of crashing and shattering glass in the background. Doesn't sound very lucky for a place named after a mirror, does it?

After hauling ass downtown, she parked in the underground garage. Layne got out of her car and rounded to the trunk, where she rummaged around for some tools of the trade. She opted for the wooden baseball bat that had rolled to the back of the compartment.

Layne could use a little stress relief today, and whatever was going on inside was likely going to give her the chance to find a healthier outlet by comparison to other available options. Relatively speaking, of course.

As she anxiously awaited inside the elevator to arrive at the designated floor, she texted Liam:

LAYNE

Handling business at the Mirror.

S.O.S. received from Diego.

Standby.

LIAM

Whatever, I'm busy.

Shut it all down if you have to.

I don't give a fuck.

She drew in an attempt at a therapeutically deep breath at Liam's indifference. Layne tucked her phone away and reassessed the grip on the wooden bat in her hand. She couldn't focus on Liam's inability to cope with problems right now; she needed to get her head in the game.

When the doors of the elevator slid open, the bland and undecorated hallway was quiet. She stalked to the end of the hall where a twin set of glossy black doors were. After punching in the master security code to allow her access, she cautiously pulled a door open to slip inside.

The Brass Mirror was just beyond the entrance. The

walls were painted gold with black accents, and red velvet chairs should have been perfectly positioned at various table setups across the space. The decor was sickeningly pretentious, and it matched the filthy rich bastards that maintained membership here to carelessly sling their funds around.

When Layne walked in, tables and chairs were in utter disarray. Poker chips were spread on the floor like New Year's Eve confetti. Multiple mirrors were in pieces around the perimeter of the room, superstitiously racking up decades of bad luck.

Grown-ass men were wrangling with one another while some pieces of arm candy were shrieking incessantly. She cringed at the high-pitched wails adding to the soundtrack of violence and destruction.

"Here we go," Layne muttered to herself. She rotated her wrist, getting a feel for the weight of the bat in her hand with a single rotation, ready to wield it where necessary.

She stomped toward the first set of grappling men, doubled up her grip on the handle, and wound up. Unleashing her swing on the back of one man's knees, it instantly dropped him to the ground.

One for the money.

It left the other man in shock, only to be greeted with her backhanded swing connecting underneath his chin. The sickening cracking of bone and shattering teeth should have bothered her, but today was not that day.

Two for the show.

Layne saw the second man drop like a fly while howling in pain as blood poured from his mouth. She pointed the tip of the bat at the first man, who was already propping himself up on one knee. "Stay." The threat of an additional strike loomed on that single word spoken.

She looked across the room and saw Diego in an altercation with a man wielding an empty beer bottle. "For fucks' sake, Diego," she cursed under her breath before navigating through the strewn-about furniture.

"Alan! Let's talk this through!" Diego spinelessly raised his hands defensively, trying to avoid getting assaulted by an empty bottle.

It took Layne one swing to smack the bottle from the attacker's grasp, sending the empty brown container towards the wall where the sound of its shattering echoed across the room. She didn't hesitate to follow up with a second strike right to his gut and a final third to his back as he doubled over in pain. He fell flat onto the floor.

Three to get ready.

Resting the bat against the front of her shoulder, she let Diego feel the anger in her gaze that she had to come down here to clean this shit up. With one hand on her hip, she scolded him. "You told me you ramped up security. What the hell happened?"

Diego opened his mouth to spout some insufficient apology, but from behind her, a hand grabbed onto the top of her bloodied bat while a large bicep wrapped around her throat, snatching the midpoint of the piece of lumber and yanking her back.

The length of the bat pressed to her throat forced her back into the brick wall of a man behind her. Her hands latched back onto the bat, pushing forward and away to relieve the pressure against her neck. Layne swung her body to the side, pushing one end of the bat up, allowing enough of a gap to squeeze out of the tight space.

Spinning around, she pulled out the small but mighty Glock, pulling the trigger for the money shot between the eyes. The bang filled the air, and everything went still. Her victim dropped to the floor with a thud, and his hand released her bat.

Four, motherfucker, let's go.

The pistol was tucked back into the holster in the back of her pants.

The wooden weapon rolled slowly across the floor towards her until she stopped it with the tip of her boot. She reached down and picked it up, only to hear a pair of hands giving slow and deliberate claps.

Clap.

Clap.

Clap.

Looking over her shoulder to see who was finding entertainment in the violent scene that had just unfolded, she was surprised to find a man who was clean-cut from head to toe. He had jet-black hair on the longer side but kept it a neat style away from his face. He had chillingly blue eyes that could either melt you down to your core or pierce straight through your heart. He stood at barely six feet tall, and his presence had an elegant command to it. If one had to guess, he appeared to be just over the cusp of forty.

The attire he had on indicated he had money—lots of it.

The suit appeared to be custom and tailored to each cut of his sleek musculature.

She completed her turn to face him, noticing he was standing only three feet away. This stranger may have been amused, but she wasn't finding the situation nearly as captivating. "Enjoy the show?" Her voice was not the least bit friendly.

Ignoring her question, the man snapped his fingers. The first two men she encountered, Alan, and any pieces of arm candy that hadn't already fled for the exit, all nodded in acknowledgment of the silent instruction they were given. They scurried from the confines of the Brass Mirror.

Finally, the stranger spoke with a silky but firm tone. "Diego, you are also dismissed. See my man outside for your payment for your inconveniences here."

Diego shamefully avoided eye contact with Layne as he rushed out of the room. She gritted her teeth angrily that he had been manipulated by another party at play here.

"Don't blame him; I made an offer he couldn't—" the man chuckled. "Well, you know the saying."

Warily, she shifted her eyes onto the man, her hand still firmly latched onto the handle of the baseball bat.

"Forgive me, and allow me to introduce myself. I'm Eric Ellis. Your new neighbor, if you will." He extended his hand out to her.

The name sounded vaguely familiar to her, which should have been an enormous red flag, but new players were always coming and going in this line of work. Sometimes, they proved themselves worthy enough to be a force to be reckoned with. Other times? They tightened their own noose and jumped from the platform.

While there wasn't some sort of monthly criminal newsletter that got distributed, Layne had heard about the new guy in town. He had snatched up a swanky corner lot and fully renovated the industrial building to convert it into a residence. It was the Upper East Side's biggest topic of conversation amongst the wealthy. What she hadn't heard was what else he had his hands in.

Layne shoved his extended hand away with the tip of her bat. "I'm not your welcoming committee."

The strength of his hand grasped onto the bat and roughly tugged her forward towards him. When he snaked an arm around her, his hold was like a boa constrictor, ready to squeeze the life out of her lungs.

"Now, that's not being very friendly, is it?" He smirked as he let his eyes wander over the features of her face.

Not showing any signs of distress, she stared into the handsome face of her self-proclaimed new neighbor. "I'm not a very friendly type of girl."

He grinned, bringing his mouth lower to her ear so he could whisper his words. "So I've heard."

Before she could snap back, he released her and stepped away to give her space. Eric walked behind the unattended bar and lifted a bottle of Johnnie Walker Blue Label, inspecting it. "I'm not here to start any wars. Instead, I figured I'd get creative in capturing your attention. How did I do?"

Still not willing to part with her bat, she watched his

every move, wondering what game he was playing. "If you were looking to piss me off, you're off to a great start."

He chuckled quietly to himself as he poured himself a drink from the expensive whiskey, he nodded at an empty chair on the other side of the bar. "Please, take a seat. I won't bite." He paused and, with a debonaire smile, said, "Unless you ask very nicely."

"I prefer to stand." Stepping over a broken chair, she approached the bar, still on high alert.

"Suit yourself." When he took the first sip from the glass, he reveled in the taste dancing across his taste buds, finishing with a slow moan of delight.

Using the bat, she laid it across the wrist of his hand, holding the glass, preventing him from taking another sip. "What is it that you're here for?"

Not making an effort to remove the baseball bat lying across his wrist, he chose to focus all of his attention on her. "A business proposition."

"I hate to burst your bubble, but I don't do business with people who come in and poach my employees and destroy my property."

Eric switched the short-statured glass into his other hand as he moved away from the threat of her current weapon of choice. "You'll have to forgive me, but I had to see for myself what I was potentially getting into. You didn't disappoint. Actually, I am rather impressed. The stories about you hardly do you any justice."

Growing tired of the banter, she contemplated just disposing of him entirely, but that's when he gave a click of his tongue and shook his head.

"Ah, if I were you, I wouldn't want to try and take my life just yet. You will want to hear what I'm going to lay out on the bargaining table."

She blinked a few times in surprise at how easily he just read her. "Then, make your point of why you're here and make it quickly, I don't have all damn day for this bullshit."

Resting one hand on the edge of the bar and leaning against it, he smiled as though he had been waiting for this very moment to answer her. "A merger. You and I. We combine our efforts and organizations, and it creates an unstoppable alliance. Right now, the O'Reilly business operations are struggling and are on the brink of collapse. After the passing of your father, which, by the way, you do have my deepest condolences, things have not been smooth sailing, have they? Your brother, Liam, is proving to be rather incapable of navigating the stressors of leadership and is leaving it all on your shoulders."

"We are getting by just fine, but thanks for the concern." Immediately, she was on the defensive as he began to verbally offend the way she and Liam had been handling things. Sure, it wasn't perfect, but Layne was working on coming up with ways to improve operations while Liam got his shit together.

Another sip of the whiskey had him licking the flavor from his lips. "Ah, ah, ah. Are you being honest with yourself, Layne? Don't you even know what I can offer you?"

She rolled her eyes, figuring he was going to try and tell her whether she wanted to know or not.

Taking her lack of protest as permission to proceed, he continued, "After Michael Franzetti did his vanishing act,

I've been picking up pieces here and there and turning lumps of coal into diamonds. With the right training and mindset, I have been able to salvage a handful of Franzetti's little worker bees. Not to mention my growing collection of assets. If you and I were to unite, I could promise you a world where you would never have to worry about cleaning up others' messes. Including your brother's."

Gradually, she was lowering her bat as her arm got tired of being at full tension while listening to him pitch himself. "Yeah, no thanks. Now, get the fuck out."

Leaving his partially drunk glass of whiskey behind, he came up to her. "I'm not looking for an answer right now. All I'm asking is to keep this conversation going. That's all. I want to help you salvage what's left of your father's legacy and turn it into something greater. He'd want that, wouldn't he?"

"Don't talk like you knew him." Her jaw tensed as she thought about how her dad might be rolling over in his grave, seeing the state of affairs everything was in right now.

Eric slowly reached out to hold her chin gently with his thumb and forefinger. "I'm not looking to be the villain in your story. I'm just trying to help us both get what we want."

Layne jerked her face away from his subtle, intimate touch. "What's in it for you?"

His lips curved into a proud smile. "What a smart girl you are. I don't have the history and clout with some of the other major top dogs across the city to pull enough weight to successfully execute my vision for my home base of operations here. The O'Reilly name is well known. If everyone knows we are working hand-in-hand, it would make both of our lives much easier. If I had your support, I could provide for an extraordinarily comfortable existence in whichever way you would prefer it."

"Let me get this straight, you want me to help you by using my connections to get you in the door with other contacts while you iron out the wrinkles in the way we are currently doing things?" It sounded far too simple to Layne. Easy ways out just didn't fall from the sky.

He grinned. "Something like that."

"Something like that, or just like that?" She knew the devil was in the details.

Eric put on the same smile that all the politicians used to pitch their false promises. "Let's make a deal here, huh? We can discuss the details further, but in the meantime, let's see if this could be a happy little alliance, hm? You can still be the force that you've always been while fulfilling your father's final wishes to settle down with a man to provide for you, and your family's business will get the support and direction it requires to thrive."

It all sounded far too good to be true, except the settling down part. When anyone approaches you with a deal out of the blue, the chances of them being a snake oil salesman are almost always a certainty. "I'll think about it."

"That's all I ask. As a peace offering and show of good faith, I will send my crew here to clean up the mess. Things will be back to fully operational by tomorrow evening."

"If they're not, I will personally ensure that you will be

wishing you were in his shoes." She warned as she motioned at the dead guy behind her.

He chuckled despite she had made it quite clear she was being serious. "My little harpy, I promise you that there will be no such need."

Eric's hand reached out to stroke the side of her cheek in an affectionate gesture. Layne snatched his wrist tightly, preventing him from touching her face again. Her emerald eyes were full of nothing but cold and emptiness.

He gave a sharp tug on his hand, causing Layne to stumble forward two steps closer to him. He ran his tongue over his lips before displaying a smirk across his mouth. "One day, you'll be begging for the soft touch of my hand."

Disgusted by the look in his eyes as he watched her, Layne released his wrist and backed away. "That's one bet I wouldn't make if I were you."

He gave a casual shrug and walked over to the two front doors, pulling one open to make his exit. Eric paused before he fully passed through it, he looked back over his shoulder at Layne. "The odds are better than you think."

He left Layne there alone in the disastrous-looking Brass Mirror.

Looking across the room at her reflection in one of the few remaining intact mirrors, a person was standing there that she didn't even recognize. Layne took hold of her bat and unleashed the bottled-up fury inside of her, taking it out on anything in her path.

A series of liquor bottles were smashed, leaving behind a river of mixed spirits along the back shelves. A framed abstract painting was another casualty of her rage-fueled assault. Layne continued to take swings at anything that pissed her off.

The final blow was tossing the entire baseball bat itself at a full-length mirror, shattering it into an infinite amount of shards. The asshole could pay for that, too.

Layne stood there alone with only the sounds of her heavy breaths, hating how tired she felt with the shit cards she was always being dealt these days.

CHAPTER TWO

A month later

"Oh yeah, baby, does that feel good? How do you like that? I bet you haven't had it this good ever." The scruffy-looking construction worker she had picked up at the bar panted against the back of her neck as he thrust into her from behind again. She hadn't even bothered to catch his name, or if he had given it, she had already forgotten.

"So good. Keep going." Layne didn't even attempt to fake it in her voice, let alone her expression. Her eyes gazed at the hand-written graffiti on the bathroom stall's partition in front of her, between her hands bracing against it. Things like phone numbers for a good time, random doodles, and names of people that were going to be together '4 Ever'.

Forever? Seemed like a pretty far-fetched concept to Layne. Nothing lasted forever in her life.

The whiny groans of the man pumping himself into her in the sole stall in the men's room distracted her from her thoughts momentarily. Layne wondered if he realized his thrusts were in sync with the tune of *Danny Boy*. How fuckin' depressing.

Her body jostled with each of the man's movements. Half of her clothes were still on, and his pants were stuck at his knees. When he came to an unimpressive finish into the condom he was wearing, she shoved him away from her, not feeling any sense of satisfaction.

Yanking her pants up and straightening out her shirt, Layne swung the stall door open.

While washing her hands in the sink, she wished she could just shower away the rest of the filth she felt elsewhere. "I've got a meeting to get to."

Reaching into her jacket pocket, she grabbed a prescription bottle partially filled with round white pills and popped one into her mouth, chasing it down with a swig of water from the palm of her hand out of the running faucet. The label on the plastic orange bottle noted to take it as needed for shoulder pain. The same shoulder pain that had subsided a few weeks after the man she had grown up calling uncle—Mick—had shot her. So much for family loyalty.

Layne needed something to dull the painful memory of the pitiful disaster that had just transpired in the dimly lit public restroom at McGregor's.

The man lingered, hoping maybe she would grace him with a more affectionate goodbye, but Layne shut it down by wiping her hands dry on the thighs of her pants and exiting the lavatory. Not so much as giving him a polite smile.

She waved a hand goodbye to Sean, who was filling drink orders as she made her way past the bar, which was currently half-full of inebriated patrons. He gave her a nod of his head in return.

Once outside, she involuntarily shivered from the chill cascading over her body as the air temperature had dropped drastically in anticipation of a hell of a nor'easter expected to hit the city in the next hour or two.

Walking down the sidewalk, she avoided colliding with other passersby as she began to send a few texts on her phone.

LAYNE

Got hung up on a few things. On my way.

LIAM

You better have good news when you get here.

LAYNE

Feeling hopeful?

LIAM

I'm as optimistic as a nun, hoping there are no sinners in prison.

Did Layne have good news for her brother? Not in the slightest.

When Layne arrived at the cemetery in Brooklyn, just slightly southwest of Prospect Park, she already saw Liam off in the distance across the sprawling terrain sprinkled with an assortment of headstones.

She had heard that Mick's family had buried him in this very same cemetery. Perhaps one day she would find out where just so she could piss on his grave. However, there were larger and much more real issues on their hands than insulting cemetery dirt.

After attempting not to trample over anyone's final resting place, she stepped up next to him and handed over a grease-soaked paper bag that had the aroma of freshly cooked french fries emanating from it. It was her attempt at a peace offering to help soften the blow of the news he wasn't going to want to hear.

Liam stood there, pulled out a fry, and bit into it. Not a gracious thank you. No words. Nothing.

He was decked out in a black pea coat, a crimson sweater, and a pair of new blue jeans. Continuing to not say a word, he just silently stared ahead, with the only sound being the crinkling of the bag each time another fry was pulled out.

In front of them was an ornate headstone with 'O'REILLY' in large letters spread across the top. Below it was the remainder of the epitaph detailing the life of a great man who had his life cut short prematurely.

"Layne, make me a promise." Her father's voice was weak from his failing body. "Promise me you'll do whatever you can to keep yourself safe. Don't make the same mistakes I've made with Liam." His hand, now frail from all the last-effort treatments he had received, reached over and latched onto her fingers. His eyes were full of sadness

and regret as this lifetime was coming to a close. "Promise me."

Clearing her throat, she tried to push her final memories of their dad from her mind and blink away the heartache in her eyes. How gaunt he had looked, how weak his grasp was on her hand, how strained his voice was, and how painful his struggles were until the morphine eased him into his afterlife.

"The good news is that we only lost a few guys." She tried to keep the positivity in her voice, but that was a trait she had always been terrible at.

Liam refused to look at her as he spoke up, "Just say it."

Layne paused, trying to choose her next words carefully. There weren't many times when she tried to protect Liam's sensitivities, but this was a rare exception.

"There's a lot of whispers, Li. I mean…*a lot.* So many that I'm not even sure it's considered whispering anymore." She cringed during the emphasis on how much chatter there had been. "You have to start pulling on the reins and cracking the whip if we are going to salvage what's left of Dad's legacy. People are getting antsy and seeking out work elsewhere. It looks bad."

"Don't fuckin' tell me how bad it looks. You think I don't know that?" He snapped at her, the anger and frustration soaking his words and finally, his glare settling at her.

She released a breath she hadn't realized she was even holding. "I know you know that, but goddammit, Liam, the ship is sinking, and you're still waiting for the captain to show up. You're the fucking captain! Show up and fix it because if you don't, I will, and you won't like how I start handling things." Her own irritation was beginning to rise up from its cage.

His brooding and inability to take charge of business matters over the last few months had been a constant, and it wasn't getting any better. Layne was doing her best to pick up the pieces, but Liam wasn't making either of their lives any easier.

His hazel eyes burned as he glared at her. "You think you could do a better job, Layne? Is that what you think?" His tone turned accusatory.

Oh, Christ, here we go. "Hell, yes. Jesus, Li, a toddler could do a better job than you are right now. Who was the one who got shit fixed down at the Mirror last month, huh? Sure as hell wasn't you!" Layne was all out of patience with her brother, and she wasn't about to spare him her thoughts on how he was handling matters. Coddling was not in her nature, especially not when he wanted to pick fights.

She may have had some help fixing up that mess at the gambling club, but she hadn't divulged to Liam her encounter with Eric Ellis just yet. Before she was willing to bring it to his attention, she needed to know more about this latest player in the city's criminal underworld. Why set herself up for another shouting match with Liam because his ego once again got bruised when business matters fell into her lap?

She had been doing her research on their new neighbor residing not too far from O'Reilly Manor. However, there wasn't much to be found out about him. The contacts who were still willing to work with her were struggling to figure out his story.

Liam squared up with her, and even given the size differential; she wasn't intimidated into backing away as he stared down at her with darkness in his eyes. He didn't say a word to her for several minutes while waiting for her to budge or look away.

Speaking through clenched teeth, he dropped his voice down low. "You don't know shit about what it takes, and you don't get to sit there on your high horse judging me. If Dad thought you had *any* potential, he would have given you the chance. Instead, you've always needed a man to save your ass when you've gotten in over your head."

The words pierced her heart, and the venom seeped into her bloodstream as he spat his verbal attack at her. The worst part was that he wasn't wrong, and Layne saw that plain as day.

Walking off, Liam pushed past her and harshly bumped against her left shoulder to serve as a reminder of the last time she had needed help. She closed her eyes and pushed the fury back down her throat into a metaphorical box to be locked away until a day when it wouldn't be contained any longer.

Today wasn't going to be that day. She hoped tomorrow wouldn't be either. Was it too much to ask to never let that day come?

The thunder echoed in the distance, announcing the approach of the storm.

CHAPTER THREE

The rain had begun to fall on the drive back home, splashing across her windshield and triggering the sensors of the automatic wipers to clear them away.

Layne had done her best not to sink into her thoughts where she could drown trying to fix everything that was wrong with her life.

When she went to pull into her garage, some douchenozzle was blocking the driveway path that had plain as day signs that said, 'Do Not Block Drive.'

"You've got to be shittin' me," she drove past her house and ended up finding an open spot around the corner. However, the storm appeared to match her current mood and picked up in intensity by the time she got out of her vehicle.

The skies opened up and unleashed a furious amount of rain that came down by the bucketful. Each raindrop stung as it pelted her flesh. Layne ran along the sidewalk, splashing in puddles that had formed in a matter of seconds as the storm drains attempted to relieve the flooding on the street.

When she did get inside her house, she looked no better than a drowned rat. Her long brunette locks were plastered to her fair skin, and there wasn't a single dry spot on her clothes. She flipped on the lights now that her home was cast into darkness thanks to the powerful storm raging outside and had devoured any sunlight.

Layne peeled her jacket off her, dropping it to the floor with a heavy splat. She shook her arms off, her grey tee clung to her upper body's every curve and swell. The drops of rainwater rolled down along her skin between the layers of clothing. She kicked off her shoes, flinging them off to the side in the main entrance's foyer.

Lightning flashed outside her windows, followed by the crackle and boom of thunder shortly after. The increased pressure of the rain crashing against the windows indicated the strength of the storm was intensifying.

She sighed as she moved to her modestly sized laundry room, leaving a wet trail of footsteps behind her. Peering inside the top of the washer, she realized she had forgotten to move the laundry to the dryer yet again. Embracing a fuck it attitude, she figured she'd wash it all one more time with a few more articles of her clothing.

The first thing to get pitched in was her damp socks, followed by her shirt, tossing it straight into the partially full washing machine. Before she could remove anything else, the lights in her house flickered, and the sound of the power cutting out caused her to curse.

Layne's eyes fought to see through the darkness as her hands reached out in front of her to ensure she didn't trip over something like a broom and die in a freak accident. She needed to find her flashlight, which she thought was in one of the junk drawers in her kitchen, or maybe she had left one in the office. After a brief debate on where she had left it, she opted to check the kitchen first.

Before she reached the entrance to the kitchen, she stopped in the hallway when something caused her to freeze up. Her steps came to a halt when one of the floorboards at the other end of the hall creaked. Layne's senses were all raised to high alert as she strained to sense any other movement or presence there in the darkness of her home.

The adrenaline prompted her heart to beat faster, delivering more oxygen to the rest of her body as she stood as still as a statue. The second she heard the rustle of clothing from someone else moving closer to her, she didn't allow herself to think before she struck.

She lunged at the shadow, and when she made contact, she ended up shoving the large body harshly against a wall. The shadow's hands grabbed for her arms, but she defensively evaded them.

Grabbing the tall shoulder of the shadow, she pulled down while simultaneously driving her knee upwards into its stomach. A set of hands grabbed the knee of that same leg and pulled her off balance, dropping her down onto her back on the floor. The impact of her back hitting the ground smacked the air right out of her lungs, leaving her unable to even gasp for a brief moment.

The shadow's considerable weight was soon down on top of her, attempting to pin her down, but she squirmed, using the leverage of her feet against the floor to roll herself over on top of what was most certainly a male shadow.

Straddling her assailant, she threw an aggressive fist at the slight outline of his head as her eyes began to partially adjust to the darkness. Her knuckles made contact, but it was a grazing strike while the size and strength of the shadow's hands shielded himself.

He bucked her off him, which caused her to fall off to the side, crashing into a small decorative table where she typically kept little odds and ends. As her body crashed into it, the table wobbled on its spindly legs and scratched across the wooden floor before it toppled over altogether.

Layne scrambled to her feet to create distance between her and the ominous shadow that hadn't been invited into her home. A powerful hand grabbed her ankle, which caused her to fall forward. Her hands broke her fall, allowing her to continue the fight to escape the shadow's hold on her.

It felt like an eternity that she had yanked and tugged to break the grasp on her ankle, but when she finally did, she broke out into a full sprint down the hall. The sound of heavy boots quickly followed behind.

Her hands outstretched in front of her ensured she didn't run into a wall at full speed. The change of the floor underneath her bare feet from wood to an area rug as she rounded a corner indicated she had successfully made it into the living room.

The bad news? So did the shadow. Layne was jerked back by her waist against the steel body of the shadow that had been so persistent not to let her get away. She screamed out in a mixture of surprise and desperation.

The powerful arms fought with her as she made it challenging as hell to restrain her there. A hand finally clamped down over her mouth, muffling the screams tearing out of her throat. Unable to compete with strength alone, Layne got pulled across the living room and forced down into the softness of her sofa cushions.

A knee forcefully pressed into her back, pinning her underneath the shadow's weight as her hands were pulled behind her and a set of cold metal cuffs clicked shut around each of her wrists. With her hands now bound behind her, she was pulled upright to sit on the couch.

She tried to stand up, only to have the pair of hands give her enough of a shove that she lost her footing and plopped right back down onto her ass again.

Layne glared at the dark figure in front of her. She hoped that he could see the dirty look she was giving.

She should have been afraid, but she wasn't. Instead, she felt an odd sense of nothingness that if this was going to be her demise, then so be it. Everyone had their day.

"Just get it over with," Layne impatiently spat the order out.

The figure crouched down in front of her, a hand came up under her chin and took hold of her jaw. Finally, the shadow spoke his first words to her.

"I need a favor." Joey's voice immediately became recognizable.

Some of the tension in her body released, hearing the soothing sound of vocals she would recognize in any crowd. The relief was quickly replaced by anger as she attempted to lash out at him with her hands, only to have the cuffs working by design to prevent her from doing so.

"What in the actual fuck? Get the hell out of my house; I don't care what you need!" She tried to get up off of the couch only to be easily knocked back down onto her ass yet again with a soft bounce against the seat cushion.

"You need to hear me out, Layney." His voice reflected a sense of calm and was collected, something that Layne currently wasn't having any of.

She shook her head in disbelief as he called her by her nickname, which she used to be fond of hearing from him. "No! No, you do not get to call me that." Layne pulled on her wrists, trying to squeeze them out of the steel restraints. "I told you that if I ever saw you again, I would put a bullet between your eyes."

Joey had the nerve to let out a small chuckle. "That's why you've got a pretty new set of bracelets on right now."

The storm outside continued to progress with several flashes of light and booms of thunder. Briefly, she got a glimpse of Joey's face there in front of her, thanks to the lightning that caused a split second of illumination.

His hands settled on the tops of her knees. "I swear, I'm just here on business. If I had any other choice, believe me, I would have taken it. Just take a moment to stop being stubborn and listen."

It may have been a little dramatic the way that she let

out a sigh and sank back into the couch, not having much of a choice other than to listen to what he had to say.

Taking her decision to relax a little bit as a green light to continue, Joey began to explain his predicament, "A job came up—"

Layne interrupted. "With your police pals?" The disdain etched over her words after recalling what had been the final straw that forced them apart a little less than a year ago. His total disregard for loyalty in assisting the boys in blue by providing them with valuable intel.

"No, I already told you that there were special circumstances with that, Layne. If you had given me the chance to explain, we could have moved beyond that."

She rolled her eyes, though she would have been surprised if he could see it in the dark.

Joey stood up and took a step back so he could sit on the edge of the coffee table in front of her. "You know what? I wasn't going to bring it up, but since I have you here, you're going to sit there and listen."

He rested his elbows on his knees as his eyes stared at her. "I was going to get pinned on some old charges that were teetering on the edge of the statute of limitations. My only options were to let them rake me over the coals for a lifetime or to find a way around it by scratching their backs. The information I fed to them when it came to anything even remotely tied to you was crafted to send them on a wild goose chase."

The volume of his voice elevated slightly as he made his final point. "I kept your ass from getting raided and diverted their interests elsewhere. I'm not going to sit here and apologize for not only saving my ass but saving yours, too. I did what I had to do."

"And I did what I had to do. I guess that makes us even." Layne hated that his explanation even held the littlest bit of weight. Even knowing she would have likely done the same thing if she had been in his shoes, she was still angry. She was always angry these days.

He stood back up and leaned over, getting in her face so she couldn't avoid what he was about to tell her. "Bullshit, you did what you always do. You shoved me away. You were the one who tossed in the towel and ran away like a scared little girl."

Swallowing the lump in her throat, she turned her face away from him only to have his hand take her by the jaw and turn her head back to face him. "What's the matter, Layne? Is the truth a little too fucking hard to hear?" His words brutally bore down on her, leaving her emotionally reeling in the downward spiral her fractured mental state was already in.

Joey had a way of making it feel impossible to hide behind her defenses and shut everything down inside of her. Layne squeezed her eyes shut, hoping to imagine he wasn't back here in her house again. What she couldn't escape was the telltale scent of the mixture of leather and sage cologne that lingered in the air between them.

Not willing to admit that he pegged the truth spot-on, she sat there silently, trying to shrink down into a mental hiding place.

It was unclear how long they both stubbornly and silently stood their ground. Eventually, she felt his hand ease up off of her face. When she opened her eyes back up, his shadow was no longer there in front of her.

There was a click and a pop, and suddenly, the power was flicking back on throughout her house. Layne squinted as the lights erased the darkness and startled her vision.

Joey walked back into the room, shaking his head to himself as he griped, "You keep so much damn crap in front of your breaker box."

Unsurprisingly, he was wearing his signature style of black cargo pants and a black shirt, but this time, he had added a black zip-up hoodie overtop of it. As she got a good look at him, she hated that she noticed her eyes drifting to the front of his pants first before roaming upward to visually consume the rest of him. Either she had *really* missed him, or he had added a few more pounds of solid bulk at the gym over the past year, and it did him damn good.

Not only did it appear he had been working out more, but there were other noticeable differences. Joey's dirty blonde hair had grown a little longer and shaggier. It suited him, and the way her body was beginning to react, it seemed it didn't disagree.

CHAPTER FOUR

The storm outside was gradually easing up, slowing to an entrancing drizzle. It was nearly reminiscent of one of those meditative sound machines.

As the evening approached, the sunshine never returned from behind the grey storm clouds. Instead, the sky sunk further into darkness.

Once Joey was comfortable that Layne wasn't going to make good on her promise to immediately shoot him, he eased her up off of the couch and spun her around. She was suddenly aware that as his hands touched her bare skin, she was still shirtless and standing there in her fuchsia bra, still damp from being caught in the rain. His fingers trailed down the backs of her arms until they met her restraints.

With a twist and a click, each of the cuffs unlatched from around her wrists.

She mindlessly rubbed each of them, easing away the

slight discomfort she had created by overzealously tugging on them earlier.

"Were those necessary?" She turned around, finding herself now looking up into his chocolate-colored eyes that easily had melted her soul so many times before this.

He must have seen something in her face, which caused him to step back and create a healthy amount of space between them. "You tell me."

Joey looked her over and raised an eyebrow. It wasn't just the soaked-to-the-bone look, but other stressors taking a toll on her physically. "You look like shit."

Rude. She tried to give him an offended look, but after the day she had coupled with getting caught in the rain, she had experienced better days. "You really know how to flatter the ladies, don't you?"

He unzipped his sweatshirt, pulling his arms from the sleeves as his muscles flexed underneath his shirt. Joey tossed it over to her. "Here. We still need to talk about my favor."

Reacting quickly, her hands caught the hoodie, resisting the urge to wrap it around her and bask in its warmth and scent.

It had been all too easy to hate him while he had been gone. Now that he was standing there in front of her, looking like ten delicious sins worth committing, she struggled to keep her thoughts out of the gutter. While her dreams had made it difficult to forget how his hands felt against her body, having him standing right there in front of her was sending sparks straight down to her core.

Layne needed to stomp out the old flames of desire,

trying to light back up. She couldn't let herself fall into this same old trap with him again.

She tossed the hoodie back to him. "I will go change. If you want to be useful, go make some coffee."

She ran upstairs to swap out her wet clothes for a pair of dry joggers and an old UCLA tee. While she brushed the wet tangles from her hair in front of her bathroom mirror, she tried to run herself through a mental pep talk. Layne was not going to let herself get caught up in Joey's charms, not after everything he had done. Recalling his betrayal, she couldn't put herself through any more pain, even if he had his reasons.

Her eyes drifted down to the unassuming bottle sitting on the counter. After ingesting one pill to take the edge off of this unexpected visit, her hand paused as she examined the container holding the whispered promise of comfort and escape. The internal debate didn't last long before she finally gave in to the temptation and swallowed one more little pill down.

When she came back downstairs, the aroma of freshly brewed coffee greeted her. Following the trail, she found Joey seated at her kitchen table, legs propped up on the seat of a chair across from him with his arms folded in front of his chest casually.

The tattoos of various images flexed across his skin. She knew each one of them well. The clocks, the ominous ravens, gloomy headstones, gothic-looking skulls, and the spread of gentle roses between all of them. The least he could have done was cover himself up so they wouldn't be such a damn distraction.

His eyes grew darker as he nodded over at the vase full of fresh blossoms. "Who sent those?"

The stems situated on her center island had been sent from Eric Ellis earlier in the week. They had come with an over-the-top designed invitation to a formal soiree he was hosting. Layne had no intentions of going to a party where a bunch of people got all dressed up just to talk shit in a classy upper-crust type of way. Thanks, but no thanks.

She noticed the dark green mug on the table and approached, lifting it to take a careful sip so as to not burn her mouth. "Why do you care?"

He scoffed incredulously. "I don't."

"Well, you obviously do, or else you wouldn't have asked." He wasn't the only one that could call bullshit when they saw it.

Her emerald eyes stared at him while waiting for him to dare and try to tell her otherwise. She took her seat on a chair across from him, drawing her legs up underneath her comfortably criss-cross style. The mug assisted in warming up her hands and getting rid of the chill the rain had set into her bones.

Wisely and predictably, Joey changed the subject. "As I told you, I need a favor."

"Oh?" She didn't hide the fact that she was delighted she was in a position of having something he needed.

Ignoring her sass, he continued, "I have a contract that's a little outside of my typical job. Less physical confrontation and more gathering of information and surveillance. Then, depending on what I find, I suspect it will end as it always does."

Listening to him explain the reason for breaking his way back into her life and her house, she waved her hand at him.

"I get it, so what do you need from me?" Forcing him to cut to the chase as she took another sip from the dark brew that he still managed to get just right with the perfect amount of half-and-half.

"Access to Eric Ellis. I heard he's going to be throwing a party under the guise of charity or some bullshit like that."

Layne coughed as the coffee started to go down the wrong pipe, and she put her hand up to her mouth, wiping away the hot liquid.

He raised a brow, dropping his feet down from the chair, ready in the event she truly was going to suffer death via coffee.

Layne shook her head adamantly. "No way." She put her coffee mug down on the table as she got up to grab a napkin to wipe her hands off. "Figure it out on your own; I don't want any involvement with this. Absolutely none."

He got up and walked over to her, his presence still holding that aura of intimidation and dominance he had always been so good at asserting.

"You owe me, just get me in there." He stared down at her intently.

Layne stepped back, bumping into the pantry door. "Damnit, Joey, I said no! I don't owe you shit. I'm not getting involved with that arrogant, self-absorbed asshole. What makes you even think I could get you in any way? I don't just get social invitations to every party on the Upper East Side."

He smirked. "So, you *do* know about the event."

Exasperated, she tossed her hands in the air. "Yes, ok? I know about it, but I'm not going. I am not playing a delicate princess for a night and have to pretend to like these people just so you can go play secret agent and snoop around for whatever it is you are looking for."

When she went to move past him to go back to the table, his tattooed hands slid around her waist to stop her in her tracks. His hold pulled her in close to him so their bodies were flush up against one another.

"Just one favor, that's all I'm asking." His voice dropped to a low tone that still had the power to make her legs quiver.

Her breath was stolen away from her when she found herself in the comfort of his touch that she had been unwilling to admit she had missed. But damn, did she miss it. Simultaneously, she was beginning to feel the ease of the two pills she had taken upstairs seeping into her system.

Wrinkling up her forehead, her hands pushed down against the strength of his muscled forearms in a poor attempt to remove his hands from her sides. "I-I can't. I won't do this."

Things began to feel like they were moving too quickly around her or perhaps too slowly. The air was too warm, but there were chills dancing along her skin. The normally welcomed fog in her head was making it a challenge to think straight. Maybe she should have stuck to just that one pill after all.

He tilted his head as his eyes carefully assessed the way she was reacting to him. "Can't do what, Layney?"

Her hands left his arms to rub over her face trying to force her brain to pull its shit together and fight against the high that was taking over. "I'm just tired. Just leave, ok?"

Joey's hands grabbed hers and easily pulled them away from her face so he could look into her eyes. It may have been the torment and hell of her life over the past year, or maybe it was her pupils beginning to constrict, but his entire demeanor shifted into a softer one of genuine concern.

He bent down and scooped one arm under the back of her legs and the other under her back as he picked her up, cradling her close to his chest.

Layne rested her head against his chest, letting the warmth of his body sedate her soul while her brain should have been telling him to piss off. She wanted to tell him to put her back down, but the words were only spoken inside her mind.

Carrying her out of the kitchen, Joey brought her up to her bedroom on the second floor. Her fingers toyed with the fabric of his shirt as she let her mind wander to wherever the pills were taking it.

"You smell like sex. Great sex." Apparently, they were bringing her thoughts straight back to the gutter.

He shot her a confused look. Normally, it would have been a welcomed compliment, but it was a sharp turn from her mood moments ago down in the kitchen.

After he approached her bed, he gently laid her down on it, and Layne's hands clung to him. "Wait." She gave a lazy smile as she stared up at him with heavy eyes. "I didn't mean it."

Joey raised an eyebrow at her words. "Didn't mean what?"

"I don't know, but I didn't." Whatever she was trying to say wasn't making sense as her body began to feel like it was floating through a cloud. She blinked, and when her eyelids opened back up, Joey was next to her in bed with a tight hold on her with, his chin resting on top of her head.

Layne curled up against him, drawing in a full breath of his soothing scent, and when she exhaled, she murmured, "You asked twice."

Her eyes closed once more as she let the opiate ease her back into a slumber where she didn't have to feel or think about the broken pieces of her life.

Joey smoothed her dark tresses away from her face as he watched her soft breaths coming and going rhythmically throughout the rest of the night.

<hr>

She stretched out her body, feeling the pull of her muscles lengthening from her fingertips down through her toes before she rolled over onto her stomach in her bed.

Hearing rustling coming from her adjoined bathroom, she lifted her head from her pillow and saw the light shining out from underneath the small crevice at the bottom of the door. A moment later, Joey stepped out, still wearing the clothes he had been in last night, sans his boots.

Layne propped herself up on her elbows as she had to

mentally try and recall the sequence of events of the night prior. "I didn't expect to see you still here this morning."

His face was as serious as she had ever seen it. "What's going on with you?" He had his suspicions, but given how hard they were for him to believe, he was willing to give her the benefit of the doubt.

So, it seemed that this was going to be a morning about picking fights. She scooted to the edge of the bed and got out, nearly stumbling over the boots he had left there on the floor. "God." She glared at the footwear that nearly killed her, then back to Joey.

"Nothing is going on with me. You're the one who decided to show up without an invitation."

She walked towards her bathroom, but he stepped in front of her, blocking her path. Both her brows perked up as she stared at him. "Do you mind?"

"Layne, something is going on with you." He made it clear he wasn't going to let her by without some sort of explanation.

"Ok." She crossed her arms in front of her chest as both her offensive and defensive mechanisms began to come out. "What's going on with me? Let's see, the one guy I was willing to trust with my soul betrayed me and lied to my face. Then, after a year, he decides to waltz back into my life, asking me to do him a shitty favor."

The anger and frustration filled her voice as she vented to him about only a fraction of what she had on her plate right now.

His eyes drifted over her, trying to assess not only her

words but her body language before he let the issue go for the time being. "So, are you going to do it?"

Briefly, she glanced up at the heavens as he renewed his request, and she prayed that whichever god was listening would grant her the patience to deal with his stubbornness that rivaled her own.

Layne sighed as she looked over at him. "You're so good at breaking into my house, why can't you just break into his?"

He shrugged unapologetically. "Not for nothing, Layney, but you don't exactly make it difficult for me. Besides, Ellis has his place built like a damn fortress. Nobody is getting in or out of there without him knowing. Not without enough time, energy, and distractions, anyway."

There he was, saying her name like that again. Growing weary of his insistence about fulfilling his request, her arms dropped to her sides, getting the feeling he wasn't going to let this go. She just didn't have the fight in her to argue with him for days, and knowing him, he would argue with her for weeks if he felt so inclined. "What's in it for me if I do?"

An amused grin appeared on his face. "Always about the bottom line, aren't you? What do you want?"

The way he asked that second question seemed to hold a lot more than what met the eye. Then, he took a step toward her, his hands running up along her shoulders and up the sides of her neck until his palms settled on either side of her face. "Hm?"

A dryness overcame her mouth as he peered down at her while embracing her face in his hands.

Days before Mick's ultimate betrayal, Layne was coming out of her bathroom after her morning shower. Joey had greeted her right outside the doorway as she exited. His hands cupped her face and pulled her in to steal a kiss from her.

After claiming her lips for a moment, he looked down into the sparkle of her green eyes. "Where was my invitation to join you?"

Layne grinned at him. "Since when has a lack of an invitation ever stopped you?"

Snapping back from the playback reel inside of her head, she found herself in the same place and looking up into the very same eyes as he held her face between his hands.

"Just... behave yourself. This isn't an open invitation for you to start hanging around all the time." Her hands came up to settle on top of each of his, trying to will herself to pull them away.

Joey chuckled at such a minimal request. "Is that all?"

"I mean it, Joey. This one favor changes nothing. I will get you into the party, but that's it. I'm washing my hands of all of this, including you. I've got enough shit going on without having to deal with yours, too." Layne had no idea why she was bothering to grant him this one favor, but if it meant that he would quickly be back out of her life afterward, then she was willing to bend a little.

He pressed his forehead against hers as his thumb stroked over her cheek. "Thank you."

She cleared her throat and finally managed to pull away from him before she made any more stupid decisions with her life. Layne hoped that he wouldn't make her regret this.

"There are going to be ground rules because I don't want to get dragged into this blindly. One," she raised a finger at him as she counted, "you need to see someone about a tux. I can't have you showing up like you rolled out of a Humvee. Two, I don't want to know what the hell you need or why you need it at the party. I want total plausible deniability. And three, all your favors are all used up after this. Every. Last. One."

Seemingly, Joey was in agreement with all of her rules as he nodded after each demand. "It's a done deal then. We can talk about specifics as it gets closer." The temptation to seal it with a kiss lingered in the air. A temptation that neither of them gave into.

After Joey got his boots back on, she shooed him off so she could go about her busy day of doing damage control around town, primarily trying to rein in Liam.

Layne did her best to convince herself that this wouldn't get messy and that it was strictly a one-time business deal. The problem was that this had all the hallmarks of going to hell in a handbasket. Wasn't that how everything in her life went?

CHAPTER FIVE

Finally, she felt like she could suck in some fresh air after Joey left her house. Fresh air that wasn't tainted by the head swirling scent of him. She made a note that if she wanted to erase evidence of his time there, she was going to need to toss all her bedding in the laundry unless she wanted him haunting any more of her dreams. Damn it, she had forgotten the laundry again, thanks to Joey's unexpected visit.

Layne was seriously questioning her mental state in agreeing to this batshit insane request from him. She shouldn't have agreed to it, but if there was anybody who wasn't going to give up, it would be Joey.

Right now's problem though? She had to deal with her brother, which was an entirely different fiasco. One that had immediate and more damning consequences.

First things first, she went downstairs and pulled the invitation to Eric's soiree out of a drawer filled with various other paperwork and takeout menus. The fancy script listed a phone number to RSVP. Well, there wasn't going to be a better time than the present.

After dialing the number from her cell, she held it to her ear while it rang. Deep down, she hoped it would go to voicemail. That was until the smooth male voice answered on the other end.

"Eric Ellis."

She mouthed the word 'fuck' and winced at the thought of actually having to have this conversation with him. Layne had been doing an expert job of avoiding talking to him after their encounter at the Brass Mirror, though it wasn't for lack of effort on his part.

"Hi, Eric, it's Layne O'Reilly."

Immediately, she could hear the smile reach his voice. "My little harpy, I've been waiting to hear from you."

She cringed at his pet name for her but swallowed her pride for a brief moment so she could get through this discussion without compromising the whole damn setup.

"Things have been hectic. Look, thank you for the flowers, but they aren't necessary."

"They were entirely necessary." He sounded far too sure of himself.

Biting her lip gently, she tried to assemble her words intelligently. "About the invitation, parties aren't my thing, but Liam thought it would be a good idea to be seen out and about rubbing elbows with the city's top-tier elite." Yes, she was lying out of her ass and may have added another item to her checklist to let Liam know what a good idea he had when she saw him later.

There was a pause on the other end of the line, leaving

Layne wondering if the call had dropped. Finally, after the awkward pause, Eric responded, "You surprised me, Layne. I expected you to call to tell me where I could shove the invite."

"I very strongly considered it." At least that part was the God-honest truth.

His laugh echoed on the other end. "Nonetheless, I will make sure that you are my guest of honor. I have been looking forward to continuing our discussion about how we can help one another. How about I pick you up tomorrow morning, and we can talk about things during a walk around Central Park?"

She pressed her lips into a hard line, doing her best to remind herself that she needed to focus on the business side of things and see past her personal feelings. "Fine, I will see you tomorrow morning, but don't get your hopes up."

Eric set a time, and they said brief goodbyes before terminating the call. Layne was already regretting her decision, but with her back up against the proverbial wall, she needed to keep her options open. Not just for herself, but for the sake of the O'Reilly legacy.

That afternoon, she sat in her dad's former office in O'Reilly Manor, waiting for Liam to show up. She looked at her smartwatch for what felt like the fifth or sixth time. He was supposed to be here twenty minutes ago.

Liam had taken over the office since their dad had passed, but it was only in the past couple of months that he began changing up the decor to fit his personal and flashy style. The formerly glossy wooden desk no longer filled the room, and in its place was something more ultra-modern with metal and thick panes of glass.

She walked over to the window and peered out across the street, watching the cars that drove by. Seeing a sports bike across the street that looked familiar, she narrowed her eyes to focus on it. However, her focus was quickly interrupted when the office door swung open forcefully.

Spinning around, she saw Liam walking in, a scowl on his face as he stomped over to his desk. His auburn hair looked like he had been running his fingers through it repeatedly, leaving the short locks sticking up in various directions.

"What are you doing here?" he said grumpily, clearly in a foul ass mood. Today was looking like a bucket of sunshine, wasn't it?

"We had a meeting scheduled, remember?" She walked away from her spot at the window and sat down in one of the two chairs across from him.

Her brother took his seat and then motioned for her to continue. "Just tell me what the hell is wrong now, and let's get this over with."

Under normal circumstances, that would have been a fair assumption, but this time, she was aiming for a more positive discussion. "There's a few things, actually, so you might as well get comfortable."

The irritation written across his face was plain as day. "Layne, I don't have time for this. Give me the shortest possible version."

This was proving to be such a stark comparison to the way their dad ran things, even when he was pressed for time, he had made others wait while he set aside time to listen to whomever he was meeting with.

She dropped the biggest item of focus. "Eric Ellis wants to discuss us potentially helping each other out. A whole 'we scratch his back, he scratches ours' type of situation."

That caught Liam's attention. "Ellis? The bougie asshole that moved here six months ago?"

She nodded. "Yes, that one. I'm vetting the whole thing; it may end up being nothing at all. He invited me to this get-together he is having so we can talk things over."

Maybe she fudged that part a little bit, but there was no reason to make Liam think that it was anything more than just idle talks. Nor did he know about Joey coming back around, or as Liam only knew him as the masked freak hired to dispose of Michael Franzetti.

To his credit, he sat there mulling it over as he sat back in his chair. His fingers lightly scratched at his chin. "What the hell does he have going on that we would need him for? You know what? Never mind, just find out. Anything else?"

She shifted uncomfortably in her seat. "Li, we need to talk about the books and client debts going uncollected. People are noticing the cracks, and—"

A bunch of commotion was heard coming down the hall, a shrill voice shrieking out words as the click-clacking of heels stomped against the floor until Kristill appeared at the entrance of the office.

Layne groaned and rubbed her forehead, seeing Liam's favorite hookup fuming with daggers for eyes.

Pointing a bony finger all accusatory at Liam, Kristill shouted. "You are a fuckin' prick, ya know that?! I want the damn money you promised me!"

Her brother rose to his feet and grabbed a decorative glass paperweight, chucking it in the woman's direction. It flew far right and smashed into the door. "I told you that you'd get the money when you did your job, you dumb whore!"

It was incredibly clear to Layne that she was unlikely to finish her discussion with Liam, at least not without getting in his volatile path and being the next person he tossed something at.

Kristill was undeterred by the flying object and was bound and determined to get up in his face. She spat her words out at him, saliva sputtering out venomously. "You're a sick bastard! I ain't sticking any of that up in my p—"

As a sister, Layne did *not* want to hear Kristill finish that sentence and hear about any of her sibling's more peculiar proclivities. However, Liam didn't allow her to finish her shouting as the sound of the violent slap of his palm across the woman's face cut off the words.

Shit. Layne popped out of her seat and scurried over between the two of them right as Liam went to lash out at Kristill once more. His face was beet-red and eyes wild with a whole new level of temper she had never seen before.

Layne ended up soaking part of his shove meant for

Kristill, which was probably for the better, considering she was likely less than one hundred pounds soaking wet. "Enough! What the fuck is wrong with you?!"

Kristill was still reeling from the strike, holding her face, which had blossomed in a bright red glow.

If Liam wanted to throw another hit, he was going to have to go through Layne. While Kristill was not on Layne's list of favorite people, she didn't deserve to be Liam's punching bag either. Fortunately, he decided to choose his battles wisely and left Layne unscathed for now.

Noticing that a couple of the guys that still worked for them were standing in the doorway to the office, staring dumbly at the scene unfolding, Layne got even more pissed off. Glaring at them, she pointed at them and then Kristill. "What the fuck are you staring at? Get her out of here!"

She shook her head as the two men finally snapped into gear and escorted Kristill out of the office and, hopefully, out of the house altogether.

Layne turned her head to look back at her brother. "Really? You've been blowing our money on *that*? Damnit, Li! I keep telling you we can't keep doing this!"

He backed up and kicked over a wastebasket that was to the side of his desk, sending it skittering across the floor into a bookshelf. "I don't need you chastising me, Layne! Learn to stay in your damn place! I've got this handled!"

"Handled?! The only thing that I can see that you've got handled is dismantling this entire damn operation!" She scoffed that he could believe that anything they had going on in their lives was being handled.

"Do us both a favor, huh?" He came up to her, his face

still flushed with enough red rage that it could have passed for a volcanic eruption. "Keep your damn mouth shut until I ask for your opinion. I'm tired of hearing you yapping at me every other day."

She should have been the one to explode, but she bit her tongue as she heard him loud and clear. Shaking her head, she made her decision. "I told you if you didn't salvage operations that I would, and you wouldn't like the way I handle things. You've left me no choice, and that's something you're going to have to deal with. I'm not going to be held responsible for your inability to step up and be a damn man. The spoiled little brat who doesn't get to play for free act is getting real fuckin' old."

Layne walked away from him. She knew what she needed to do. If she was going to survive in a world where the other big bad criminals fed on the weak, she had to strengthen her position. She couldn't rely on Liam any longer. If her family name was ever going to command the respect it once had under Scott O'Reilly's leadership, Layne was going to have to be the one to step up and make the hard sacrifices.

CHAPTER SIX

In a rare instance of waking up before her alarm wailed, Layne had been trying to fend off the headache nagging at the inside of her skull all night. The events that transpired the day before with Joey, Eric, and Liam had left her mind unable to turn itself off.

When she did finally get out of bed, she got ready for her outing with Eric. She stared at her clothes hanging up inside of her walk-in closet. Layne internally debated as to what she should wear to meet with a potential ally who appeared to have the hots for her. She couldn't deny that at least he was a sight worth looking at in return.

After spending far too much thought on it, she opted for a pair of skin-tight jeans that flattered the shape of her legs and the curve of her ass. They had always been her favorite pair. Matching the jeans with a light blue sweater with a low-cut v-neck was a compromise between casual and flirty. Not to mention a little bit of warmth, given the shift into the crisp autumn air that was falling over the northeast.

Layne swept her hair up into a loose bun, only a few rogue strands falling away from the bundle of chestnut locks at the back of her head.

Once she was downstairs, while she was draping a black knit scarf around the back of her neck, the chime of the doorbell sounded. Unhooking her coat from a rack on the wall, she swiftly slid it on before answering the front door.

Standing there on the other side was her potential new business partner, Eric. His eyes lit up when he saw her, and he held out a cup of coffee for her. "A peace offering for springing this on you last minute yesterday."

Trying not to let on that she appreciated the coffee too much, she managed to only give him a polite smile before accepting the steaming cup of joe. "Thanks."

After locking up her house, they walked a few blocks over until they approached Central Park. People were casually walking along a paved path, some with their dogs, others with their strollers, and some training for their next big 5k.

Layne took a sip from her coffee, noting that it had notes of nutmeg and vanilla in it, a satisfying combination with the richness of the dark roast. It was fancy, much like Eric, but still appreciated for its caffeine content.

She looked over at the man who was determined to find mutual ground with her. "Well, you have me here. What's your proposal?"

Eric wasn't dressed nearly as formally as he had been when they first met. He was wearing a navy pullover sweater with a lighter blue shirt underneath and a pair of khaki pants that fit his lower body perfectly.

He smirked as Layne cut right to the point. "I hoped for us to get to know each other on a more personal level before diving right into business discussions."

Her eyebrows lifted briefly before she gave a partial laugh. "I don't bring my personal life into my business if I can help it." She walked off the path onto the lawn that had the beginnings of fallen leaves sprinkled indiscriminately across it. The blustery air carried nature's little messengers of the season change to and fro.

He followed beside her. "Your life is your business, and soon you're not going to have either if drastic changes aren't made."

She stopped and turned to face him, not appreciating the way he pointed out the seriousness of her situation. "Are you trying to intimidate me?"

He shook his head. "Not at all, but you know as well as I that the state of things will make you and everyone tied to you a weak and easy target. I don't want to see that happen."

Layne narrowed her eyes at him. "Why should you care?"

Eric leaned in and dropped the volume of his voice as though he was going to share highly confidential information. "Call me a bleeding heart." He smiled at her before he walked to a bench set underneath a line of trees and motioned for her to take a seat beside him.

Stupidity generally wasn't one of Layne's top traits, and it would be stupid of her not to be skeptical of his motives. After following him to the bench, she continued to stand.

"Alright, let's get personal then." Her eyes reflected her consideration of the next move she needed to make in this game of dangerous and violent real-world chess. "Bleeding heart or not, this isn't solely a business move for you. If it was, you'd be speaking with Liam. So, why me?"

Impressed with her assessment, he nodded.

"All due respect, your brother isn't cut of the same cloth as your father was. You, on the other hand, very much are."

Her expression shifted slightly, indicating she didn't quite believe him. "Says the man who hardly knows a thing about me."

Eric grinned and leaned back against the bench as he spread his arms along the backrest, and he locked arctic blue eyes on her.

"I know enough. Besides, I know that an alliance between us would send a strong message to the other factions. Together, we could be a force to be reckoned with. Isn't that the type of respect you deserve? Your father had it."

Layne hated that he was laying out a game plan that was not only beneficial but made sense. She finally opted to take a seat next to him but was sure to leave a comfort-able amount of space between the two of them. There was no sense in letting him get the wrong idea that she was particularly keen on this. She drank from her coffee cup as she let the entire concept of both a personal and business merger soak in.

"Just spit it out. What are the terms?" She stared straight ahead, her eyes focusing on the scenery of buildings jutting into the skyline.

His hand reached over and rested on top of her leg, just above the knee. "For starters, we could make it clear to the public eye that we will be working together very closely. Then, we can discuss how you'd like to tie the knot."

His touch immediately snagged her attention and shook something up inside of her. When her head turned to look at him, he seemed to be positioned closer to her.

"Gee, you go all out on a proposal, don't you?"

Eric's hand slid up her leg gradually. "Are you saying 'no'?"

She grazed her teeth across her bottom lip as she brought her face in closer to his.

"I'm saying you're going to need a hell of a lot more than a two-minute elevator pitch and a cup of coffee to convince me to say 'yes'." Layne straightened up and pulled back from him. When she decided to stand back up to distance his touch on her leg, his hand grabbed hers to encourage her not to leave. His hold was firm but not painful.

"Give me a chance to show you how you can have everything you've ever wanted and more than you've dreamed of. But, let's face it, you don't have much time left to make up your mind." He was pointing out what she had been trying to avoid thinking about. Time.

After her encounter with Liam yesterday, she had even less time than most people knew. The painful realization couldn't be hidden from her eyes, knowing she was running out of options and the train was running out of track.

Eric keenly picked up on it and stood up, releasing her hand and running his hands over the yarn of her scarf draped around her neck. He wrapped his hands up in the material and used it to tug her in closer to him.

Looking up into the devilish charm of his face, she knew he was more aware of how precarious her position was than he was letting on.

His face neared hers while his silky tone offered unspoken promises. "We can take the world by storm, my little harpy."

She wanted to choke on the air around her. Damn him. Damn her. Damn it all. Damn everything to hell.

"I will have an answer for you by the time I see you at the party at the end of the month." That at least seemed like a decent amount of a delay for her to figure her shit out. Miracles happen all the time, right?

He whispered into her ear with a purr. "I look forward to it." The softness of his lips left a light caress against the side of her face as he uttered his words to her. Layne's heartbeat quickened, and when she turned her head, his mouth was right there, hovering over hers.

"If I were you, I wouldn't disappoint me." His hold released from her scarf, letting the ends fall back down into place before giving her a little more room to breathe.

Eric had insisted on escorting her back to her house after they had carried a lighter topic of conversation. He told her about the renovations on his house and the way he was getting to know some of the other faction heads planted across the city.

As they left the park, Eric took ahold of her hand and quickly crossed the street to avoid getting run over by typical New York drivers. Walking by various parked vehicles along the street, Layne failed to notice that they walked by a black sports bike with a helmet resting on the seat. A helmet with decals representing a skull-like smile across the front of it.

After arriving back on her front steps, Eric managed to sneak in a quick peck on her cheek before he went on his way. Something in the way he had looked at her before he left indicated there was far more to his interests than he was divulging to her.

Layne was left wondering whether tying herself to Eric was grabbing onto a lifeline or was it an anchor that was going to pull her down into the depths of the ocean? There was only going to be one way to find out.

CHAPTER SEVEN

Each day following her outing with Eric, a new bouquet of fresh stems was delivered to her house. Today's delivery was a unique set of blossoms wrapped in black florist paper. It was a mixture of roses and lilies, but it was their coloring that made them so eye-catching.

The starburst-shaped lilies had deep violet hues on the edges of the petals that grew lighter in a gradient effect towards the pistil in the center. By contrast, the tightly wrapped rose petals were a lighter shade of purple on the outside that darkened with each layer until they were nearly black in the center.

A shining silver card was tucked inside with a hand-written note which simply read:

My little harpy.

With all these deliveries, it was making it difficult to

take her mind off the choice she was going to have to make in a few weeks. Not to mention, her house was beginning to smell like a florist as she tried to find a spot for each new delivery.

Layne chose to put this newest set of flowers inside her home office, arranging them in a vase that was centered on one of the shelves of her bookcase.

As for the other man weighing heavily on her mind, if Joey had been snooping around and keeping tabs on her, she hadn't caught him in the act...yet. After catching a glimpse of a sports bike outside of O'Reilly Manor the other day when she met with Liam, it left her questioning if she was just being paranoid, hopeful, or maybe both.

He was particularly adept at lingering without making himself known, she had learned that very early on after their first encounter. However, she still hadn't been able to fully anticipate his next steps, and that's what drove her crazy the most. Joey was capable of living in her blind spot when he wanted, and she hated not being able to get ahead of his every move.

As far as she was aware, he was behaving himself and keeping his distance. He had left her a new number to reach him at so they could talk over some of the more mundane details of getting him into the Ellis residence on the night of the party.

Layne pulled out her phone and texted his contact number.

LAYNE

Did you get your tux?

JOEY

Just got back from the fitting.

LAYNE

Are you still set on meeting me at the party instead of picking me up like a gentleman?

JOEY

You know I don't do the knight in shining armor act.

I will leave that to Prince Charming.

Even though she hadn't heard his tone, it was clear he had some opinions on Eric's affections towards her in referring to him as a prince out of a fairy tale.

Word was making its way through the grapevines around that Ellis and Layne had some personally driven interactions. Undoubtedly, Joey's tap into the criminal underworld hadn't spared him that knowledge. Unbeknownst to her, he may just have been seeing more than he was letting on.

LAYNE

Well, if you're late, I'm going in without you.

JOEY

Layney, you should know by now I'm never late.

LAYNE

Yes, I know you're obsessed with punctuality.

JOEY

(. . .)

Layne saw the text bubble that indicated Joey was typing a response, but one never came. She waited a few minutes before giving up and determining he thought better about what he wanted to say to her.

Frustrated yet mildly curious, she contemplated calling him out on his unsent thoughts. However, knowing Joey, he would just ignore the inquisition. She sighed and decided she desperately needed a distraction from all of this before her thoughts drove her crazy.

Good thing she at least had plans to go dress shopping with Rebecca in an hour. Girl time always proved to be an escape from the wild chaos of her life.

After a long period of silence, there was finally a sign of life. "I look like a pumpkin that's been rotting on the porch for two months too long!" Layne shouted out to Rebecca from behind the curtain of the dressing room of the boutique dress shop.

She yanked the curtain to the side and stepped out to confirm that the dress she tried on did indeed make her look like a deflated pumpkin—from the aggressive shades of orange to the poofs in all the wrong places of the sleeves and the awkwardly shaped bustle.

With a glass of champagne in one hand and her phone snapping photographic evidence in the other, Rebecca was crying in a fit of laughter.

Dryly and unamused, Layne spoke, "I'm glad you find this amusing." Layne gave a huff and a sigh as she tugged at the itchy tulle of the gown. "I don't even know why I even care, I don't even want to go to this damn event."

Her best friend sat there on the velvet bench across from the dressing room and put her phone down for a moment to wipe a few tears away from underneath her eyes, attempting to speak coherently between her giggles.

"I-I… hope it's a—" Rebecca chuckled again before sputtering out her thought, "it's a H-Halloween party!" She deteriorated back into side-splitting laughter for a moment before making a more serious effort to compose herself.

Layne stood there, not finding the humor in this hideous gown, her arms crossed in front of her. "Ha-ha." She came over and took a seat next to the one person who had always been there to support her no matter the hopelessness of the situation.

She leaned over and rested her head on Rebecca's shoulder. It gave her bestie pause, and she sobered up from her amusement over the ridiculous gown.

Straightening up, she wrapped an arm around Layne's shoulders and drew her into a reassuring hug. "There are plenty of other stores, Layne. You'll find something. There's plenty of time; the party isn't until the end of the month."

"It's not the dress." She frowned while debating how much she was going to be a disappointment to her lifelong friend.

"What is it, then?" The concern was evident in Rebecca's voice as she tried to look at Layne's face to assess just how big whatever was plaguing her was.

Layne raised her head and shook her head as she looked

at her hands in her lap. "Same shit it always is. My life is a mess, and I don't even know what to do with it anymore."

"Is Liam being an ass? More than normal anyway?" Rebecca moved her eyebrows questioningly.

Giving a partial crack of a smile at the lovely thought of if that had been the only thing weighing on her, how it would be so much more manageable. "Obviously that, but it's not just that. Everything keeps stacking up, and nothing seems like the right choice anymore. Meanwhile, for every one thing I patch up, three more things fall apart."

Rebecca handed off the rest of her bubbly to Layne, who didn't refuse to consume the dry beverage.

"Well, if I know anything about you at all, it's that you eventually figure out what it is that matters most to you. You're one tough cookie, and you'll figure out how to make it all work out the way it needs to in the end." Rebecca offered her up a hopeful smile, and her pale blue eyes still held concern for Layne's demeanor. "You can't expect to fix everything yourself. You're one person, Layne. A hell of a badass bitch, but you still only have two hands to work with. It's ok to accept help every now and then."

Layne was incredibly grateful that Rebecca knew how to give some of the best advice without prying too much for the details. Communicating the unique complications of her not-so-legal life had never come easy to her, and there were days when it hurt too much to say all the words out loud.

Not to mention, the less Rebecca knew about the business side of things, the better. There was no need to expose her to things that could potentially drag her into the same danger Layne wrangled with on a day-to-day basis.

"I can't tell you how much I appreciate you. You've always been the sister I never had." Her arms wrapped around Rebecca, giving a strong hug.

While her friend returned the gesture, she laughed in response. "Thank God for that, or else we both would be the queens of the insane asylum. I'm not sure the world would have been able to handle it if we had been born sisters." Her words teased in an effort to lighten the mood.

Layne chuckled, imagining just how fucked they both would have been had they grown up together in the same household. At least one of them deserved a chance at a typical life.

Drawing back, Rebecca patted Layne's hand. "Now, please, for the love of God, get out of this dress so I don't go blind."

In full agreement, Layne didn't need to be told twice. She returned to the dressing room and discarded the eyesore of a gown.

Finally, after a few more dresses were tried on and immediately pitched, Layne found the one worthy of wearing in public.

Rebecca whistled in a catcall as she stared in awe at the chosen grown. "If you don't buy this one, I will never speak to you again. The way it fits, you would even have the Pope worshipping the ground you walk on."

Layne stared at her reflection in the mirror, turning to capture each angle of the way the material fit her figure. It had been a while since she had felt this stunning and undeniably beautiful. She smiled confidently to herself, imagining the look on *his* face when he saw her the night of the swanky soiree.

———

After squaring away all the details for the dress to be tailored to fit her height and size, Layne and Rebecca got to enjoy some lunch out on the sidewalk in front of a small Italian spot. Despite the cooler air of the fall outside, the restaurant had set up heaters to allow diners to enjoy the fresh air a little longer.

Layne stabbed her fork into the oversized meatball, cutting away a bite-sized portion and dunking it in the extra sauce and the mound of burrata. "This place has the best damn meatballs." She shoved the fork into her mouth and gave a satisfied moan.

Rebecca grinned as she also helped herself to the meatball appetizer they were both sharing. "You know," her friend looked at her from across the table, "I'm proud of you."

Layne lifted a brow. "For what?"

Her bestie gave a warm smile. "Not that I need a reason, but the way you—"

Whatever it was that Rebecca was going to say was cut off by the sound of a man yelling from a passing car. "Your time is almost up, you Irish cunt!" Followed by shots ringing out, shattering the front glass window of the restaurant.

Before her brain had time to process the words, Layne

heard the firing of bullets. Dropping everything in her hands, Layne reached over and grabbed Rebecca's arm, pulling her down onto the ground. Protectively, Layne lay on top of her, flinching at the sound of each pop.

When the only sounds left were people screaming in a panic, Layne pushed up onto her feet to try and get a look at the vehicle as it took off down the street. The only thing she could make out was the white, blue, and red stripes of the Russian flag on a sticker in the back window.

Now that the threat had passed, she leaned down and helped a shaken-up Rebecca to her feet. "Are you okay?" Her friend gave a slow nod.

Layne stood there breathing heavily as the harsh reminder of the O'Reilly family's standing in this city was plummeting. Today was just a warning, if they had meant to take her out, they could have. But, if she didn't do something soon, Liam and she were going to be at the top of every criminal organization's hit list.

CHAPTER EIGHT

"Mr. Ellis is right this way." The host led the way through the hall down to a private box suite there inside Madison Square Garden. The space could have easily hosted ten or twelve people, but instead, it would just be the two of them.

Eric had been insistent that they continue to be seen together for appearances' sake. It was always about appearances, wasn't it? Money and power, and what you did with it. This was especially true among people in their line of illegal dealings.

Originally, he had tried to convince her to go to the New York Ballet, which was a hard pass for Layne. She had nothing against seeing people in tights and tutus weightlessly glide across a stage, but it was far too stuffy of a way to spend a night out.

His alternative suggestion of seeing a rock music concert at the Garden seemed far more appealing, and it was a bonus that she wouldn't have to get dressed up.

Instead, she opted for a set of flattering and snug jeans fashionably torn in a few places across her thighs and a small black tank that had multiple straps crossing over her back and a glimpse of her smooth stomach depending on which way she moved.

Layne's hair was styled into a few edgy braids that fed into a teased ponytail for additional volume and sass. The makeup she opted for matched the rest of her, dark and edgy. Since she didn't anticipate kicking anyone's ass tonight, she had put in a pair of gold hoop earrings in each ear. Under normal circumstances, they just weren't practical when there was a risk of getting them caught up and torn from her lobes. Not something she wanted to experience; she would rather take a bullet to the shoulder. Oh, wait…

When she arrived in the suite, every beverage she could order was available for consumption. Multiple hot trays of food were on display, along with various cold platters. She'd never have to worry about eating for the rest of the week, given the sheer amount of food laid out for just the two of them. If nothing else, Eric was excessive in everything he did.

Eric greeted her immediately, wrapping his arms around her in a hug before pulling back to take in the sight of her with a smile. His right hand gently drifted over her shoulder, his fingers caressing along the shiny scar from where Mick's bullet had entered her body last year.

Self-consciousness caused her to draw her shoulder back from his touch over that grim physical reminder that would never disappear.

He spoke with words filled with awe. "I will never stop being amazed at how much you take my breath away."

At least he was making an effort to stay in her good graces, or maybe he was just hoping that it would help sway her decision in his favor.

She noticed he was dressed down the most she had ever seen him, yet there was still an air of sophistication wrapped around him, from the designer jeans to the plain long-sleeved tee that was sure to cling to the fit outline of his upper body.

His hand dropped down to the small of her back as he guided her over to the bar. "I wasn't sure what you'd feel like drinking, so I made sure there would be a little of everything." If this was his definition of a 'little bit,' she was scared to see him go all out.

Setting her small black purse on the countertop, her eyes scanned the beverage collection before she selected the tall can of *Brooklyn Brewery* Brooklyn Lager from the mini-fridge. "I see that." Her finger popped the tab, prompting the smooth sound of the metal opening up and the quick fizz of the pressure release.

After taking an initial taste of the brewery's flagship beer, she offered him a light smile. She should have felt a sense of awkwardness, but instead, he somehow managed to keep things on the lighter side.

The lights dimmed inside the suite as the remainder of the venue darkened in anticipation of the opening act taking the stage.

Layne walked over to the two nearest seats, with Eric

following behind her. Expectedly, he took the seat to her left after she sat down.

Continuing to indulge in a couple of beers over idle conversation, Layne propped her booted foot up against the empty seat in front of her while the band she hadn't ever heard of continued its opening set. What had started as light topics of conversation began to take a turn into more serious things she had been avoiding.

"Layne, I need to know how things are business-wise," he urged her.

"Until you're on a need-to-know basis, Eric, I can't get into it with you." She shook her head, hoping he would leave well enough alone.

"I can't help buy you time if you don't let me." The weight of his arctic blue eyes were on her, even though she was avoiding looking at them. His hand reached over and turned her face toward him. "Let me help as a show of good faith that I'm serious about investing in all of you."

Briefly, she met his eyes but was quick to find another reason to escape. "I need another drink." She left her seat, tossing the empty can into a trash bin on the way back to the fridge. After pulling out the next beverage for herself, she reached into her purse that had been sitting there on the counter since she arrived and pulled out her emotional support pill bottle.

Beer was not going to numb her nearly enough to deal with Eric's probing. Just like it was nothing more than popping an aspirin for a headache, she swallowed down the tablet, chasing it with the freshly opened lager.

Layne returned to her seat, knowing that he was still

waiting for her to provide the necessary details he had asked for. She turned in her seat so she could face him as her hands focused on the cold of the beer can between her palms.

"Things are not great, but I'm sure you already knew that. Funds are getting tighter, and it's getting harder to rely on people to stay in line. The list of people working for us is getting shorter by the day. I can only do so much trying to clean up the messes." She slowly dragged in a breath as her thoughts jumped to the last mess she had tried to clean up, thanks to Liam running his mouth to one of their oldest clients on the books. Not to mention the warning she had been given by one of the Russian families.

With another long sip of the slightly hoppy beer, she made an effort to lock all those problems away for another day.

That's when she noticed that Eric's gaze had turned into something more serious as he took in the words she had spoken. His hand reached over and eased the can from her grasp and set it off to the side.

"All you have to do is give the word, little harpy, and I will make it all better." Eric placed his hand on the back of her neck and drew her in closely. "I promise. All you have to do is say 'yes.' I won't even ask you to add a 'please' with it."

Now that the main act had shown up, the inside of MSG was only lit up on the bottom floor where the stage itself had come to life, and fans were screaming in excitement as the first chord erupted across the speakers. The remaining notes of the song followed, but Layne barely noticed over the roar of her resulting self-medication taking hold from behind her eyes and spreading quickly like a violent invasion of her senses.

Not thinking clearly, let alone wanting to think at all, her senses and inhibitions were quickly fading. Instead of committing to one problem of giving him a definitive answer, she committed to another. She latched her mouth onto Eric's. Taken by surprise, Eric gave a pleased smile into the kiss as Layne made the first move, and he was more than happy to embrace the connection with her.

Quickly, he drew her into his lap while his mouth feverishly captured hers and wrangled for dominance. Layne straddled his lap, feeling the growing erection press up against her body.

His arm wrapped around her body, tightly pulling her slender figure up against him while his hips pushed up against her to feel their clothed bodies rubbing against one another.

The more she kissed him, the more her head swam, relying on his hold to keep her in one place. Her lips ran along the line of his jaw as she tried to focus on what she was doing here with him. His cologne filled her nostrils, reminding her of a forest just after the break of dawn, but what it was missing was the scent of sage that she craved the most.

Eric pushed her hips down on him forcefully, eliciting half a moan to be exhaled into his ear, which only encouraged him further. His mouth ventured down to the juncture where her neck met her shoulder, and his teeth sank into her flesh in a possessive bite intended to leave a red ring behind on her unbroken flesh.

Layne didn't feel a whole lot on so many levels, especially in that moment. The result was her poor choices, leading to exactly what she had been after an escape from all the stress and pain in her life that had nowhere else to go. Her hands held onto his shoulders for stability, her face pressed into the side of his neck as she succumbed to the high taking over.

He grasped onto her and stood to shift and swap their positions. He placed her back down on the seat in a way where she was on her knees and the front of her body was up against the backrest.

Layne latched her hands onto the top of the back of the seat, using it like a handlebar for support. Eric's hand slid around to the front of her stomach and down to the waist of her jeans. His fingers pushed the button free, and as he slid his hand directly down the front of her, the loose zipper slid down on its own.

His other hand wrapped itself in the length of her ponytail and tilted her head back enough so he could growl his words into her ear. "I can't wait to hear how you call my name."

Her eyes were barely focused; the ceiling looked hazy from this angle. Yet, she didn't care. She was getting the distraction away from the cruel whispers of her past and current traumas.

Eric's fingers dove deeper between her skin and the fabric of her thong until they slid against the wetness of her slit. Her mouth parted in a breathy moan. He didn't make her wait long before two of his thick fingers found her entrance and buried deep inside of her.

"That's it, baby. You're going to give yourself over to me."

A sensation of pleasure mixed with the sedative effects of her impromptu cocktail of pills and beer. Seeking an even further high, her hips moved her body against his hand.

The heel of his hand stroked over her clit every time he thrust his fingers back into her. At first, the rhythm was slow and predictable, but it quickly began to elevate to something more. His touch was claiming her wet pussy, and she was encouraging it as a means to her own unraveling.

Her sweet moans grew more intense, though overpowered by the loud music of the band blaring across the speakers throughout the building. Layne's body shivered from the escalation of pleasure marking the approach of her release. "Mm, I'm gonna… come…"

"Go ahead and come all over my fingers. Show me how much you like it when I make you squirm, my little harpy. And, when you're done, you're going to do it again for me until I'm all you can think about." The tips of his fingers curled and pressed against the spot deep inside of her, causing her body to bear down around him as she cried out in release.

The sticky, sweet arousal from her body coated his fingers that continued to massage against the sensitive spot they had found, extending the lustful ride she was getting.

The surge of oxytocin gave a brief reprieve from the

haziness of her thoughts. As her chest rose and fell due to the breathlessness, she attempted to get up off the seat.

He withdrew the hand from inside of her, only to release her ponytail with his other hand and press down on her shoulder to keep her right where she was. "Not yet, I want to see what else your hot little pussy can take." Eric brought his fingers to his mouth, sucking the taste of her off of each one.

"I need a minute." Mentally or physically, she wasn't even sure.

That's when some prying eyes decided enough was enough, and a strip of light cut into the suite as the velvety privacy curtain slid to the side.

Layne's eyes tiredly looked at the intruding figure and saw Joey walking into the room. She questioned if she was seeing correctly. Maybe she was dreaming again, and things were going to get really hot in here.

He was wearing a white shirt with the black outline of a skull on it underneath, a thin black jacket with the sleeves pushed halfway up his forearms, and a pair of slim-fitted deep blue jeans on his muscled legs.

Eric stepped back from Layne as if he hadn't just been fingerfucking her moments ago. "Private suite, asshole."

Joey's jaw clenched tightly as he approached the two of them, his size and build overshadowing Eric easily. He glanced down at Layne, his brown eyes set in a stony, cold look. "I'm Miss O'Reilly's personal security, asshole."

An arrogant and judgmental scoff immediately came from Eric. "As you can see, she's fine." He leaned down and turned Layne's head to face him as he slowly assaulted her mouth with his lips for a moment. "Isn't that right?"

Images of snapping Eric's neck flashed through Joey's mind. "She's had enough fun for the night." He shoved himself between Layne and Eric.

A spark of anger rose in Eric's eyes. "That's not your call."

Now, Joey was imagining all the other creative ways he could send Eric to the grave in the most spectacularly gruesome way. If he didn't need Eric alive for his current job, he would have acted on his urges without hesitation.

Layne pushed up against the seat, underestimating just how woozy and uneasy on her feet she was. Her legs trembled underneath the weight of her body and caused her to stumble.

Joey's strong hand immediately caught her by the upper arm, ensuring that she remained upright. The first flicker of emotion reached his eyes in a fiery glare at Eric. "The fuck it's not. She's done here."

When her eyes finally found Joey's, she recognized the indication that a dangerous shift in his demeanor was quickly approaching. It was not something that would easily be quelled if pushed too far.

Still being supported by Joey's hold on her, she looked over at Eric. "It's fine. He takes his job a little too seriously." Her eyes tried to give an annoyed glare at Joey, but it fell flat when she didn't have enough energy to expend on it.

Eric stepped around Joey to come around in front of Layne. His hand touched her cheek, paired with a smile filled with future promises. "Next time, we will pick up where we left off." He leaned in to give her another kiss.

Before their lips made contact, Layne was pulled to the side as Joey's hands guided her away with a gentle firmness. "C'mon, you have a busy day tomorrow."

On her way toward the exit, Layne snagged her purse. The strength of Joey's hold never faltered as he led her out, keeping her supported on her own two feet.

He shook his head at her, but it was his lack of words that was the loudest.

CHAPTER NINE

The ride home in Joey's car was all a blur for Layne. She leaned on him as he walked her inside her house. After he got her upstairs into her bed, he took a seat in a chair in the corner of her room. Leaning over with his elbows on his knees, he buried his fingers in his dark blonde hair. A shaky breath escaped his lips as Layne lay there quietly breathing while she slept off the sedative mix she had ingested.

He dropped his hands down to hang between his legs as he lifted his gaze to watch Layne's chest rise and fall. A grim darkness of realization slid across his pupils while he clenched his teeth together, and a series of thoughts plagued his mind and conscience.

The hours passed, and soon, the sun chased away the night. Joey was still seated in that very same chair. His jacket draped over the arm of it.

Layne was beginning to stir, her feet kicking at the

sheets wrapped around her legs. When she cracked a look and caught sight of him, she slowly sat up. "Have you been sitting there all night?" Her hand rubbed the sleep from her eyes.

He looked at her and blatantly ignored her question. "What the fuck are you doing?" A simple and direct question.

It was a hell of a rude way to be spoken to when you were just waking up.

Layne popped up an eyebrow at his question; confusion shifted across her face. "Waking up on the wrong side of the bed, apparently. Christ."

He rose from the chair and came to stand at the foot of her bed. Joey reached into his pocket and pulled out her prescription bottle that had been in her purse. "What. The. Fuck. Are. You. Doing?" Each of his words punched out with a level of irritated sternness and demanded an answer from her.

Deep down, she knew what he was asking, but hell, if she was going to make things personal between them. Layne was still set on trying to get him back out of her life as quickly as possible after their business together was over.

She scooted to the edge of the bed, stood, and reached out to take the bottle from his hand. He held it out of her reach.

"You went through my things?" She scowled at him. "You need to learn how to mind your own damn business." She attempted to grab the bottle from him once more, unsuccessfully.

"Layne, I don't know what the hell you are thinking, but this?" He shook the container, rattling the pills inside. "This ain't going to fix it."

"It seems to fix everything just fine." She glared at him, wondering what the hell he knew about what she needed fixed in her life. He had been God-knows-where for the past year, and now he wanted to act like he had a right to give his opinion on how she handled herself.

He then laid down a demand. "You're going to stop with this bullshit. It's not you."

She outright lifted both brows before she laughed. "That's hilarious coming from you. What would you know about me? A person can change a lot in a year. You're just pissed because I'm not tripping over myself and landing on your dick."

Suddenly, the prescription bottle went flying from his hand and crashed into the wall, where it popped open and the pills scattered across her bedroom floor. Joey reached over, grabbed her by both of her arms and pushed her up against the back of her closet door.

His eyes flashed with a mixture of unfamiliar emotions, even to Layne. Staring up at him in shock, she didn't even resist as he held her still.

"This isn't a fuckin' game, Layne! If I thought I could fuck some sense into you, I would already have you bent over and taking my cock until you couldn't remember your own goddamn name."

"Maybe you should try anyway." Her voice set on making it clear she was just trying to push his buttons.

He growled as he gripped her jaw with the strength of

his hand and tilted her head up towards him as his mouth fought the temptation to consume her despite being a breath's distance away. "I'm not going to so much as put my mouth on you until you start listening to me like the good girl I know you can be." God knew he wanted to, though.

Stubbornly, she glowered at him. "Well, if you're not going to at least do that, then get your hands off of me."

He didn't budge as he silently stood there for a moment while his eyes gazed over her face while he struggled with his thoughts about the destructive path she was on.

There was a trickle of frustration as he murmured, "Were you just going to let him fuck you last night?"

A slap to her face would have been less of a surprise than this very personal inquiry. "So, that's what this is really about?" Her temper was already on a low simmer, but now he had just added fuel to her fire.

"You're all pissed because I'm giving someone else the time of day? Well, fuck you! If I want to go around screwing half of Manhattan, that's *my* business. You had your chance!" She jerked herself against his grasp.

He willingly let go of her but didn't back away. "Layne, this isn't you. None of this is." His tone softened as it was made clear that his brute force methods weren't working.

"Why? Because fucking a guy that isn't you is so hard to believe?" Layne rubbed her fingers against her temple as her head began to ache at the unexpected stress so soon after she had woken up.

Joey realized that she was going to dig her heels in on

this, making it an uphill battle. He had made a promise to her once to never let her lose herself. He needed to make good on that promise. He took a moment to find a little more calm within himself before speaking again.

"Look, why don't you go downstairs and get yourself some coffee? Then, we can talk about next steps with Ellis." He wasn't going to apologize for confronting her, but he knew when things were going to be on an unproductive path. The last thing he needed was to push her further in that direction.

She looked skeptically at him as he began to backpedal on everything that had started this argument. Layne deeply questioned her sanity in not just telling him to shove this favor up his own ass without an ounce of lube.

Not saying another word, she spun on her heel and left her bedroom to head downstairs.

Once she was gone, Joey drew his hand back, ready to smash it into the wood of her closet door. Pulling back in restraint last minute before contact, he gently rested his fist against the hard surface and leaned forward, pressing his forehead to the door as he squeezed his eyes shut. Feelings of guilt, helplessness, and frustration weighing down on him.

A few minutes later, he picked up the mess of pills from her floor and flushed them down the toilet. He knew it would only be a temporary solution, but it was one band-aid on the dam that was about to burst. If there was going to be any hope of pulling her back from the ledge, that band-aid was going to have to be enough for now.

When he got downstairs, the smell of freshly brewed coffee filled the air. Not finding Layne in the kitchen, he wandered from room to room until he noticed her sitting on her back patio. Moments later, he arrived with his own mug and took a seat in the cushioned chair next to her.

Layne had her legs tucked up underneath her to the side as she cradled the steamy beverage between her hands. Her eyes didn't even lift from watching the curls of steam rise from the top of the hot liquid.

He cleared his throat, deciding to break the silence and push past the awkwardness hovering between them. "Once we get inside at the party—"

"He wants to merge our organizations." She cut him off with her matter-of-fact statement.

"What?" Joey blurted out at the tidbit she just dropped on him.

She felt the heavy air enter her lungs as she breathed it in, and the weight remained even after she exhaled. Swallowing down a small sip from her mug, she finally looked over at him. "It's a cutthroat business, you know that. So, why don't you start by telling me what you need to get in there for?"

After setting the mug down on the small table in front of him, he sat back in his seat. "Thought you didn't want to know?"

"Want and need are two very different things, Joey. I don't have the luxury anymore of choosing what I want." And it was slowly killing her from the inside out, one shitty situation at a time.

She sat back and thought about each time she had to

take another hit to her sanity. Over the past year alone, she had been dealing with betrayals left and right, deaths, and escalating tensions not just between her and Liam but across business relationships as well. There had been no reprieve in sight and no way out as she felt her world closing in around her. Some days, she thought about how she wished someone would just hire a hitman to come find her.

Immediately, she pushed the morbid thought back into the deep recesses of her mind and tried to get her head back in the game. That's what her father would have expected, right?

His face grew solemn as he thought about what he had been hired to do. "Eric's into some epic shit. I mean, this goes beyond just the city limits. At best, it's statewide. At worst? Potentially international."

This was just turning out to be a spectacular fucking morning, wasn't it? "He's an overachiever? Not surprised." Making light of the situation was the only tool she had at the moment not to crumple in on herself.

"That's why I need to get in there; my client needs to know how widespread things are. The things that they're claiming he's done, and what he is doing…" Joey shook his head, visibly disgusted.

"I will get you in the door, but you keep things discreet. I don't want this coming back to haunt me in a week or even a year."

"Discretion is my middle name." In fact, they both knew it was not. It was Elliot.

Attempting to circle back to their discussion upstairs,

his hand reached out to rest on her thigh. "Layne, I know a lot has happened since last year."

She looked at her watch, seeing that it was time to avoid getting into her mushy feelings. "I have work to do today. I don't have time to sit and talk about the weather." Layne stood, allowing his hand to fall away from her leg.

His dark brown eyes were still glued to her, trying to figure out how to get past any imperfections in the invisible wall she had constructed around herself. After a resigned sigh and running his hand over the back of his head, he rose from his seat.

"Call me if anything changes." He didn't mean just with Eric, either. "I'm never far away."

She simply nodded at him and watched as he walked back inside to see himself out. The second he was out of sight, she flopped right back down into her chair, trying to suppress the quiver tugging at her chin. Layne drew her knees up in front of her and buried her face into them as the tears began to leak from her eyes.

After taking a few minutes to coil back up her self-control, she firmly pressed her lips together to start locking her feelings back down. Lifting her head from her knees, pulled out her phone to see a few missed messages.

ERIC

Thought about you all last night.

I haven't been able to focus on anything else this morning except what you're doing to me.

I will see you again soon, little harpy.

She stared at the screen, her fingers hovering over the onscreen keyboard. She shook her head and locked the screen. That could be dealt with later, just like everything else in her life.

CHAPTER TEN

She blew out a breath harshly. "Bianca just put him on the phone." Layne's fuse was running short as she held the phone to her ear while sitting inside her office at home.

The polite yet stern voice of the woman on the other end repeated itself. "Mr. Corelli is unavailable. I can take a message if you'd like to leave one for him."

Layne gave a soft growl as she summoned the last of her patience. "Bianca, I swear on all that is holy, if you don't go get Andrew, I will come down there myself. We both know he's standing right there next to you. Tell him if he doesn't get on the phone with me, I will make a special delivery to the *New York Times* pointing out his inability to properly file taxes because he's too busy jacking off to underage girls."

There was a pause as the call was placed on hold. Just when Layne thought she had been disconnected, a male voice came on the phone.

"Hi, Layne." Andrew almost sounded like he was expecting a pleasant conversation. Oh, how wrong he was if that was what he thought.

She leaned back into her seat, feeling partial relief that he had finally grown a pair to talk to her. "Where's my money, Andrew? I'm all out of patience."

He began to rattle off the excuses. "There's been some unexpected business expenses, and I was going to send it to you."

"The fuck you were. I'm getting tired of the bullshit. If I don't get it today, I'm going to be pissed that I have to come down there and get it myself in whichever creative ways I come up with."

There was a long pause followed by a defeated sigh. "Look, I didn't want to say anything, but another, um, business partner approached me."

She sat up in her chair. "What do you mean someone approached you? When?" Layne didn't want to jump to any conclusions and needed him to spell it out to her as plain as day.

Andrew cleared his throat on the other end of the line. "I am working with Russell Spencer now. He said if you had any problems with it, to take it up with him."

Russ Spencer and his crew were one of a few factions that had been not so quiet about speculating on the end of the O'Reilly era. Once word had gotten out that the great Scott O'Reilly was on a massive health decline, Russell began making moves to take advantage of the shift in leadership. The bastard was playing with fire and beginning to pick off their income sources one by one. It seemed that Andrew was the latest acquisition.

Layne didn't even bother to try to hide her displeasure at this news. "Believe me, I'm going to take it up with him." She hung up on Andrew without a further word.

"FUCK!" She tossed her phone down onto her desk in front of her. Monetarily, this was a hit they couldn't afford to take. Layne leaned over, her elbows on the edge of her desk, as she put her head into her hands. Her fingers scrunched up and got lost in her silky locks of chestnut hair as she tried to wrap her brain around this devastating blow.

She shook her head and pulled open a drawer on her right, seeing a spare bottle of pills nestled inside. Her eyes stared down at the easy escape that was calling out to her. The image of Joey losing his shit on her was still fresh in her mind.

Layne grunted as she slammed the drawer shut, leaving the pills untouched.

***

Still riding the coattails of anger and frustration, she slammed her car's shift knob into park after coming to an abrupt stop in front of a large retail storefront. Layne got out of her car, slamming her door shut so hard it would have likely amputated any fingers that got caught in it.

She was not giving a shit that she should have done the political thing and called Russell Spencer first before showing up here. If he was going to underhandedly start stealing her business, then she was going to step foot in his territory without one fuck given.

Was it stupid? Yes. Did she care? No. She also should have gone to Liam first, but she wasn't in the mood to add to her long list of things that pissed her off today.

Layne walked into the retail storefront, ignoring the girl at the cash register scrolling through her phone. Layne stomped towards the backroom and past all the iconic New York heart-laden merchandise on the shelves, Statue of Liberty souvenirs, and Empire State Building toothpick holders.

She shoved the door open, walking through the stock area full of plain cardboard boxes. In front of her was another door, but this one required an electronic keycard access. One of her fists began to pound on it repeatedly. "Open the goddamn door!"

She looked up at the camera mounted right above the door with a deadly glare set in her eyes. "I'm not fuckin' around! Open the door!"

An audible click was heard as the electronic lock was remotely disabled. She didn't waste a single moment before swinging the door open and walking inside a long hallway until she came to one more door. This one was left wide open.

When she stormed into the office, she was greeted by three of Spencer's associates and Russ himself perched on the edge of his desk. Russ was a stocky middle-aged man who may have been averagely handsome in his prime, but these days, he carried a little extra weight around his midsection, and his hair was noticeably thinning despite being clipped close to his scalp.

A small screen on the far right wall had the black and white CCTV feed where they undoubtedly had seen her coming to unlock the door for her. The remainder of the room was set up as a small meeting space with a plain table and chairs designed to hold up to six people, a mini fridge off to the right corner, and Russell's desk centered along the back wall.

There was no stopping her; she approached the man responsible for her foul mood. Without hesitation, she grabbed a handful of his polo shirt in one hand and let the fist of her other hand propel toward his face. "You snake-like motherfucker!"

Her punch was a glancing blow as he realized that she was actually crazy enough to spring an attack on him physically, and he raised an arm to block it. Chaos immediately erupted inside the room, with lots of yelling filling the air.

When the first punch didn't land to her satisfaction, she wound up and threw as many more as she could muster in her fit of rage before two of the men struggled to pull her off of their fearless leader. Even as they grabbed her arms and dragged her back, she spat at Russ, the saliva making it onto his shirt.

The hands on her arms were gripping her tightly, but Layne's eyes never left Russ's face. He looked down at his shirt and shook his head before he got up off his desk and stepped in front of Layne.

After a call from Andrew, Russ had been expecting to hear from her. What he hadn't expected was this unhinged visit. "Did your father teach you nothing? No fuckin' respect." His words almost sounded like he pitied her.

Russell's hand grabbed a handful of her face, squishing her cheeks in his hand. A switchblade was pulled from his pocket and sprung open to expose the sharp edge of metal. He tapped the tip of the knife against her bottom lip.

Still trying to catch her ragged breaths from her outburst and the rush of adrenaline pulsing in her ears, she tried pulling her face back from the sharp threat, teasing the softness of her lip with whispers of violence and pain.

He pulled the blade away, compressing it back into the handle until the locking mechanism quietly clicked. "If you were anyone else, I'd be teaching you a little bit about respect. But, I'm going to give you a pass this one time only, Layne. You come into my damn territory again looking to start a war, I will make sure you get one, and you won't win. Do you understand me?" His hand still latched onto her face, digging into her skin uncomfortably.

"As long as you understand that if you ever approach any of my clients ever again, I won't only bring the war to you, but I will have half the city at my back when I do." Her arms jerked against the grip of Russ's men, holding her back.

"Those are big words coming from a little lady. You don't have the resources, everyone knows it. It's just a matter of time before what's left of Scott O'Reilly's grand enterprise is dismantled, right down to his two brats." His hand finally released her face, but the red marks of his hold remained on her skin.

Layne's eyes held all the warning they needed to.

"Tread lightly, Russ. I'd hate to put you at the top of my list."

He shook his head in disbelief and waved his hands at his two men on either side of her. "Please escort Miss O'Reilly out before she makes any other brash decisions today."

The two goons pulled her out of the room, her feet barely able to keep up with their steps as they guided her out a back entrance that led to the alleyway behind the building. She was given a harsh shove, sending her stumbling and nearly losing her footing until she caught hold of a chain link fence dividing this property from the next. The steel door shut behind them as the two men retreated back inside.

Layne's fingers curled around the thin ropes of metal of the fence and pressed her forehead to the cool links as she shut her eyes briefly. Her world was on the brink of collapse, and she felt powerless to stop it. One more client ripped from the O'Reilly books today meant two more were likely to follow. At this rate, they were going to be lucky to hold their ground for another couple of months.

CHAPTER ELEVEN

After her encounter with Spencer, she had been trying to pull her head back inside the game. As brash as it had been, Layne didn't regret storming into Russell's office and letting him know that she wasn't going down without a fight.

The event at Eric's house was only a few days away, and Liam's lack of leadership was going to sign both of their death warrants. It was quickly becoming clear that she couldn't run this business on her own, especially not without Liam's aid.

Layne sat on the floor of her dad's old office, now having been taken over by Liam. The house was empty most of the time since he had refused to give up his studio down in Tribeca. However, business was still conducted here. Well, what little business they had these days.

Surrounded by boxes, Layne pulled out piles of papers that appeared to be just thrown haphazardly into each box. She guessed that Liam had been the culprit and hadn't wanted to deal with any of the paperwork. The least he could have done was to keep everything organized in the boxes. Instead, she had to figure out why her great-grandmother's recipes were in folders labeled bank accounts.

She sighed as she dug through each piece of paper, her eyes scanned for anything that might be useful. Layne didn't even know what would be useful at this point, but she wasn't going to leave any stone unturned. Her dad had been old-fashioned, and he may not have left a paper trail for the less-than-legal aspects of his business, but everything else was done in a cold hard copy.

Layne sighed as everything seemed to lead nowhere. No useful contacts, no strategies, and no words of wisdom. A recipe for soda bread was not going to be the lottery ticket she needed. She sat there staring blankly at everything laid out before her, waiting for the answers to leap out of their hiding spot.

Her thoughts were disrupted when she heard the sounds of the front door opening and quickly slamming shut. Lifting her head at the intrusion, she pushed herself up onto her feet and stepped over several piles of documents.

Liam nearly ran into her when she got to the door, neither of them expecting the other to be there. She extended her hands out to brace herself in the event of an actual collision. Fortunately, all that resulted was a small bump into one another.

"What the hell are you doing here, Layne?" Her little brother already had a tone in his voice, making it clear he didn't appreciate her presence. His eyes looked beyond her and saw all the boxes and papers in disarray on the office floor. "What the fuck is this?"

She shrugged. "I'm going through Dad's things, looking for anything that might be useful."

Liam pushed past her, going to the nearest box and peering inside of it. "This is all trash; I should have just burned it all after the funeral."

He stepped away from the cardboard banker box, carelessly walking over some papers left on the ground on his way over to the wet bar built into the bookcase along the back wall.

While his back was turned to her, she began to clean up the mess she had made. One knee on the floor while she packed the papers back up, a blue letter-sized envelope slipped out from between a few other pages. It was seeing her name sprawled across it in her dad's handwriting that truly caught her eye.

Glancing up, she saw that Liam was still busying himself and opening up a fresh bottle of booze. Layne took the envelope and slid it into her back pocket. Quickly, she wrapped up cleaning the floor of the remaining disaster.

"While you're here, I got a call this morning," Liam spoke up before turning around and sipping whichever high-proof liquor had called to him today.

Layne finished stacking a few boxes on top of each other off to the side of the room. "From the therapist you haven't hired yet because you don't think you need one?" Not that she should have been one to talk, given her own mess she was actively ignoring.

He ground his teeth together, biting back the urge to

immediately lose his shit. No, he was biding his time on this. "It was from Russell Spencer."

Oh, *that* call. It had only been a matter of time before word got back to Liam, being that he was technically the O'Reilly man in charge. Out of professional courtesy, it wasn't unexpected that in events where another faction's associate stepped out of line, the big guys ended up hearing about it.

She crossed her arms in front of her chest. "Go ahead, Liam, say what you're going to say about it."

As he did, he waved his hands around in corresponding gestures with his words. "Who the hell do you think you are? Acting like you're the damn head of this family, making stupid as fuck decisions like you have the authority to do shit. Why can't you just leave everything alone and stay out of things?"

"Because I'm trying to clean up your inability to get shit done, Liam! How many times do we have to have this conversation? You want to sit back and let things roll. Do you know where that has gotten us? Our guys, the few we have left in our ranks, are coming to *me* to put out fires you should have made sure never existed. So, yeah, I may have made a stupid decision with Russ, but it's because I'm *tired* of playing this game with you."

He forced the glass in his hand down onto his desk with a loud clunk that threatened to put a crack in the bottom of the drinkware. "Get the hell out! I don't want to see your face in here again."

Layne goaded him. "Or what? What are you going to do, Li?" Her eyes locked on his every move.

He took the bait and stalked his way towards her. When there was little room between them, he forced his arms out in an explosive shove.

Fortunately, she had seen it coming a mile away and dodged to the side. She grabbed his non-dominant arm with both her hands and painfully twisted it behind his back while bending his wrist at an awkward angle. To further make her point, she shoved him forward face first into the door. Her foot came up and struck down on the back of his knee, causing him to automatically drop to the floor. Layne released his arm during his fall to his knees.

For extra measure, she grabbed a handful of his hair and drew his head back to look up at her. "I've learned how to play with the big boys, Liam. It's about damn time that you did, too." She thrust his face forward again, letting it collide with the door before she stepped back from him.

Liam howled out as he sat back on his ankles, his hands going up to his face where a superficial nosebleed had begun from the two collisions against the door.

She left him there, hoping he would have some sense come to him after that. Layne was doubtful, though. If Liam hadn't had his moment of grand enlightenment by now, she found it unlikely he ever would.

Once she was back in the driver's seat of her car, she sat there trying to focus on her several deep breaths after dealing with Liam's inability to do anything but manage to piss her off. She wanted nothing more right now than to take the edge off of things and lay in bed in a beautiful foggy haze to escape from the hell she was dealing with day in and day out. After Joey had verbally laid into her before disposing of most of the stash she had on hand, she had been trying to go without.

Reaching behind her into her back pocket, she retrieved the blue envelope she had discovered amongst the other papers. Her eyes looked over the curve of each letter of her name in her dad's elegant penmanship. A breath caught in her throat as thoughts about how much she needed him there right now crept into her mind.

"Layne, you will never have it easy in this business. All the odds are stacked against you." Her father solemnly looked at her as he sat up in his bed after yet another surgery.

She frowned, waiting for him to try and convince her to leave this lifestyle behind. Go get married, have a kid and all that bullshit.

He gave a reassuring smile instead. "But, that is what will be your greatest strength. Nobody pays attention to the team that has to overcome a fifty-point gap. Take advantage of that."

Hastily, she shoved the envelope into the center console between the two front seats. She needed to be anywhere else right now but here. She needed to be somewhere where she could clear her mind. Layne needed a place where all the noise of her thoughts weren't overwhelming her.

"C'mon." Joey kept a hold of her hand and led her towards the quiet and unoccupied beach.

It was a welcome reprieve from the constant noise pollution of Manhattan. Joey released her hand so he could hide both his hands in his pockets as he stared at the last bit of sun reflecting off the water as it sunk lower in the sky.

"It's not much, but I like to come here when things get too heavy."

Layne smiled at her memories replaying in her head. The recollection of their first date together stirred up a warmth deep inside of her chest. She started up the engine of her car and drove off. Maybe a trip over to that quiet little spot in Brooklyn would do her good.

CHAPTER TWELVE

The Saturday night of the party came a lot quicker than she wanted. A pit had been growing in her stomach since the moment she woke up that morning.

All day, she had been pacing her house, wondering what the hell to do with her time. She had tried everything from reading, streaming a bunch of shows she needed to catch up on, and even attempted cleaning the house. None of it lasted very long before she felt compelled to move on to the next thing.

She stared at herself in the mirror and murmured. "Get your shit together." Her father had always been able to sternly direct her to what she needed to do, even if she didn't listen all the time. Now, she was left without that looming guidance in her life. It was only the lingering memories that haunted her, serving as a reminder of whose daughter she was.

One of the silver linings of having a wide open

schedule for the first half of the day was that she could take her time getting ready. It also served as a perfect storm to overthink everything right down to the most meaningless details.

Layne preferred her hair down but kept it styled so one side of the dark chestnut locks was pulled back away from her face with some strategically placed pins. She brushed on some makeup, going for an elegant evening look with a seductively smokey eye and a flirty shade of dusty pink on her lips.

Pulling her dress off its hanger, she shimmied into it. The silky fabric was unforgiving in how it adhered to the curves and lines of her body. The regal shade of purple complimented her fair skin, which there was plenty of it exposed to capture the attention of any wandering eyes.

The dress was a halter-style gown that left her back fully open, down until the material wrapped around the roundness of her ass. The strap around her neck was embroidered with tiny shimmering crystals that dove down into a steep neckline.

The remainder of the dress fell into a narrow skirt with a slit just high enough to be considered a classy display of the flesh of her leg and, more practically, allow for more ease of movement.

Lastly, the outfit wasn't going to be complete without a little bit of safety insurance. She latched a thin strap to her upper thigh where a dagger was slid into the sheath. If shit went south tonight, she refused to be playing a game of 'could this random item be used as a weapon'?

After picking out a small clutch and strapping on her

heels, she met her driver outside of her house. He held the door to the back seat of the SUV open for her with a heart-warming smile. "You look radiant, Ms. O'Reilly."

The older man with silvery grey hair, Artie, had been working for her family for years. She didn't make a habit of using his services too often, but on a night like tonight, where appearances were everything, she opted for the car service.

From everything she had heard about the guests in attendance, there were going to be some of the most impor-tant names in criminal organizations across the city coming together under the guise of raising funds for charity. It wouldn't be all the big bad guys there, of course. Politi-cians, financiers, judiciaries, and others amongst New York's social elite would also be in attendance.

"Thanks, Art. You've always had the kindest things to say." Her hand gave his arm a gentle squeeze while she sweetly smiled at him before sliding into the back seat. The door shut behind her, and moments later, he was driving her to the Ellis residence not too far from where she lived. It was only about ten minutes further uptown. A little too close for Layne's tastes, but she wasn't about to pack up and move on Eric's account.

By the time Artie pulled up, where others were also unloading from their vehicles, she was a solid ten minutes late. Still socially acceptable in her mind and by elitist stan-dards. Layne wasn't in a rush to kick off this evening, which she had been dreading ever since she agreed to it.

While she sat in the back seat, she wrestled with her nerves that refused to settle down. This should be like any other job she had ever had a hand in. Joey's presence should have been inconsequential. However, she still found herself spending far too much time thinking about his involvement in tonight's affairs instead of thinking about Eric's proposition to salvage the O'Reilly family business.

The back passenger door swung open, and instead of being greeted by her driver, she noticed Joey standing there with his hand reaching out to her.

Her breath caught in her chest as she saw him dressed in the sharp lines of a tux, a crisp white shirt underneath the black jacket, and a corresponding black vest and tie. The way it fit the muscles of his upper body reminded her of the delicious gift underneath all that packaging. The creep of his neck tattoos peeked up past the top of his collar, and the ink on his hands was easily visible. It was the only indication that he wasn't in the same class as the rest of the pompous assholes in attendance.

Layne did her best to remember to breathe and not appear as shell-shocked as she felt seeing him all cleaned up for once. But, damn, could that man wear a tux.

Stubbornly, she ignored his offer of assistance, gathering the lower half of her dress and stepping out onto the sidewalk on her own accord. The length of her dress fell around her legs down to her feet, which were set in a sparkling set of heels encrusted with shimmering crystals that matched the shine of the crystals on her halter straps.

He dropped his hand back to his side, but his eyes never left her. Joey didn't usually break the serious façade when it came to his work, but in this case, Layne did manage to pick up on the subtle shift in his brown eyes. A shift that told her she wasn't the only one with a view worth appreciating. His tongue subtly swiped across his lower lip, an act that one would expect while eyeing a particularly decadent dessert.

"You're late." A slight edge of frustration could be heard hanging off the end of his words.

Layne gave a nonchalant shrug with a smile, knowing how it was eating away at him and how she was not bothered in the least about her tardiness to this little affair. "I guess you should have come picked me up if you wanted me to be on time."

After she was out of the car, he shut the door and stepped up to join her at her side. His arm wrapped around her lower back, pulling her in close to his side as he leaned in and whispered, "Remember, I'm still here as part of your security detail. Which as I recall from the last time I kept my eyes on you full-time, you were extremely satisfied with my services." His charismatic smirk stretched across his face.

As people walked past them on their way up to the front door, Layne plastered an over-the-top saccharin smile on her face. Tonight was all about wearing an invisible mask that told a story that not only did she want to be here, but she belonged here. That included upkeeping the premise of Joey being part of her security.

She didn't even look at him as she quietly responded. "I'm in four-inch heels, a dress that wants me to be ten pounds lighter, and my escort is breathing down my neck. You're asking a hell of a lot right now for me to look satisfied with *any* of your services."

His voice dropped down to a dominant tone, with his words teasing along her skin. "You used to like it when I did things to your neck."

Uncontrollably, her cheeks flushed a delicate shade of pink before her hand slapped his chest, and she managed to slither away from his arm that wrapped around her. "Stop dicking around."

Joey smirked, noting that he had managed to get under her skin. "Interesting choice of words."

Layne shook her head while trying to keep things between them strictly business. After all, that was the agreement, wasn't it? She would help him tonight, and then he would be on his merry way.

Quickly ending the conversation and moving straight on to the matter at hand, she followed the rest of the guests dressed to the nines into the obscenely luxurious private home of Eric Ellis.

It was situated on a prized corner lot and was previously an old printing house that had undergone massive renovations that turned it into a residential space to be admired by the city's deepest pockets.

What most people failed to notice was the extensive security on the outside. Cameras were tucked into various corners at multiple angles, turning the home into a fortress. Nobody was coming or going from this place without it being captured on video. At least, mostly nobody.

When Layne and Joey both approached the entrance, there was a delay in movement as everyone was checking in with event planners to ensure no unwanted or uninvited party guests tried to sneak their way in.

Joey stuck close to her, only a step behind, and even then, she could still feel his gaze roaming over her body. Despite all of her conflicted feelings, she couldn't deny that having him here with her put a part of her soul at ease. Something she hadn't felt in some time.

When it was finally her turn to check in, she smiled pleasantly at the woman who looked like she was typically as quiet as a mouse. Her condensed facial features were speckled with a few light freckles, and her brunette locks of hair were tied back into a short but low ponytail.

"Name, please?" Yup, Layne was right, the woman's voice was soft as a whisper in a confessional booth.

"Layne O'Reilly." While the woman began scrolling through an iPad with names on it, Layne took a glance at the entryway. The gothic style decor was a little over the top for her tastes, but it was better than the same boring old-money style that most of uptown was accustomed to.

The woman looked up from the screen and looked at Layne and then over at Joey. "I'm sorry, Ms. O'Reilly, but I don't see a plus one next to your name."

Joey stepped forward to intervene, but Layne rested a hand on his bicep as a signal for him to back down.

"Oh, he's not my date, he's my security. I didn't realize I needed to register him; I thought it was already taken into consideration."

The poor girl looked like she was on the edge of tears as an apologetic look crossed her face. "I do apologize, but we can't allow anyone inside who hasn't been pre-cleared. Mr. Ellis' orders."

This wasn't off to a great start at all. Right as Layne

was about to choose some stronger words to make her point to this delicate little rose, she heard Eric's familiar voice as he approached. "Laura, it's ok." His hand patted the woman's shoulder and motioned for her to continue checking in other guests.

The host himself was done up in a tailored tuxedo that was all black right down to the shirt. His hair was slicked back except for a small piece that was having no part of compliance with the rest of it. With all the darkness wrapped around him, the blue of his eyes particularly stood out more than normal.

He turned to Layne and stood there, taking his time drinking in the image of her all dolled up. An image that he surely thought was solely for his benefit.

Eric's eyes memorized every fine detail and curve that was on public display. His lips parted in awe, drawn in by the vision in front of him.

"My little harpy, you do not disappoint." He exhaled a breath while his gaze remained locked on the vision that stood before him.

His hand reached out to take hers, bringing it up to his mouth, where he pressed a lingering kiss to the back of it. The gesture got minutely more intimate when his eyes lifted to stare at her as he did so.

The presence standing at her back was getting restless as Joey cleared his throat loudly.

Hearing the grumpy disruption behind her, Layne slid her hand out of Eric's slowly. "Eric, I didn't realize that I needed to register my security for the evening. I hope it won't be a problem."

The icy hue of Eric's eyes looked past Layne at the familiar tall and well-built man accompanying Layne. Judgment and condescension settled across his face. Their prior standoff at the rock concert while he was enjoying Layne's company had left a sour taste in his mouth.

He was quick to shift back into a man full of incredible charm the second he returned his look to Layne. "Of course not. Though, I will say there was no need for it. You have my full protection while you are here."

Joey interrupted. "It's not your job to keep her protected."

Eric gave a light shrug. "No. I suppose you're right; it's not. Not yet, anyway."

Starting to suffocate with the tensions growing in the air and the amount of testosterone being pissed around, Layne awkwardly tried to change the subject and move things along.

"I'm sure you have other guests to greet, I don't want to keep you from your obligations." She preferred he kept busy with all the other guests for as long as possible.

Eric gave a nod of appreciation that she recognized he had other duties to see to. "I look forward to us picking up our conversation later on the arrangement we've been discussing."

Before anything more could be said, a rather heftily round man came up to Eric and slapped a hand on the back of his shoulder. A rowdy greeting followed before immediately diving into a conversation about the renovations that were done to the recently acquired building.

Layne took the window of opportunity to scurry further

inside, heading towards the stairs that led up to the next floor. According to the signage, that's where the primary party spot was.

As for Joey, he didn't let her get too far ahead of him. "What did he mean by 'not yet,' Layne?"

She gave an irritable sigh as she began to conquer one step at a time without tripping over her dress. "How the hell should I know?"

Once they were on the second floor, he pulled her by her elbow off to the side to peer into her eyes, looking for a better response from her. "Tell me what he meant. I'm not asking twice."

She glanced around in paranoia that someone would overhear them, so she kept her voice down to a whisper, hoping that Joey would do the same. "Even if you did ask twice, I wouldn't have anything to tell you. Now, I got you in here, go do whatever it is you came here to do."

There was no sense in getting him worked up and involved in her business affairs. He was here to do a job, as was she. The only difference was that his job was hopefully short-lived, while hers had more permanent consequences.

As she pried her arm out of his hand, Layne saw Joey's hands squeeze into tight fists in either anger or frustration — she couldn't tell which it was.

"This conversation isn't over," he warned. Knowing how well Joey let go of things, she knew damn well that he was going to continue poking the bear until he got a response. "I won't be far," he added before walking off.

Layne watched as he stepped away from her, blending

into the hustle and bustle of the other guests who were also making their way towards all the festivities.

After Joey's departure, the tension in her body eased up momentarily while her emerald hues relaxed. With her thoughts becoming less clouded by his presence, she realized she desperately needed to drink half the bar if she was ever going to survive this evening.

CHAPTER THIRTEEN

I t had been a painful and tedious task of playing all the social elitist games of fake smiles, fake pleasantries, and fake laughter at terrible jokes. Layne had spent the last forty-five minutes fielding conversations with various other guests. Some of whom she knew and others who were introduced to her.

Did she care about any of the pretentious assholes? Not a single ounce of care was to be found within her. But she had put on a smile that left her cheeks sore and aching for the sake of keeping a strong front. The last thing she needed to show was weakness while surrounded by representatives of various criminal factions that were in attendance.

Servers were constantly coming around offering beverages, collecting empty glasses, and providing a variety of hors d'oeuvres for those needing something to soak up the freely flowing booze.

There was live music playing primarily classical tunes,

and if the songs weren't Beethoven or Mozart, they were classical renditions of modern melodies. The room's vaulted ceilings that seemed to go on forever made for acoustics that would have any musician swooning.

Most of those chattering away with small talk or even more serious conversations stuck to the perimeter of the room, while others danced to whatever was being played at the moment.

Finally breaking free from a conversation with an elderly man that couldn't hear for shit, Layne found her way to the bar. She ordered another glass of wine from the swamped bartender and stood there thirstily drinking down the chardonnay.

From behind her, a hand slid down over her bare shoulder with fingertips that caressed the back of her arm. She spun around to see the man who had invited her there. Eric's face was full of excitement. "Here you are. Follow me; I have something I would like to show you."

Eric offered his arm to Layne, who reluctantly took it as he guided them to a pair of glass french doors. Opening one and allowing her to step outside first, she saw the balcony had an artist's dream view of the expansive Central Park.

As dusk was fading into evening, it was eating away at the sky in shades of oranges and reds before fading into darker hues.

Layne sipped from her wine glass as she placed a hand on the edge of the balcony's rail, taking in the sight.

With Eric at her back, his hands rested on her bare shoulders as he looked past her at the picturesque scene laid out before them. He whispered into her ear. "I will never grow tired of this view." The meaning behind his words was layered with more than just one view he was enjoying.

She tried to keep the tension at bay as it was clear he wasn't just talking about the beauty of nature doing its thing. Her head turned towards him. "Never is a strong word."

"Yes, it is." He didn't apologize for using it, though.

Finally, she fully turned to face him, noticing that they were the only ones enjoying the privacy of the balcony. "I figured you would be busy mingling with all your guests."

"I'm only concerned with spending time with one very important guest here tonight. I hope you don't mind." His grin held a touch of cockiness that it still wouldn't concern him, even if she did mind.

He continued, "I was hoping we could talk a little more, away from any nosey eavesdroppers."

Swallowing more of the expensive vintage in her glass, Layne prompted him with the obvious question. "About?"

Eric gave her a chiding look. "Don't be coy; you know exactly what I would like to talk about. I met with one of my associates downtown earlier, and there are a lot of unhappy folks with the way the O'Reilly Enterprise is handling things. I know you are doing your best to do damage control, but time is of the essence if you're going to make a move—if *we* are going to make a move."

She looked down into her wine glass, watching the small ripples of movement as she swirled the liquid around idly inside the glass. "I know."

"Tell me how to make this comfortable for you. I have already promised that you would never be without anything you ever need. We can rise together and establish a choke-hold on the other factions who are threatening to overthrow your family and everything it's ever stood for." His hand moved under her chin and gently lifted it so he could remove her focus from her beverage.

Hesitation was not just in her voice but in her body language as well. "It's a big decision, and I don't want to make it lightly."

"I don't expect you to." He nodded and then decided to switch up his strategy. He eased the wine glass out of her hand and placed it on the ledge behind her. "Dance with me."

"I don't dance, Eric." Her heartbeat sped up with panic over the idea of sharing a close space with him on the dance floor in front of so many pairs of eyes.

Despite her reluctance, he took her hand and led her back inside and onto the dance floor. "I do, and I make a point to share at least one dance with a beautiful woman during these parties." He found a spot in the middle of the floor, turning to face her with a look meant for a predator to lure in its prey.

He slid his hand around her waist onto the bare skin on the small of her back and forcefully pulled her in toward him until the fronts of their bodies were touching. His other hand, by contrast, lightly held onto hers.

Intuitively, she rested a hand on top of his shoulder as she found the space between them entirely gone. The music playing in the room transitioned over to a slow and haunting tune. One that seemed to tell a sad yet dark love story with its minor notes and dramatic crescendos and decrescendos.

Eric took the lead by beginning to move them across the dance floor, never once easing up his hold on her. His captivating blue eyes bore down on her, intent on maintaining all of his focus on her. Seeing the way he seemingly ignored everything else around them, Layne never once thought about her feet.

He brought his mouth to her ear as he whispered, "You promised me an answer tonight."

Briefly, she closed her eyes as the moment she had been dreading finally arrived. Layne had to make her choice. A choice she had never wanted to make for herself. A choice the person she was years ago would have never considered.

Her mind recounted each struggle up until this point. Liam's incompetence. The lost ranks of employees. Financials circling the drain. Clients flocking to other organizations. The warning shots that had been fired. Everything was piling up. How much longer before it was game over?

When she opened her eyes back up, revealing the depths of her green hues, he granted a moment of air from their tight hold as he raised her arm and twirled her around in a slow and elegant circle before drawing her back up against him.

When she came back into his hold, she saw a familiar pair of eyes watching from the depths of the crowd. Eyes that tugged heavily on her heart. Eyes that were full of darkness at what they were witnessing. Joey stood back, but even from where Layne was, she could feel the heat radiating off his emotions.

"I know what I promised." That was all she could respond to Eric with, trying not to allow herself to get distracted.

His hand inched lower along her back until it reached where the smooth material of her dress began at the top curve of her ass. Boldly and without hesitation or permission, he continued his exploration with his fingers. His fingertips slipped down between her skin and the dress, grazing over the hem of her seamless thong just underneath.

His voice had a rasp to it as he spoke quietly to her. "That's not an answer."

With his fingers still lingering inside the back of her dress, her mind struggled to stay in the moment. Layne felt a warmth in her core begin to spread underneath his touch. Her nipples strained against the fabric of her dress as they stiffened into peaks.

She knew her world was crumbling, and she couldn't stop it on her own. It felt as though she was a frightened mare out in the wild, and a lasso was already tied around her throat.

Layne glanced past Eric's shoulder while they continued to move slowly together to the tender notes of the song. The invisible mask she attempted to maintain broke, and her eyes betrayed her as they filled with dread and panic. She searched for any sign of Joey in the crowd.

Whatever was reflected in her eyes, Joey didn't like it the moment he saw it. He abruptly began to push towards them, creating a path for himself through the crowd.

Not realizing that she and Eric had gradually come to a

standstill as the song faded to the next, his hand released its hold on hers and turned her face to force her attention back to him. "Look at me and give me an answer. No more stalling."

His demand held something new in it, something laced with a promise of death. It was a tone she was very familiar with in all her years in this lifestyle. The promise may not have been a threat from him, but there was no mistake that death was knocking on the O'Reilly door. Eric was just the one offering her a way to chase away the nightmares.

Her words felt like they were choking her while getting lodged in her throat. "Yes."

Eric tilted his head inquisitively, looking for clarity. "Yes, what?" The man wasn't stupid; he just wanted to hear her say it in no uncertain terms.

The sinking feeling in her stomach grew heavier. "Yes, to the merger and this alliance." Layne swallowed down her stubborn pride. "I'll marry you."

A victorious smile curved over his mouth as he whispered against her lips. "You're all mine now, my little harpy." He leaned forward so his mouth could territorially claim her lips while his arm squeezed tighter around her.

Things were abruptly broken apart when an arm came between them, prying Layne and Eric away from one another. Joey protectively pulled Layne back, putting himself between her and Eric.

Joey held his ground there with his eyes filled with a level of possessiveness Layne had never seen before. Fury was simmering underneath the surface as he kept it aimed at Eric. His jaw was tightly clenched as he spoke through his teeth. "Miss O'Reilly, unfortunately, needs to leave for the evening. A business matter has come up requiring her attention."

As the reality of what she had just done sank in, she made a futile attempt to shake off all the feelings that were crashing like relentless waves into her. The room began to feel too crowded. Layne backed up a step, nearly knocking into another guest before she turned and quickly headed for the exit while Eric was otherwise distracted by Joey.

As for Joey, when he went to follow after her, Eric's hand clamped down on his arm. An equally vile look was directed at Joey. "Let's get one thing straight. As of right now, she's mine to handle as I see fit. What she does is my concern, not yours."

Instead of giving in to the temptation of physically demolishing Eric's face and devolving into a blind rage, Joey gave a dark smile in amusement. "I don't give a fuck what you think you're entitled to. Touch her again, and I'll kill you. I won't just kill you, but I will make sure that you suffer an unfathomable level of pain before you beg for me to end your life."

Roughly, he shoved Eric's hand away and left to follow Layne.

When he managed to get eyes on her, she was already at the front doors pushing against several people coming back inside from having a smoke.

"Layne!" He called for her, hoping to get her to at least wait for him.

She never heard him through the roaring of her inner monologue that was screaming inside of her head. Her thoughts told her how much she had to do this for survival while simultaneously berating herself for being so damn stupid in agreeing to be at a man's mercy.

When Joey caught up to her, he didn't immediately say a word. Instead, his hand dropped down to take hers and guide her to where his Challenger was parked in an empty church parking lot. Layne let him guide her to the lot across the street. The plan had always been for him to drop her off at home after the party, just that the night had ended much sooner than either of them planned for.

He opened the passenger door for her to get safely settled. Joey pulled his suit jacket off, balling it up and forcefully tossing it into the backseat before he got into the driver's seat. He slammed his door shut with a force that rattled components inside the dash.

Layne wasn't sure what to say to him or where to even begin to explain what she was doing, if he even cared. Her emerald eyes watched him as he backed out of the parking space, and the tires squealed against the pavement as he left the lot.

His hands yanked at his tie, loosening it around his neck enough to unbutton the top couple of buttons of his shirt. Joey's breathing was heavy and ragged as he replayed what he had just witnessed at the party. It wasn't just what he saw, but the reading of how her lips moved to speak words to Eric he would never understand the reasoning for.

"Joey—"

He cut off her words. "What the fuck are you thinking?! Do you even know what type of monster Eric Ellis is?" His eyes parted from the road for a second to shoot a glance at her.

Trying to keep her voice calm enough for the both of them, she spoke quietly. "You don't understand; my hands are tied here. It's the only option I have. I can't sit around and wait for a miracle that is never coming."

His hand squeezed onto the top of the steering wheel. "You're not doing this."

She reached over and put her hand on top of his while he held onto the gear shifter. "I am doing this. I have to. I don't know why the hell you're so bent out of shape about it. You came back for your one favor, which, by the way, you're welcome."

His eyes looked down at her hand that was touching his, covering up the sprawling tattoos etched into his flesh. Joey made a sharp turn and pulled into an empty parking garage. He accelerated up the ramp of each floor until they reached the top level on the roof.

"What are you doing?" She stared at him questioningly as he pulled into the cement structure.

He parked the car diagonally across several spaces and got out. Layne flung open her door and met him in front of the Challenger, the headlights left on and cutting through the darkness of the night.

Now, she was beginning to slip as her anger started to rear its head. "What is your problem, Joey?!" Her hands shoved his chest, only for him to stay solidly planted on his feet as his eyes were locked on her. The rage she had seen in his eyes earlier now had melted into a softer burn.

"It's you. It's always been you." His statement was

calm, but the words had a storm brewing behind them. When she tried to shove him again, he wrapped his hands around her wrists. "He doesn't deserve you."

She knew better than to struggle against his grasp. "And you do?"

He took another step closer to her, still restraining her wrists in front of her. "I've made some mistakes, but I'm not going to let you fall further down this spiral."

Layne rolled her eyes that he thought she was having any sort of spiraling crisis in her life that she couldn't handle on her own without his help.

"Roll your eyes again at me and see what happens, Layney." A soft growl rolled over his words. A growl that prompted several goosebumps to flitter across her skin.

Her teeth scraped over her bottom lip as his taunt had her body reacting with a heavy sense of arousal between her thighs. No matter how long it had been, he had always managed to get her body to respond with the slightest of actions or words.

She rolled her eyes at him.

CHAPTER FOURTEEN

Unsure what caused her to instigate him, Layne didn't have long before he reacted. Joey's hands dropped their hold on her wrists and pulled her face to his. His lips crashed against her mouth with a blazing kiss filled with pent-up emotions.

As she released a small gasp, his tongue took advantage and slid into her mouth to devour her taste. The electricity between them felt incredibly familiar, but now there was an edge of something else in how he touched her, tasted her, and held her.

She couldn't tell who was breathing the air out of whose lungs as they stood there on the roof of the empty parking garage.

Each movement he made prompted a chain reaction of sensations throughout her body. His hands roamed down over the front of her dress, making a momentary stop as they settled over her breasts. The palms of his hands aggressively kneaded each of the supple swells on her chest. She leaned her body into him, encouraging him to continue.

Joey's lips broke away from hers. "I told you once before, I *always* fight for what's mine. I lied. I will bring the fires of hell earthside if it means keeping you in my arms." His eyes lit up with an inferno of need for the woman standing before him.

He dropped his hands down to her waist and guided her backward. When she felt the front bumper of his car against the back of her legs, he picked her up and laid her down on the hood. The metal pressed against her bare back was still warm from the engine underneath.

Still craving more of him, she grinned. "Do you really think hellfire is going to keep me here with you?"

His eyes assessed what was laid out in front of him. Joey took one of her feet and ran his hands down the length of her leg slowly. The slit of the dress fell away up until its stopping point a couple of inches above her knee. "I don't know, Layney, but I'm going to find out."

Grasping a hem on each side of the slit, he yanked in one forceful motion to tear the fabric further up until it ripped all the way up to her hip.

It took Layne by surprise, and she should have been angry about how he just ruined a dress that had cost a small fortune. Yet, all she could think of was how she had wished he had torn it right in two.

With the night air whispering over the freshly exposed skin of her thigh, her black sheath containing her blade was revealed on her upper thigh. Joey immediately took notice and gave a playful smirk. "Look what we have here."

"A girl has to be prepared for anything. You never know when a man in a mask might show up." She smirked right back at him.

His hand unsnapped the knife, removing it from its holding place. Expertly, he twirled it in his hand while examining it, the look on his face made it obvious he had more than just thoughts of admiration for her weapon.

Joey dragged the tip of the blade along the inside of her thigh, letting the sharp edge threaten to split her flesh with any wrong turn or too much pressure.

She held her breath as she watched the steel tip hover over her femoral artery before continuing to move further north. Carefully, he hooked the knife underneath the thin garment that was a poor excuse for panties. With one upward motion, her underwear was sliced at the perfect junctures to fall away from her body.

While he licked his lips in anticipation of what was laid out before him, Joey tossed the blade to the side; it clattered as it hit the concrete.

"Joey," she began to warn, "this—us, can't—"

He leaned over; his hands pressed against the hood on either side of her as he slid a hand up over her throat. He gripped it firmly without depriving her of anything as he stared down into her eyes. "I need you to stop thinking so much, Layney."

She lost her train of thought as his face hovered above hers, leaving her lips parted around stubborn words that never made it out.

His hand fell from her throat and buried into her hair along the back of her head; he pulled her head up so that she could meet him halfway. Their kiss connected and exploded like a busted dam of emotions. The more she tasted him, the less she cared about anything or anyone else in the world.

His free hand rubbed down over her side until it found the exposed flesh of her hip. Layne moved her hips in an effort to motivate his hand to move exactly where she needed it most.

Her hand grabbed the tail of his tie, pulling on it to keep him there, hovering over top of her as she deepened the kiss further into an abyss of passion. Their tongues danced with one another, reacquainting themselves with each other's sinful tastes.

Breaking the connection of their mouths briefly, Joey nibbled on her bottom lip. "Tell me this is what you want." His finger teasingly grazed along her slit, purposely avoiding her aching clit.

Moaning quietly, feeling his touch so close to the small bundle of nerves between her legs, she tried to capture his lips again, only this time, his grasp on her hair prevented her from closing the distance.

Joey knowingly smirked. "Tell me."

Her eyes gazed up at him, already feeling breathless with need and desperation. "I want all of this. I've always wanted all of you."

"There's my good girl that I've missed so much." He took her mouth against his again while his finger stroked over her sensitive arousal, rewarding her with a jolt of pleasure.

Her moan got lost against his mouth as her hips drove against his touch. Layne's hands furiously worked to loosen his tie entirely to get to the remaining buttons of his shirt and the corresponding vest. With each button coming undone, Joey's fingers worked over her sex more fervently, making her concentration on the menial task increasingly more difficult.

By the time she released the last button, it caused his shirt to fall open to expose the rippling muscles of his chest, which had collected several more tattoos since she had seen it last. It was difficult to make out the designs in the dark of the night, but the one that stood out the most was a shamrock drenched in blood located directly over his heart.

Layne's mind wandered with questions as her fingertips delicately drifted over the red and green that stood out on his pec.

Before she could expend any more thoughts on his additional ink, three fingers were shoved deeply inside of her. Her hands latched onto his open shirt, scrunching up the fabric in her fists. A sound of straight pleasure was ripped out of her mouth and swallowed up by the stars themselves.

Joey's fingers curled up to massage over the particular spot deep inside of her each time he thrust his digits into her body. Her hips bucked against his hand while his thumb continued to circle over her throbbing clit.

The promise of release was descending on her, but

before she could get a taste of it, he withdrew his hand from between her thighs.

"No, no, no. I was so close." She groaned in frustration the moment her orgasm began to settle back down into her lower stomach.

He pulled back, and the sound of his belt unbuckling could be heard now that he wasn't coaxing moans out of her. Joey grinned. "I know, but I need my cock to feel how hard you're going to come for me."

Reaching into his boxer briefs, he pulled out his hard length. His chocolate-colored eyes were filled with raw desire as he saw her on the hood of his car, soaking wet with need. His tatted-up fist wrapped around his cock and stroked himself twice while enjoying the sight of her laid out before him, ready for the taking.

Lowering himself down on top of her, he taunted her with the tip of his hardness pressing against her swollen clit. Kissing her a little more gently this time, he ran his thumb down over her bottom lip.

"Are you going to run away from me this time, Layney? Or are you going to finally open yourself up to me?" Joey's voice was as soft as that kiss he had just laid on her.

She shook her head. "You know it's not that easy."

Sternly, he responded. "I asked a question." He rubbed his length against her, prompting her hips to press against him with a deep yearning and the sound of her whimper.

Trying to keep her thoughts straight was proving to be quite the challenge as he distracted her even more so with his mouth nibbling along her throat one possessive nip at a time.

"I can feel how wet your pussy is against my dick, how much you want me inside of you. How much it wants me back where I belong." His tongue teasingly licked along the hollow of her throat near her collarbone.

Layne's back arched slightly, pressing up against him as the warmth of his mouth worshiped her skin. She gave him the answer they both needed to hear. "I won't run from you."

A spark lit up in his eyes. "Damn right, you won't. After I'm done with you, you'll be lucky to walk." He rammed himself fully inside of her, unleashing any final bit of restraint he had been clinging onto.

Her body jolted against the hard metal of the Challenger's hood underneath her as a moan came straight from the depths of her center and was swallowed up by the night sky. The vehicle's suspension shifted with each shove of himself into her body.

Layne's fingers dug into his back as the ecstasy she had been pining for since he had been gone was now coming to her full force.

Clear as the evening sky, Joey had been craving this as much as she had. His breaths ran hard as her inner walls wrapped around his shaft, welcoming him deep inside of her.

As she locked her legs around his waist, the skirt of her dress fell away from her lower half, draping against the front of the car. Her body trembled against him, her mouth dragging kisses anywhere she could plant them between her pleasure-laden moans.

"Joey! You're going to—I'm going to—" Layne cried out as the swelling tidal wave began to break its crest.

"That's it, fuckin' come for me, Layney. I want your pussy to fuckin' welcome my dick back home." Pumping his thickness even harder into her, repeatedly hitting the sweet spot relentlessly, her words had only incited him to continue the deliciously sinful assault between her thighs.

New stars came into her vision aside from the ones speckling the blanket of the universe above them. Her release overcame her and spilled onto him, threatening to send her to a blissful existence not on this planet.

He clenched his teeth as his own body began to shudder, feeling Layne's tightness squeeze around him even tighter. Joey's movements began to grow less and less controlled before he groaned out in a feral roar as he gave one final shove of his cock into her as far as he could get. His peak was reached as he spilled himself deep into her body with several spasms of his cock.

Collapsing down on top of her, he laid his head against her chest, hearing both his own heartbeat pounding away inside of him alongside Layne's pulsing heart against his stubbled cheek.

As her body began to relax from the height of her climax, he lifted his head to stare at her lazily. "You still with me?"

Layne nodded with a smile, feeling nearly cross-eyed from the intensity of the orgasm. "Mmhmm, barely, but I'm here."

He smirked. "Such a good girl for me." His hand ran over the side of her face affectionately.

The cool breeze on the parking garage rooftop should have sent a chill through her body, but all she could feel was the heat and passion still burning in her veins.

Layne knew it had been far too long since he had been gone, and now that he was back, she wasn't sure she had the strength in her to ever set him free again. Consequences be damned.

CHAPTER FIFTEEN

After their mind-shattering romp on the hood of Joey's car underneath Manhattan's night sky, he drove her back to her house. Things stayed light conversationally between them, with zero mention of Eric and what all of this was truly going to mean, if anything at all.

Layne could have begged him to stay the night with her and make her forget all about her life's chaos, but he had to take care of a few things related to his adventures inside the Ellis residence. She tried to mask the disappointment on her face, and whether or not she had failed miserably at that, he hadn't let on.

While alone in her bathroom, she removed the last of her makeup and tossed the sullied cotton pad into a wastebasket. Layne stared at herself in the mirror as her dark thoughts began to creep back into her head. Why was it that her life had to always come with complications? Couldn't a girl just work for a criminal organization and eat her cake, too?

She promised she wouldn't run, but she also needed to keep the family business alive. Liam was useless. Eric was her only lifeline, and she had agreed to tie herself to him. Joey may have ordered her to stop thinking so much while he ravished her, but now that he wasn't there? She couldn't stop thinking about the harsh reality of life looming over her. One night with Joey didn't change her circumstances.

With a mixture of intense emotions trying to surface, she squashed them all down deep inside of her. To aid in that endeavor, she popped a pill to make her forget they existed and ensure she didn't toss and turn all night. Joey may have disposed of the stash she had on hand in her purse, but inside her medicine cabinet, she had another bottle with a few tablets still remaining.

The very next morning, she heard some loud voices and power tools outside of her bedroom window. It sounded like it was not just coming from the back of her house but the side and front as well. If this had been midtown, she wouldn't have thought anything of it, but it was typically far quieter this time of day in her neighborhood.

Her bare feet walked across the cool wooden floor of her bedroom as she pushed the sheer curtain to the side to see what the hell was going on out there.

Surprise didn't begin to cover what she saw, which led to her stumbling over her own feet as she ran downstairs to the front door. She swung it open wildly to begin raising all hell on earth.

The poor workers got a hell of a sight when she

appeared in the doorway of her home. Her long locks were still a tangled disaster from sleep and leftover hairspray from the night before, and she was barefoot and wearing nothing but a pair of bright green boy shorts coupled with a black tank.

"What the fuck is going on here?!" She stared at the men on ladders by her windows and near her front stoop. They were all carrying electronic equipment, wires, and various tools.

Despite the brisk autumn air pulling a shiver from her scarcely clothed body, she stepped down onto the front stoop to get a better assessment of the work being done— work she hadn't requested.

The men all looked dumbfounded while sharing glances amongst themselves and not sharing any answers with her.

That's when Eric rounded the corner, waving with his hand to the men to continue their work.

"Layne, I'm so sorry, I tried calling but didn't get an answer." He didn't sound one bit of fucking sorry to her.

One man uninstalled one of her security cameras mounted near a window. Layne couldn't believe her eyes, and she pointed at the guy. "*Hey*! What the fuck?!"

Eric softly wrapped a hand around her arm. "Why don't we go inside and talk, hm? I will explain everything."

She looked down at his hand touching her and then up into those stark blue eyes he had. Sliding her arm out of his hold with a glare, she walked inside, not caring who saw the lower curve of her cheeks peeking out from the bottom of her panties.

The front door closed behind Eric as he began to dial up

the charm, mistakenly thinking that it was going to make her ok with strangers doing work on her house, which she hadn't approved.

"You want to explain what the hell those guys are doing with my security cameras?" She crossed her arms in front of her chest, not particularly caring how little clothing she had on at the moment.

Eric softened his look while trying to reassure her. "The security system you have is inadequate. Now that we are coming together, your safety is my utmost concern."

Bullshit—an anosmic bloodhound would still be able to smell it a mile away.

He was wearing a black dress shirt left untucked; the sleeves rolled up to his elbows, and a pair of jeans that looked like they had never seen a day of wear and tear. Eric stepped up to her, placing his hands on the edges of her shoulders.

"After you left last night, I was made aware of a concerning incident that occurred in my private office upstairs."

Her face softened up as her curiosity was piqued. "An incident?"

A sigh passed through his lips. "Two of my men were killed."

Immediately, her mind was back on Joey, but this time, it was what had brought him to the party in the first place and his disappearance to take care of some business matters. That jackass was supposed to be discreet, and he left two bodies behind? The back of her brain was furious at him. Joey better have a damn good excuse.

"By who?" If he had any suspicions, she figured she would be dead by now. That's what she would have done in his shoes.

Trying to be reassuring, he offered up a smile. "I'm still looking into it. It appears whoever was responsible was looking for something. Until I know more, as a precaution, I am having my top-tier security system installed here."

She shook her head. "That's not necessary; I am more than capable of dealing with anyone that wants to break in here and start shit with me." Well, mostly anyone.

When she went to step back, his hands tightened their hold on her. "As my future wife, it is very much a necessity." His voice grew more stern with her.

Her nostrils flared slightly, seeing that he thought he was going to be the proverbial man of the house. "Eric, let's get one thing straight. We're not married yet, and when that day comes, let's get one thing very, very clear." Her voice mirrored the same level of rigidness as his. "You *will not* be making any decisions for me."

With a firm shove, she removed one of his hands and shook off the other as she stepped away with unfriendly eyes targeted at him. Eric watched as Layne distanced herself. Switching up his approach, he softened his face.

"You're right; I should have said something. I apologize for that. However, I will not apologize for doing my best to keep you safe from any potential threats. It's now my responsibility since we have come to our agreement to be bound to one another."

As much as she wanted to lay into him about protecting his assets, she swallowed it down into the base of her stomach. Layne reminded herself that she needed to be smart in handling this situation and her alliance with Eric. Personal feelings needed to be shoved aside.

He presented her with an offer. "How about I make it up to you? I will take you out for a night, and we will forget about work and just focus on getting to know one another."

Layne peeked out a window at the workers beginning their installation of new cameras on her property. Part of her wanted to scream out her annoyance and frustration. The other part? She wanted to just give up and sink into a deep, dark, black hole. He may as well have shoved a tracking device up her ass.

"How does that sound, my little harpy?" Eric stepped up behind her, his hands trailing down along her spine before pausing at the small of her back. He rested his chin on top of her shoulder so she could feel the light caresses of his breath as he waited for her response. His hands began to knead the tense muscles along the bottom of her spine.

Layne couldn't explain why the world felt so much smaller around him. Maybe it was the fact that she didn't have a better way out of the current predicament the O'Reilly organization was currently stuck in.

"Sure." She craned her neck so that she was able to discreetly maneuver away from the proximity of his touch. It did little to persuade him to back off. When she turned around, he stood there in front of her like a wolf assessing its latest meal.

His hand lifted and settled lightly on her cheek. Despite

the light touch, it felt heavy with something else - something more ominous.

So many thoughts bounced around inside of her head like an erratic ping-pong ball, overwhelming her. How was Liam going to react? What did this mean for her and Joey? Was she doing the right thing?

All the unanswered questions tugged on her heart to a point where she wanted to reach into her chest and tear it out in a move of utter desperation and hopelessness.

Whether it was the conflicted expression on her face or merely an affectionate gesture, Eric leaned forward and brushed his lips against hers. The newest of conflicts went to war inside of her as she felt like a hostage in a cage she had helped build for herself.

Tilting her head down before pulling it to the side away from him, she stepped away. "I have some work to get done." It was absolutely a lie, but a necessary one if it meant ending this unexpected visit. Layne scraped her teeth over her bottom lip as she scrambled to quickly rebuild her typically tough exterior and abolish any displays of weakness.

Eric allowed Layne to pull away from him but maintained a careful eye on her. "Of course. My men should be wrapping up outside in the next hour."

Layne nodded, having nearly forgotten about the new shackles being set up on her life with Eric's men installing a brand new surveillance system on her home.

After he left, she trudged back upstairs, pulling herself up one step at a time by the railing while trying to bear the weight life was taking on her. She just needed something to make it more tolerable. She needed something to make the world stop spinning. She needed something and anything to make her stop feeling.

Once she was in her bathroom, she struggled with the child-resistant cap on the prescription bottle. Her lower lip was trembling as she fought back the feelings that were growing heavier on her conscience.

Finally, the cap popped loose, and the second the pills were washed down her throat with a handful of water from the bathroom faucet, there was a sense of relief. Something was on its way to help relieve the pressure valve.

Still in bed well past dinner time, she woke up under a heavy fog. Attempting to shove the duvet from her body felt equivalent to moving a stubborn elephant. It took well over another hour before she could gather enough function-ality to check the messages on her phone.

Several missed calls. Missed text messages. Unread emails. Social media notifications. Before she could wrap her head around where to begin catching up, her phone began buzzing with an incoming call—Liam.

Wearily, she brought the phone to her ear as she answered. "Yeah?"

His voice was the most serious she had heard in some time. "We need to talk."

"What else is new?" She wasn't feeling up to putting up a front at the moment.

Her brother grumbled. "Meet me at McGregor's."

"Now isn't a good time." Her head was pounding.

"Fuck that shit, it's a good time for me. Meet me there in thirty minutes." He hung up on her.

Great, now she had to be a functional human being, all for the sake of trying to appease Liam.

Layne pushed through the sluggish feelings and managed to get out of bed, dragging herself to the shower in hopes that the steamy streams of water could melt away the remnants of her faded high.

Afterward, she slid into a comfortable pair of jeans and a loosely fitted sweater.

Liam would just have to cope with the fact that she would be arriving forty minutes later than he wanted her to.

CHAPTER SIXTEEN

To her surprise, McGregor's was hosting a slew of people when she arrived. She walked inside, pushing past the folks who were spilling into the main pathway while waiting at the bar for a beverage.

As she got to the backroom, she noticed a few familiar faces. In particular, Liam was chatting with a couple of his friends while Kristill was perched on his lap. Either she had forgiven Liam, or he had made it monetarily worth her while to crawl back to him. Layne didn't care for either of those scenarios, but there were bigger issues than her brother's volatile involvement with an escort.

With an arm around the hooker's waist, Liam polished off the last of his milk stout. Layne approached the table, and it didn't take long before Liam dismissed the rest of the crew surrounding him.

Kristill leaned over and whispered something undoubtedly dirty into his ear before rising off his lap with a salacious grin. "Don't take too long, baby." Her teeth nibbled

Liam's ear and tugged on it before releasing the flesh and walking out into the main room.

"Well, if I needed a reason to feel like puking my brains out - that may have been it." Layne shook her head, still unclear of what Liam ever saw in that girl or what Kristill saw in him.

Liam raised his view to stare at her, remaining silent. Layne took it upon herself to occupy the seat across from him while waiting for him to say something. When he didn't immediately speak up, she took it upon herself to start the conversation. "You're the one who wanted to meet."

"Did you really do it?" It seemed like such a simple question, and yet she was unable to comprehend where it was stemming from.

"Do what?" She sat back in her seat, balancing the chair on the back two legs for a moment. A waitress brought her over a light ale that she typically ordered on days when it wasn't the date of her mother's death. Layne gave a brief and polite smile at her before taking a sip.

Liam finally cut to the chase. "Marry Eric Ellis?"

A small spray of beer exited from between her lips, followed by a cough as the back of her hand came up to wipe across her mouth. "What? Fuck no!"

The expression in Liam's eyes remained unchanged and full of judgment. She quickly gathered her senses and shook her head. "No, not yet, anyway. Li, look, you have to understand where I'm coming from—"

He interrupted her, "—you have my blessing."

Her words trailed off as she looked as shell-shocked as

she felt. Layne sat there wondering if her hearing was possibly deceiving her. "Wait, what?"

He shrugged. "I think it's a good idea. You have my blessing."

"*Your blessing*?" She lifted a brow in confusion. "I don't need your damn blessing. Besides that, I'm not sure your blessing means a damn as of lately."

"Shit is going south, and Eric has the means and desire to fix things. If that means you have to finally pull your weight around here, then so be it. I expect I will get appropriately compensated." He made it sound so simple. So matter of fact. So businesslike. So… easy. Not to mention entirely archaic.

"Compensated? That's the part you're worried about?" She rose from her seat, resting her hands on the table as she glared at him. "I'm putting my ass on the line here to try and salvage what Dad built from the bottom up, and you're worried about getting *compensated* while you sit back and get your dick warmed by some two-bit hoe?"

Liam shrugged again, seemingly unbothered and unfazed.

Irritated didn't even begin to describe the feelings bubbling up inside of her. She tilted her head as she stared at him suspiciously. "Where did you hear this anyhow?"

"He hasn't exactly been keeping it a secret, Layne. He's already making it known that anyone that crosses us is crossing him." Her brother looked the most relieved he had looked in months. It rubbed her the wrong way that he could just so easily be ok with this arrangement where he didn't have to put in any effort.

"Great." She didn't hide the displeasure from her voice that word was making its way around in less than twenty-four hours. She rubbed her forehead as her tumultuous thoughts made it ache. Why did everything feel like it was moving far too fast?

Her phone began vibrating in her pocket, and when she pulled it out, she immediately recognized the number. A sensation of butterflies filled her stomach. "I have to take this."

Liam waved her off to go do as she needed. Layne answered the call, pressing the phone up to her ear as she began to walk away from the table. "Hey, give me a minute to step outside."

Before she passed by her sibling, his hand reached out and paused her. "Just don't fuck this up, Layne."

That was rich coming from him, the same person who had been fucking up his own shit since he was born. She glared at him before she pulled away to cut through the crowd toward the side exit into the alleyway.

Once the fresh air washed over her, she let out a sigh of relief.

"Are you still there?" Joey's voice on the other end of the line brought her thoughts back into the present. Feeling an overwhelming sense of pressure and loss of control of her life tugging at her soul, she blinked back some tears as she looked up at the dark sky. She pressed both of her lips together tightly as she worked on reigning in all the emotions threatening to spill over the ledge.

He spoke up again, this time more concern evident in his voice. "Layne?"

She leaned back against the side of the building, her hand clutching onto the phone in her hand tightly. Her exhale was a little shaky, but she managed to at least respond to him. "Yeah. I'm here." She swallowed past the knot in her throat.

His voice tried to lull answers out of her with its husky tone. "What's wrong?"

Not that he could see it, but she shook her head and cleared her throat, trying to shake off the emotions. "Nothing. It's just been a day."

"Layney—"

She cut him off. "Why did you call?"

After a sigh of resignation that she was going to avoid answering his question, he responded to her. "We need to talk. I will come pick you up."

"I'm not at home." She looked down at the ground and kicked an empty beer can across the alley.

"I know." He always seemed to find his way to her, no matter where she was.

Feeling like she could push past the swell of emotions she had felt moments ago that had threatened to swallow her up whole, she moved away from the wall and walked towards the sidewalk.

"Of course, you'd know that." Not hiding the lack of shock in her voice. "Meet me right outside the 50th Street Station." It wasn't too far from McGregor's, making it a convenient spot to have him meet her, only a block and a half away.

During that walk, she was able to mentally string herself together, desperately hoping it would stay that way.

When she got to the end of the block where the subway station entrance was, she immediately recognized Joey straddling his black sports bike, patiently waiting for her.

One boot-clad foot pushed the kickstand down before he got off his ride and walked over to her. He was wearing a dark pair of jeans that hugged over his broad thighs and his black leather jacket that always mixed in with his cologne in a delightful and intoxicating combination of scents.

Despite her efforts to keep a mask over her feelings, what he saw when he looked at her prompted him to pull her into his chest and wrap his arms around her without hesitation. His arms squeezed around her firmly, encasing her in his warmth.

Layne wanted to push him away so she didn't lose herself to something she wasn't sure she could shut down once it started. Despite wrangling with the side of her that wanted to maintain a strong front, her hands squeezed onto him tighter, and she buried her face into his chest a little more.

All the pieces she had just tried gluing back together inside of her were starting to show indications of faltering. A shudder shook her upper body as a quiet sob broke through. Layne had tried to stop it before it came out, but his embrace provided a sense of safety more than any security system ever could. Another sob soon followed, and her body lightly trembled against him. The tension could be felt all over her body as it fought against this breakdown that was currently taking its toll on her.

His hands worked gentle rubs along her back to try and

erase whatever torment she was suffering. Joey's hard exterior managed to provide her with a soft landing spot for the emotions that were at war inside of her.

With people passing them by and going about their lives, Joey stood there holding her for as long as she needed at that moment. He was going to try to soak up anything and everything that was weighing down on her by physical touch alone.

CHAPTER SEVENTEEN

Joey had the sense not to ask her any questions before they arrived back at his place.

His unit hadn't changed much since the last time she had been there. It still had the same minimalist decor representative of how little time he spent in the quaint apartment. There were no photographs or anything else that made it feel personal. It was clear that if he had to up and move, it wouldn't take long to pack it all up.

The bottle of whiskey was set down on the center island of the kitchen in front of her at her request.

Layne sat there on a kitchen stool, her head held in her hands with her fingers tucked into her hair. When she finally looked up, she saw his puppy-like brown hues locked on her and filled with concern.

"Stop staring at me like I'm a wounded animal." She hated it when her emotions got the best of her, except for anger. She was more than happy to embrace that one any day of the week.

Her hand reached out, pulled the bottle closer to her, and removed the cork. Taking a swig straight from the bottle, she let out a sigh as the smooth burn traveled down her throat.

Joey came around from the other side of the island and pulled out a seat for himself. Perching on the stool, he turned to face her.

"What did you want to talk about?" Her eyes drifted over the label of the whiskey bottle to avoid any more looks of pity in her direction. Angel's Envy. The bottle had an outlined design of feathery wings down the backside of the clear glass container.

His hands reached over and grabbed her legs, pulling her so the stool swiveled to rotate her to face him.

"Last night." His hands remained latched onto her legs.

Her eyes reluctantly looked over at him. "The part where you left two bodies in Eric's house or the part where you railed into me on the hood of your car?"

From the draw of his deep breath, it was clear he was summoning as much patience as he could. "Layne, I get there is a lot of fucked up shit going on. You gave me your word last night that you weren't going to run from this, from us."

"I'm still here, aren't I?" It sounded bratty, even to herself. "You told me you just needed to get into Eric's house to go poke around and look for information. You dropping bodies was not part of the plan. Do you realize how stupid that was? If Eric knew that it was you or that I had any knowledge of what was going on, I'd be six feet in the ground by now or worse."

Her temper was beginning to roll, and it felt better to embrace it than some of the other feelings trying to resurface. Layne lifted the bottle of amber liquid, and before she was able to bring it to her mouth again, Joey's hand grabbed her wrist and stopped her.

"First off, I didn't have a choice." He pulled the whiskey from her grasp and set it to the side out of her reach. "Second, he's not going to lay a hand on you."

She gave a short laugh of disbelief at how delusional Joey was to think he was going to step in and be able to protect her. That may have been the case a year ago, but it sure as hell wasn't the same world she was living in now. "Good luck with that."

He perked a brow at her. Before he could comment, she continued her thoughts, "In case you missed the memo, we're going to tie the knot so that Liam and I aren't executed in a horrible and grotesque display of fucked up dominance across the city's factions. Eric's ready to charge full steam ahead on this little agreement we have. He was at my house this morning, fucking around with my security system, all in the name of ensuring my safety."

She stood up to walk away from him, but his hand curled around her wrist and tugged her back so she was standing between his legs while he sat there on his stool. Joey's other hand came up to hold onto her chin so she could stare at him while he spoke calmly to her. "What did I just tell you? That twisted motherfucker is not going to lay a goddamn hand on you."

Attempting to refrain from rolling her eyes at him, she shook her head in disbelief. "What makes you so sure of that?" Her eyes searched his face for any hint that he had a miracle stored away.

"Because, Layney, you're mine, and I'm not sharing. Now, sit your pretty ass down so I can tell you what I need to say."

"And if I don't?" She was being a challenging pain in the ass, but she didn't give a damn as her words began to come out hot. He had signed up for this the moment he stepped foot back inside her house, asking for a favor. "Are you going to come at me again like you did when you told me that I should stop taking pills? They're the only thing that is keeping me fuckin' sane right now as I deal with all of this bullshit. If I'm not dealing with Liam's unhinged ass, it's Eric or you, or maybe the fact that I have to worry about getting shot at in public on any given day. You haven't been around for the past year, so news flash, people change, and I'm doing what I can to cope."

Joey's gaze darkened as Layne indirectly admitted that her coping mechanism of using pills hadn't ceased. He stood up to his full six-foot-two height, towering over her. "Give me a reason to remind you that I don't ask twice."

Maybe it was the whiskey, or maybe it was the mounting pressures she was dealing with, but she straightened up, not willing to back down this time. "You talk a big game."

He nodded as he considered her response. Joey's hand came up along the back of her neck until he had a handful of her hair in his grasp. He tilted her head back so that she was looking up at him. "Suit yourself." He spun her around until she was bent over the top of the counter.

Stepping up behind her, he sealed his hips up against her ass. Even through the thick jeans, she could feel the swell of his cock begging to be freed. Leaning over and whispering into her ear, "We're going to have this conversation whether you want to be my good girl or not."

The next thing Layne felt after he took a step back was the sharp sting of his palm landing on her ass. It was his way of ensuring he had her undivided attention. It elicited a sudden squeak from her, and when she tried to stand back up straight, his hand slid down from her hair and firmly pressed between her shoulder blades so she remained bent over the counter for him.

He continued to explain himself to her. "As I was trying to tell you, I had no intention of taking out two of Ellis' men. They were unfortunate but required casualties. If I hadn't indisposed them, you and I both wouldn't be here right now."

She pushed back against his hand, but he kept her pinned there. "That still doesn't make up for—"

Joey's hand came smacking back down onto the same spot on her ass, this time a little more vigorously. "I'm not done yet."

His hand reached around and tugged hard enough on the button of her jeans that it popped off entirely. It caused the sound of a light dink against the floor when it landed and rolled away. Joey made quick work of her zipper before he shoved the jeans down over her ass, exposing the bare flesh of her cheeks and the thin strip of material between them. A light flush of pink on the one side from where his hand had made contact twice already.

Layne wiggled underneath his hold. Her teeth pressed into her lower lip, finding herself getting heated at her center despite wanting to take her anger out on him. She then parted her lips to say something, and before any sound came out, Joey cleared his throat as both a warning and a reminder.

"Now, about last night. There was a small snag in what I was able to get my hands on, and I'm going to need your help to get it." He dragged his hand down along her spine to join his other hand as they both slid down over the curve of her exposed rear until they settled between her legs. He applied pressure, spreading them open at his command.

He continued talking while his fingers toyed with the narrow and stretchy material of her thong. He ran two fingers along the soft material up to the waistline and down all the way to its midpoint, where he felt her arousal dampening the underwear. "However, before we get to that," he gave a tug on the strip of fabric, allowing it to tug against the more intimate parts of her, "I'm laying down my rules."

Layne felt his fingers so close to her body, which was already begging him to explore further. Her eyes looked back at him while her hips pressed into his touch, hoping to get more of his attention.

He pulled on the back of her thong before releasing it to lightly smack against her skin. It was followed by the sound of his belt coming undone and the zipper of his jeans sliding down.

When he leaned over, his hard cock teasingly pushed between her thighs. Joey placed one hand on either side of her bent-over body on the countertop and leaned against her back close enough that his breath wisped at the skin on the back of her neck. "Rule one," he rolled his hips so that his length rubbed against her. "No running. I don't care how hard things get. If you run away this time, I will hunt you down and drag you back a thousand times over until you realize I'm all in and I'm not going anywhere."

Layne swallowed hard, whimpering at the sensation of the heat of his body so close but not giving her the touch she wanted. The pace of her breathing ticked up a notch.

"Two," he slid his hands down over her arms until they rested on her wrists, putting pressure on her hands to stay where they were. "No more damn pills. If you want an escape, I will fuckin' worship your body in every way I know how until you can't even find it in you to scream out to God anymore."

She pressed her lips together, squirming underneath him at the discomfort of his second demand to knock off her reliance on the prescription drug to wash away her stress.

He pressed a kiss to the side of her neck. The sensation seemed to draw away her anxieties for a brief moment. "Finally, my favorite, rule three." He paused and smirked down at her. "No more of these." His hand traveled down to the side of her hip, his hand wrapped around the waist of her thong and forcefully tugged. The material easily gave away under the sudden onset of force.

Layne gave a light gasp followed by an excited smile.

He dropped the now useless article of clothing to the floor. "Any questions?"

She pushed her hips back against his thick length. "When does all the worshipping begin?"

He grinned, already knowing by the feel of the warmth of her soaked pussy rubbing over him that she was very much looking forward to being taken. For added measure, he rubbed his aching cock against her slit. Her arousal left a sheen of desire along the top of his shaft. "If you had been a good girl, I'd already have you riding my dick."

He pulled back and tucked himself back into his pants despite the way he wanted to get another hit from his addiction to her body. "Since you wanted to mouth off, you're going to have to wait."

As he pulled away from her, her body's anticipatory tension tanked. Every part of her felt lit up like a firework about to be launched toward space, only to have the fuse fail before the fun could even begin. At first, she frowned in frustrated disappointment; then, she furrowed her eyebrows at him for leading her on. "You can't be serious."

With a sigh, she tugged her jeans back up, only zipping them since the button suffered a glorious end to its functionality.

He walked over to the freezer and pulled the bottom drawer open. "As the grave."

Joey reached in and grabbed a pint of Baileys Irish Cream flavored Häagan-Dazs and lifted it for her to see. "Go sit on the couch, Layne." So demanding, wasn't he?

"Ice cream is not really what I'm in the mood for."

After retrieving a spoon, he walked up to her, capturing her chin with his fingers, and gently kissed her. "Next time, don't make me ask twice." He grinned unapologetically.

After she begrudgingly went and sat on the sofa, she tried to ignore the desire that was screaming at her between her legs. Layne drew her legs up onto the couch with her, criss-crossing them.

He joined her and handed her the pint of ice cream and the spoon before sitting down next to her. Comfortably, he leaned back and rested an arm along the back of the dark grey sectional. The dark brown of his eyes settled on her as she opened up the frozen dessert and began to dig in. Despite the dirty looks she was giving him, Joey could have watched her like this all damn day.

Layne moaned quietly on the first taste of the ice cream as it danced across her taste buds. It had been far too long since she had indulged in this particular sweet treat.

Discreetly, Joey adjusted himself at the sound of her approval. It was going to be a long evening if she kept that up. By making his point to her there by the kitchen counter, she wasn't the only one who was being left unsatisfied here.

After Layne finished her pint of ice cream, Joey internally questioned how the hell it was possible to be so painfully hard watching a woman enjoy something as innocuous as a little frozen dessert. The idea of jerking off to find relief didn't even appeal to him when she was sitting right there, so close to him.

With the television on some show about two brothers and the family business, Layne curled up into Joey's side. He dropped his arm around her shoulders, keeping her close. His fingers traced small and senseless patterns along her arm as they sat there, just enjoying one another's presence.

He looked down at Layne. He parted his lips to say something, but before the words came out, he shut his mouth after thinking better of it. A few more moments passed, and he finally spoke up. "I will raise all hell for you, always. Don't ever question that."

When she didn't respond, he shifted to lean over and take a peek at her face. Layne's eyes were shut as she was soundly asleep in his embrace. Joey kissed the top of her head and carefully maneuvered her, doing his best not to wake the little Irish beast in the process.

He shifted her into his arms and carried her into the bedroom, where he got her tucked in. He joined her moments later. His fingers tucked a strand of her hair behind her ear as he leaned over and whispered a few words to her, knowing she'd never know of his confession to her come morning.

CHAPTER EIGHTEEN

I t had been a rare occasion that she hadn't needed to rely on a pill to sleep through the night. The only thing that had been nagging at her was the deep ache between her legs after Joey had withheld himself from her. Even then, she had just felt at peace and calm as she breathed in the natural scent of his body mixed in with the familiarity of the last remnants of his cologne with notes of sage.

That wasn't the only pleasant smell that had her feeling at ease as she began to wake, the scent of food cooking filled the unit. When she was finally ready to open her eyes for the day, she found herself alone in Joey's bed. First things first, she hit the bathroom, where she found one of his tees neatly folded on the counter for her. Opting for the comfort of an oversized cotton shirt versus her jeans and sweater, she made the quick wardrobe change. As expected, his shirt swallowed her petite body up.

After emerging from the bathroom, she breathed in the scent of freshly cooked bacon that was hanging heavily in the air as an indication of the promise of breakfast. Layne shuffled out of his bedroom, rubbing the sleep away from her eyes as she came into the kitchen. She was greeted by the view of Joey standing in front of the stove, wearing a pair of grey sweatpants barely hanging onto his body at the hips.

The display of tattoos spilled over his shoulders and upper back and down along the sides of his ribs. She stood there in awe, her eyes appreciating the view. Her core between her legs also appreciated it very much, especially as she observed where his exposed skin stopped at his lower back, and the waistband of the sweats began as they barely adhered to the curve of his muscled ass.

Joey moved some eggs around in the frying pan with a spatula, and without looking over at her, he spoke up, "See something you want?"

Her thighs pressed together, reminding her that she was without her pair of panties he had so politely disposed of last night. "Maybe. What's on the menu?"

She grinned and walked over to his side, taking a look at what he was preparing. The scrambled eggs were just finishing up in the frying pan; there was a plate full of bacon, and pancakes were stacked on another plate.

It pulled a smile onto her face, seeing that he had gone to the effort to cook for her. Typically, she got her breakfast from whichever bagel shop was convenient.

Joey set the spatula down and turned to face her, giving

her a more complete view of his toned physique. The lean lines cut around each muscle group on his upper body. Each tattoo decorating his skin was on full display for her to appreciate, from the sprawling mosaic over his arms, across his chest, and down to the "Chaos Addict" words scripted along his side.

The newest addition to his ink collection was in plain sight. Placed directly above his heart, the curves of the shamrock graced his pec as the crimson blood dripped from the emblem of luck just past his nipple.

He captured her face in his hands and drew her mouth up into an adoring kiss. "How did you sleep?"

She couldn't help but keep smiling up at him. "I would have slept better if I had gotten what I wanted last night."

His smirk flicked onto his mouth.

Before he could respond, the sound of her phone vibrating and the corresponding high-pitched tone rang against the kitchen counter where she had left it the night before. Layne walked over and frowned, seeing the name on the screen. "Eric." Her eyes glanced over at Joey, who didn't seem to have a change in his demeanor.

She slid the answer button over and placed the phone to her ear. "Hi."

The smooth sound of Eric's voice was strained as he spoke on the other end of the call. "Good morning. I didn't see you get home last night."

Joey approached her and took her by the waist, lifting her onto the edge of the counter. Layne swatted at him for fucking around while she was trying to have a damn conversation. What was Joey's response? He gave a mischievous grin and placed a finger to his lips as an instruction for her to remain quiet.

At first, Layne was confused about his intentions, but then he pressed her to lay back on the counter. He pulled her by her legs to the edge before spreading her legs apart. The t-shirt got caught up underneath her and remained pushed up around her stomach. Her half-naked body was fully revealed to him, making her arousal quite obvious from his perspective.

"Layne, are you still there?" Eric's voice echoed in her ear.

Her attention was drawn back to the voice on the other end of her device. "Yeah, I'm still here." Layne's brain struggled to recall his initial commentary, thanks to her attention being drawn elsewhere.

Eric repeated himself. "You didn't come home last night when I checked the security footage."

Joey leaned over and hungrily lapped up her arousal along her folds, with his tongue flicking over her sensitive bundle of nerves. Her hips jolted at the sensation, and before she could squirm away, his hands clamped down onto her thighs to steady her.

Her heart was hammering away inside of her chest as she choked down a gasp.

"No, I didn't." Layne's words purposely remained short as she spit them out.

That vague response didn't seem to satisfy Eric as he continued talking. "Where are you? I want to make sure you're okay."

She pressed her lips together in a hard line as Joey began to assault her pussy with his mouth. His teeth nipped at her clit while the scruff on his face continually brushed against her. Layne placed a hand on her forehead, trying to focus and maintain her composure while her thoughts felt scattered.

"I'm fine. I stayed at a friend's."

At the mention of the word 'friend,' Joey raised an eyebrow, then snickered quietly to himself. He removed one hand from her thigh and pushed two fingers deep inside of her.

Layne slapped her hand over her mouth as she nearly cried out at the pleasureful intrusion of her body. Joey continued to lick and suck at her most intimate bits. Her hips were unable to stop themselves from grinding against his touch.

"Are you sure you're okay? Let me send someone to come pick you up," Eric pressed on.

Joey's fingers curled inside of her, stroking over the special spot that drove her insane. Her face was flushing while her heart felt like it was loud enough to drown out Times Square on New Year's Eve.

She removed her hand from her mouth briefly. "No, no. I'm already on my way." As much as she wanted to set him straight about checking in on her, she just wanted to get him off the call.

That's when she felt Joey's teeth bite at her swollen bud. A squeak squeezed past her throat before she was able to muffle herself. Her eyebrows furrowed together as it became a struggle to keep all the pleasure bottled up inside of her.

Joey's hand gave her inner thigh a slap as a warning to keep her sounds to herself. She looked down at him with a silent whimper.

Eric's voice was barely audible in her ear over the sound of the blood rushing in her ears as it all traveled south to her center. "I need you to tell me these things, my little harpy." While he explained the importance of him knowing where she was at all times for her safety, Joey didn't ease up on devouring her.

The tattoos on his fingers disappeared inside of her every time he pumped them into her body. His tongue drew circles over her delicate pleasure button, occasionally drawing it into his mouth and sucking harshly on it.

She writhed under the overwhelming weight of desire and ecstasy building up inside of her and was unable to be vocalized. Her voice was strained as she did her best to wrap up the call with Eric. "Can I call you back? You're breaking up."

Noting that Layne was trying her best to end the conversation, only encouraged Joey to ante up. He pulled his mouth from her and licked the flavor of her body from his lips. It gave Layne a small window of relief, but it wasn't long before his hand reached up and sealed down over her mouth.

That's when Layne felt him shove a third finger deep inside of her as he picked up the pace of penetrating her body there on his kitchen counter.

Her hand grabbed the wrist of Joey's hand that was

pressed over her lips. She wasn't sure if she wanted to pull him away or keep it there as sensations began to quickly escalate inside of her.

She thought she heard Eric say goodbye after she promised to call him back, but she wasn't sure of anything at that moment. The several moans that managed to slip from her were muffled against Joey's hand while her body looked for its release.

Out of the corner of her eyes, she noticed the call ended on her cellphone. Her hand dropped it down onto the counter in relief. Her sounds of approval were still muffled as he coaxed her body closer to her climax.

His eyes flickered at the uptick of noise against his palm. "Did I tell you that you could make a sound yet, Layney?"

Her face looked at him pleadingly while her hips rode against his fingers with a strong need to hit the approaching peak. Layne's whimpers vibrated against his palm.

Just before she spilled over the edge of sensual release, he removed both hands from her and pulled her upright. She panted heavily as the wave of pleasure began to ebb.

The second she was face to face with him, he pushed his fingers into her mouth with her body's wet arousal coating them. Layne hungrily sucked on his fingers in the same way she wanted to put her mouth on other parts of him. She watched the lustfulness fire up in his eyes as she did so. Her tongue slid over every inch of each finger, being sure not to leave any part of her desire behind.

Joey growled as her mouth sucked the taste of her own body off his fingers. "That's a good girl, cleaning up after yourself." He then withdrew his fingers and snatched her up off the counter. Her hands grabbed onto his shoulders, and her legs wrapped around his waist.

Her mouth kissed along his jaw and down over the spread of his tattoo of raven wings along his neck. "You better finish what you started."

"Mm, and if I don't?" With his hands grasping her by the curves of her ass, he carried her over to the fridge, where he pressed her back up against it, letting the hard bulge straining against his sweats press up against her bare pussy.

Her teeth playfully nipped at his lower lip, tugging at it. "I may need to hire someone to abduct you and bring you to an abandoned building so that I can have my way with you."

His grin widened. His movements shifted to tug at the waist of his sweatpants, allowing his cock to spring out, already locked and loaded, ready for her. A drop of precum glistened at the tip. "As much as I would like to see you try," he lowered her hips so that his head pressed against the entrance of her pussy teasingly, "I'd rather be the one doing the abductions and having my way with you."

"Mmhmm. Just shut up and fuck me." Layne leaned over and locked her mouth onto his.

She didn't have to tell Joey twice; he pushed himself into her slowly to enjoy the way her body felt as it welcomed his cock's invasion. He groaned as Layne's moan vibrated against his mouth.

Layne immediately felt a wave of pleasure as he fully sank into her. Her hips pressed back against him while he filled her. She tilted her head back slightly as far as the fridge door behind her would allow as she let the sensations overcome her.

He took his time laying kiss after kiss along her skin, starting along her jaw and traveling toward her neck. His hips slowly pulled himself back from her body before reentering at the same speed. Joey wanted to enjoy each moment of savoring her body. The neck of his tee on her tiny frame sloped down to expose her left shoulder. Joey's mouth found the shiny bullet-sized scar on her shoulder. He swiped his tongue over it, lapping over the healed gunshot wound to try and erase the bad memories associated with it.

Her hands ran over the tops of his shoulders and down onto his upper back, where her nails dragged across his skin. The way his length paused up against her sweet spot had subtle chills of desire running over her body.

As he continued to press that slow and decadent assault on her body, it was more than skin-deep. The feelings welling up inside of Layne weren't anything that she was accustomed to. It was a slow burn of desire that wasn't just tugging deep and low in her core. No, it was a tugging of feelings and warmth inside of her chest.

"Joey…" Her breathy voice whispered as she brought her eyes to meet his.

Using one hand to support her, he lifted the other to take hold of her face and passionately kiss her. Their bodies continued to grind against one another. It was a much different pace and swirl of sensations than the other night on top of the parking garage. This was something far more intimate.

It was unclear how much time passed, but each push into her brought her right up to the edge of release. Joey's hands tightened up on her legs that remained locked around him. "Layne," his words were spoken against her lips. "I've missed everything about you."

She pressed her forehead up against his while her lips caressed over his between each heavy breath released. "I haven't been able to breathe without you." Her clutch on him tightened up as her body shook as it spilled over the edge and crashed into complete ecstasy.

When her body tightened down around him and her flood of desire coated his cock, he shuddered, and the apex of his pleasure was unleashed. Joey pushed himself deep within her, trying to plow past the physical limitations as his release filled the depths of her body.

They both remained there, heavily breathing in each other's embrace. Layne slumped forward, her face buried in the crook of his neck as she held onto him for dear life. With an arm underneath her ass for support and one around her back, he stepped back away from the fridge. He inhaled the scent of her dewy skin below her jaw, planting several more kisses on it as they both came down from their orgasms.

After they both were adequately recovered, Joey made sure to reheat the breakfast he had prepared for her. He carried a plate over to the modest kitchen table where Layne sat. Her plate was full of a little bit of everything for her to feast on after expending all their energy on one another. She smiled up at him, a smile that hadn't left her face since the second he had given her a hell of a way to wake up this morning.

"Can't have you leaving here hungry," he stated as he set the plate down before her.

Layne couldn't even imagine eating, given how satisfied she already was. "I don't think you have to worry about that."

CHAPTER NINETEEN

Layne hated it, but now she had confirmation that Eric was watching her every move a lot closer than she anticipated. It left her feeling paranoid about how far he was willing to take things. Not to mention that Joey was going to have to be extraordinarily careful about his visits to her house.

Yesterday's breakfast with Joey had left her feeling renewed and refreshed in so many ways. For a small amount of time, he had managed to melt all her worries away. However, there was still the unsolved complication of salvaging her family's floundering business operations.

Feeling more optimistic than she had felt in some time, she was ready to take on this new day. She tossed on a pair of dark leggings with her knee-high boots and a cozy sweater knit with loose stitches so one got glimpses of the ivy tank top underneath. Her hand grabbed her coat and keys on her way out the front door.

As she stepped outside, she was greeted by two men dressed in boring black suits coming up the walkway to her door. Layne hadn't been expecting company.

"Can I help you?" She hoped not. Layne was planning a pitstop at Rebecca's to borrow a book, *Warlock: A Strange Grove Novel*, that had been recommended to her before meeting with the skeleton crew that still worked for the O'Reilly organization. Now was not the time to be asked about her satisfaction with her cable service by some salesmen.

Both men stopped, blocking her pathway. The taller man with a dark olive complexion nodded at her without so much as a smile. "Yes, Mr. Ellis has requested you join him for lunch."

Layne tilted her head, unable to hold back the look of disbelief that he had actually sent his people for this. "You can tell him I already have plans."

When she went to sidestep them, they stepped along with her, maintaining an obstruction. She sighed and shook her head. "I don't have time for this. Get out of my way."

The slightly shorter of the two men reached out for her arm. "We must insist you come with us, miss."

Layne jerked her arm away before he could lay a finger on her. "This is fuckin' ridiculous." She pulled out her phone and dialed Eric's number.

As if he had been expecting her, he answered immediately, sounding far too cheerful. "Hello, Layne."

She glared at the two suits in front of her. "If you had called, I would have been more than happy to tell you I already have plans today." Her tone did not hide any of her annoyance at the absurdity of the situation.

"If you had bothered to call me back yesterday, we could have discussed this. I'm afraid today's lunch isn't optional."

Great, Eric was going to be pissy about not getting a phone call, and Layne didn't do well handling fragile feelings. She drew in a deep breath, trying to weigh her options. "It better be a quick lunch." She ended the call.

Again, the shorter one reached out to take her arm, and she fired a glare at him. "Unless you want to part ways with your damn hand, I would keep it to yourself."

He paused to consider if she was bluffing or not. It seemed he was a smart man when he extended his arm away from her to indicate for her to follow them both to a sleek black sedan. The engine was still running while being double-parked in front of her house.

After they escorted her to the vehicle, they let her into the back seat while they both took up seats in the front. The entire twenty-minute ride had been in complete silence. Not even the radio had been turned on.

When they parked the car in front of a tall office building and killed the engine, Layne pulled on the handle to let herself out. Nothing happened. The fuckers had the child door locks on, preventing her from getting out on her own accord. Bastards.

If she hadn't been pissed off about this change in plans already, this was the needle on the bitter Irish girl's back. The taller man opened the door for her, and after she exited the car, they led her inside the building with large glass windows reflecting the damn near blinding sunlight.

After a stroll through the lobby and an elevator ride to the forty-eighth floor in awkward silence, they brought her to a corner office with a picturesque city view. An L-shaped desk on one side of the room and a leather sofa on the other, with two chairs and a table opposite it.

She noticed a few silver carryout containers on the oval table in the seating area. At least he didn't plan a six-course meal like she had expected from him.

Layne stepped inside and noticed that she was all alone. The door shut behind her, allowing privacy from any prying eyes of anyone else potentially passing by.

She tossed her coat over the back of one of the chairs and walked over to the massive windows, crossing her arms in front of her chest as her eyes took in the view. Layne didn't want to admit how she could stare at the beauty of the city she had grown up in all day long.

The office door opened up again, prompting her to glance back over her shoulder to see Eric walking inside with a folder in one hand and a coffee mug in the other.

He was dressed in a grey suit with a black shirt and tie underneath the jacket. Eric offered her a polite smile, seeing she had arrived, as he set everything down on his desk. "Ah, there you are. Glad to see you came to your senses."

He walked over to her like he had given her a choice to be here. When he placed his hands on her arms and leaned over to place a kiss on her mouth, Layne turned her head so he got her cheek instead. There was one mouth she wanted on her right now, and it wasn't his.

Noticing her evasive turn, he seemed surprised. She stepped back from him, keeping her arms crossed in front of her. "I'm giving you the benefit of the doubt that you somehow had a temporary moment of insanity and thought I could be summoned like a pet."

"Is that what you think that was?" He inquisitively looked at her before shaking his head and immediately moved on. "There are some business items that need to be handled. I thought we could have lunch together while we finalized a few minor items."

Eric walked back to his desk and grabbed the folder he had walked in with. He brought it back to her and handed it over. "I need you to sign these."

Opening the folder, she saw page after page of legal documents. Eric circled her until he stopped at her back and looked over her shoulder. He was close enough that she could feel the heat of his body hovering at her backside.

"What are these?" Her eyes skimmed each page, looking for the keywords of what each page entailed.

He rubbed his hands over her upper arms while his mouth came up to her ear. "Those, my little harpy, are what is going to save your family's business."

As she got to the final page in the batch of documents, Eric's hands dropped down to her hips. "And that one there is where we make it all official." Boldly printed across the top of the page was the certified heading for all New York State Government documents, and underneath it were the cold black letters spelling out *Marriage License.*

Immediately, she shut the folder. "I need my attorney to look these over."

He reached over her to ease the folder out of her hands. "With what money are you going to pay a lawyer? Not only that, but time is going to be of the essence. I've heard that Russell Spencer isn't very happy after a little stunt you pulled. I'm not a miracle worker. These agreements are going to be the only thing that gives enough leverage to avoid a major catastrophe."

Word got around quickly, and she shouldn't have been surprised that Eric already got wind of it. Coming back to stand in front of her, he traced a finger down her cheek, and it dropped under her chin. "Sign the papers, Layne." The blue of his eyes shone a little brighter from all the natural light pouring in from the windows.

Layne gritted her teeth. The very thing she had been against all her life was staring her in the face. She had never wanted to marry a man for strategic financial and business purposes. "This is happening really fast; I don't feel comfortable with this."

Eric pushed the matter without hesitation. "My little harpy, I can't promise the second you leave here that someone won't try to erase the O'Reilly name from the map. I don't want to wake up to the front page running an article that the Upper East Side lost a young woman to a horrific random act of violence." The strength of his hand shifted to latch onto her chin. "If you give a shit about yourself and your family, sign the papers."

With her forehead wrinkled up in torment as he made the veiled threat that wasn't too far off of reality, she understood the looming harshness of reality ready to descend upon her. Her hand pulled the folder back from his possession. "Get me a pen."

After she had a pen in her hand, she began initialing some pages and signing others. Most of the documents were typical arrangements tied to assets and liabilities. When she arrived at the last page, she paused at the sensation of a heavy weight settling in her stomach.

All her personal information, alongside Eric's, was already listed there. There was just one last remaining field for the signature of the bride. Even the alleged officiant and witnesses had signed. Layne forced the pen to glide across the paper:

Layne Nicole O'Reilly

She dropped the pen and stepped away from the desk she had been using. This was what was going to be what kept Liam and her from being swallowed up whole by the city's criminal factions, all waiting to pounce on them. Layne should have felt a sense of relief. Instead, all she could feel was intense suffocation.

Eric looked over all the papers, double-checking that she hadn't missed anything. Afterward, he approached her with a delighted smile. His hands cupped her face and, without any hesitation, lowered his lips onto hers. He clutched her face there in his hands while he deeply kissed her, drawing it out far longer than it should have lasted.

When their mouths parted, he grinned at her. "Congratulations, Mrs. Ellis."

The post-nuptial lunch had been some sushi from a five-star restaurant that Eric had splurged on in celebration of the joyous event. While he had been in great spirits, Layne didn't have much of an appetite and merely picked at the rice of her spicy salmon roll.

"Now that everything is official, the process of fixing all the fractured pieces of the O'Reilly organization can begin. I will personally reach out to the heads of all the major entities to make sure it is clear that no one is to make a move against you. If they do, they will have hell to pay and me to answer to." Eric was making a lot of bold promises, and she only hoped that he could deliver on them and it wouldn't eat away at her spirit from the inside out.

Layne finally gave up on her lunch and rose from her seat across from him. "I told you I didn't have time for a long lunch."

He put his chopsticks down on his plate and quickly wiped his mouth with a napkin before rising from his seat. "I thought you'd be a little more eager to celebrate."

Eric came over to her and wrapped his arms around her waist. "Maybe even pick up where we left off at the concert before your security guard rudely interrupted us." The words he spoke were eager to try and manifest his desires.

Before she could knock him off track from his train of thought, he drew her in so their bodies were flush with one another. Her hands braced against the front of his chest. She should have had no problem blinking an eye at a potential good time, but something in her was holding her back. That 'something' had many tattoos and a voice that sank into her soul.

A delicate smile lifted her lips as she looked up at him. "I haven't been sleeping well, and all of this caught me by surprise. Maybe we can celebrate some other time."

There was tension in his hands that were resting on the top curvature of her ass, but it released quickly as he rebounded from his clear disappointment. "That sounds like a great idea. I would rather we have all the time in the world to enjoy the moment. We can make an evening out of it, or perhaps, an entire weekend."

Layne prayed that her face masked her true feelings on the idea of turning this into a celebration with him.

His hand came up to the back of her head as he dropped his head down and made sure to savor, sharing another kiss with her. When he released her, he grinned. "We'll talk soon about all the fun we're going to have together."

Before she left his office there on the forty-eighth floor, he had offered his men to drive her to where she needed. Layne adamantly declined, citing that she preferred to walk, given Rebecca's condo wasn't too far and she could use the fresh air and sunshine.

The elevator ride down to the ground floor felt like it had moved at a snail's pace. When the doors opened up, the anxiety that had been building up during the descent of all forty-something floors was quickly coming to an insurmountable peak.

She hurried through the lobby in hopes that the outside air would provide relief. Instead, what should have been a refreshing late autumn day felt too warm and muggy. Or, maybe, it was just her disgust with herself.

Her palms began to feel clammy while her face paled.

The twisting and spasming of her stomach was the only warning she needed. Layne ran over to the nearest trash receptacle and wretched up the little amount of lunch she had consumed into it.

The very thing she had been fighting against most of her life just became her reality.

CHAPTER TWENTY

For better or for worse, things over the next week moved quickly. Eric wasted no time in meeting with various figureheads across the city. One of those meetings is what had her pacing back and forth inside the office at O'Reilly Manor.

To hammer out some final details on the business end of matters, Liam needed to be involved whether she liked it or not. She tried to convince her brain to settle down while she waited. She wiped her palms against the thighs of her jeans before adjusting the bottom hem of her burgundy blouse.

"The office is right in here." She heard Liam say on the other side of the door before it opened up, halting her pacing.

In walked Liam, followed by Eric close behind. While Liam had chosen comfort over business, wearing a pair of jeans and a hoodie, Eric had gone with a more polished and professional look. He wore a charcoal set of pants with a matching vest overtop a light blue dress shirt and a navy tie.

Eric's eyes immediately landed on her. "There she is." He walked to her, smiling in excitement at her presence. Layne allowed him to greet her with a gentle kiss that left her feeling a little on edge, given the discussions that were about to take place.

Noticing her apprehension, he moved his mouth to her ear, where he whispered. "It will be painless, I promise." He followed it with another kiss on her cheek before he left to take a seat across from Liam. She doubted that any business discussions between the three of them would be painless.

Liam was already behind his desk, firing up the computer. He looked over at Eric. "Let's talk about what I'm getting for allowing you to marry my sister?"

Layne did her best to stifle her snort that Liam had anything to do with this. He had no authority to claim he had allowed this whole damn order. Now, his only interest was what kickbacks he was going to get. Apparently, her sound of disagreement hadn't been quiet enough, seeing the way that Liam's glare was shot over at her.

Sitting back with an aura of collective ease around him, Eric laced his fingers in front of him. "I don't think I was very clear over the phone. You're getting my help in bolstering your team of men, which seems to have been dwindling in numbers over the last six months. Not to mention investing my money in fixing the financial woes it seems that you have gotten into. For me to do that, I'm going to need you to provide me with account information and get me authorized to manage funds."

Her brother's face faltered slightly as he realized that things were not as he had imagined. Liam's hand rubbed over his jaw as he pondered how he could twist this around selfishly.

Layne spoke up, interrupting her brother's slow turn of the cogs in his head. "Li, this isn't the fuckin' middle ages. You're not getting a lump sum payment for bringing a woman to market."

"Did I fuckin' ask you? You shouldn't even be here anyway," he snapped back at her.

Eric straightened up in his chair. "Look at it this way: she won't be spending a dime of your money, she will be spending mine on whatever she pleases. That's savings directly in your pocket. You'll even get to sell her house once she moves in with me or keep it for yourself, whatever you choose."

There was no hiding the immediate attitude change on Layne's face at the mention of moving in together and giving up the home she had earned through all her hard work. "What?"

She stepped over to Eric's side, staring him down. He looked up at her and grinned. "You look so surprised; I figured it was understood that eventually, you'd be living with me under the same roof. It would look a little strange living separately, don't you think?"

A partial laugh mixed with disbelief came bubbling out of her. Before she could verbally lay into him for the assumption on his part, he quickly reiterated himself.

"I said *eventually*." As if that was supposed to soothe her temper.

Liam interjected, "Yeah, Layne, he said *eventually*. Don't get your panties in a twist."

"Shut the fuck up, Li." Besides, she didn't have any panties on to get in a twist.

Eric steered the conversation back to his original points of interest, discussing timeframes for getting him access to all that he required to sort things out.

While the boys discussed the finer details, Layne's thoughts wandered to Joey's role in all of this. He still needed Layne's help in gathering some key pieces of information out of Ellis for his contracted job. Based on everything he had told her, there were one too many skeletons hiding in Eric's closet.

When her mind lingered back to the present, Liam was talking very animatedly on the phone. "What the hell do you mean I'm not authorized on the account?!"

She blinked a few times, wondering if she had heard him correctly.

Liam continued to berate the poor representative on the other end of the line before he hung up in a fluster. "Bitch." He looked over at Eric with instant regret that he had lost his temper without thinking about how it would look.

Clearing his throat, Liam shifted in his seat. "They must be having some sort of shitty system error. I will get things sorted and everything to you."

"I hope, for your sake, it gets figured out quickly." Eric pushed himself up out of his chair after taking a peek at his watch. "Based on that, I think we've discussed everything we can for today. I will be in touch by the end of the week so we can finish wrapping up everything here."

Layne's eyes remained critical while assessing each of the expressions tugging at her brother's face. She only drew her eyes away when Eric took her hands in his. He lifted them both to his mouth, where he affectionately laid a kiss on each set of her knuckles. "We still need to schedule that celebration we talked about." He gave her a wink.

"Of course." She was too bothered by what she had heard from that phone call to argue. "I will see you to the door, and we can talk about it soon."

Layne left the office with Eric to accompany him back to the front door. A few minutes later, she returned to the office, closing the door behind her and staring at her brother, who was sitting there with his hands buried in his short, auburn hair.

"What the hell was that about?" She stared at him.

Liam looked up at her with the gravity of the situation finally hitting him and showing in his eyes. "How should I know? The dumb bitch said I wasn't authorized to discuss details on the account!" His words were getting defensive.

"Goddamnit," she sighed and tried to think through all the potential reasons for their access to be restricted. "Did you have the right account number?"

"Yes! Do you think I'm stupid, Layne?!"

"How are you even just now finding out that you aren't authorized on the account? Haven't you been using it?"

There was silence.

Her tone grew stern. "Liam?"

He finally responded in a hurry of words. "There hasn't

been a reason! I've been busy. Besides, the money has been going out as fast as it's been coming in."

Layne threw her hands up in the air. "Are you kidding me? Busy fucking off?!"

She walked over to the desk and placed a hand on it while her other hand pointed at him. "You have to fix this! This is your screw-up, not mine. I don't give a damn how you do it, but make it right."

"What do you want me to do?!" He threw his hands up in the air.

She shouted back at him. "Dad showed you the ropes and put you in charge, Liam. You should know these things and at least have a clue what to do. You wanted me to stay out of this shit, and I have. I have sacrificed enough of myself for this family for one week!"

When her phone rang, her irritation was already on a warpath. She saw Joey's name pop up on the screen, and she answered. "Joey, it's not a good time. I will call you when I finish dealing with Liam's fuck up." She hung up abruptly, not waiting for his acknowledgment.

"Who the hell was that?" Liam's eyes narrowed at her.

She shook her head. "None of your business."

He stood up and walked over to her to yank the phone right out of her hand. Layne turned and clutched onto it while using her other hand to shove him away. He grabbed her arm, and they both wrestled with one another until the phone slipped from her hold.

"Liam, give it back!" She was unable to reach around him as he turned and began tapping on the screen.

"Really? Mom's birthday is your passcode?" He

scoffed. "Predictable." He shook his head as he began sliding his finger across the screen and tapping away.

He pulled his shoulders back as he pulled up a picture from her albums. Liam turned and showed her what was on her screen. Layne pressed her lips together, immediately recognizing the picture she had taken with Joey after their breakfast together. The memory of it was clear as day.

After getting dressed, she noticed his skull mask hanging over the edge of his laundry basket. She picked it up and dangled it in front of him. "Maybe next time you could wear this." Her eyes sparkled with playful excitement.

"Be careful what you wish for. That mask comes with a lot of other conditions," Joey smirked at her.

"Oh? I think I will take my chances." Layne stretched the mask over her face and pulled her phone out on selfie mode to see how it suited her. "It almost looks better on me than it does on you."

Joey came up behind her, wrapping his arms around her waist while laying a kiss against her neck. Her thumb snapped the selfie of them together with her in his infamous mask.

The sound of Liam's harsh words brought her back to reality. "It seems like I'm not the only one who is fucking around."

She stood there quietly, not feeling that she owed him any sort of explanation.

"Is this who I think it is? The masked freak that dad hired to take out Franzetti, and you couldn't keep your whore mouth off of?"

Layne shrugged at him. "Does it matter if it is?"

"Yes! You want to sit here and criticize me while you're off fucking two guys, one of which I might remind you has our business by the balls!" Let Liam's throwing of figurative stones begin like he hadn't wet his dick in half of all of Manhattan.

Both of her brows lifted now that he wanted to step up to the plate. "Oh, now you want to be concerned about the state of things? Where was this attitude six months ago?"

He tossed her phone back at her. "I told you not to fuck this up with Eric, and this is your idea of playing it safe?"

Her hands fumbled for the phone that was carelessly returned to her. "This is my idea of doing what I have to in order not to lose my shit. You can take this holier-than-thou crusade and shove it up Kristill's ass or whoever is the flavor of the week."

Deciding she wasn't going to stand there and listen to him bitch at her any longer, she turned for the door before she decided to shoot the last member of her blood relatives.

Before she stepped out of the office, she got her last words in. "Just fix the goddamn account, Liam."

After the door shut behind her, all she heard was his rage-filled roar as something smashed against the closed office door, shaking it upon impact.

***

"Stop!" Layne giggled as Joey leaned over and buried his face against her neck, playfully nipping at her skin. The short hairs of the dark blonde scruff on his face tickled against the delicate skin of her throat.

They sat inside his Challenger parked at their quiet little spot near the water in Brooklyn. He was leaning over the center console, unable to control himself from showering her with attention to try and erase the mood Liam had put her in. His hand slid up along her inner thigh toward the center of where her legs came together.

"I'm trying to have a serious conversation!" Trying to fight back the smile on her face as she squirmed in her seat.

Joey smirked as he muttered against her neck. "So am I."

"Bullshit." Her hips jolted as his hand finally found the apex of her jeans. Finally, she grabbed his hand to pause his efforts temporarily. "Liam was off his rocker level of pissed."

He finally drew his head back and looked at her unbothered. "Fuck him. He's a whiny piece of shit." Joey wasn't Liam's biggest fan, not many people were. What else was new?

Before he dove right back in for another taste of her, she turned in the passenger seat to look at him with all business in her eyes. "I don't need him doing something stupid and interfering."

He exhaled, trying to bring the blood flow back up to his brain as he sat back on his side of the vehicle. "He may be a selfish prick, but he's not completely stupid, Layne."

She nodded, still not feeling at ease. "Let's just say this plan works, and you can get what you need from Eric's house this time. Then, what?"

"You let me worry about that." Layne had heard that from one too many people before and hated hearing it out of his mouth. It felt like she was just being placated and kept out of the loop.

Before she could roll her eyes at him, his thumb and forefinger captured her chin so she could look into his eyes. His eyes shone a slightly lighter shade of brown with the sun beating in through the windshield.

She didn't bother hiding her concern weighing down her voice. "And you're okay with all of this? I've seen the way you look at Eric."

Joey smiled at her lightly. "I'd be more than okay if you just so happen to become a widow at the ripe old age of twenty-six." He leaned over and captured her lips to lull them into a slow and drawn-out kiss.

When he pulled away, he looked back into the stunning green eyes he had fallen for time after time again. "Look, Layney, it's a piece of paper. It doesn't mean shit."

"And you're not the least bit remorseful that you're putting your hands all over a married woman, are you?" She grinned at the thought of it.

He leaned in and growled into her ear. "I plan to use more than just my hands."

"Promise?" The question posed to him was full of hopefulness.

He grabbed her and pulled her to his side of the car and into his lap. Layne faced Joey as her legs straddled him. His hand ran up along her spine until he could grab a fistful of her soft locks of hair and tugged her head back. Joey leaned over and dragged his lips down the center of her exposed throat and over her chest. Each kiss was more sensual than the last as they reached the exposed swell of her cleavage. His other hand slid in the opposite direction down her back until his hand squeezed a handful of her ass.

She pushed her hips down over the quickly growing erection. Each seductive movement of her body against him caused him to groan against her. Her hands grasped onto his head, letting her fingers get lost in the newer and longer length of his hair.

Joey didn't take long to make good on his promise to use more than his hands on her. Hell, if he was going to let her enter the lion's den without knowing who the real king of her jungle was.

CHAPTER TWENTY-ONE

The first snowfall of the season had taken hold of Manhattan. It was a light coating that barely interfered with daily life, but it added an extra touch of wintry beauty across the city.

Powdery white flakes clung to parked cars, signage, and street lights. While it was a gorgeous sight tonight, she knew that it wouldn't take long to turn into a sullied mess of sloppy gray debris on the sidewalks. But for now? She could appreciate the view seated by the restaurant window. She was sitting at a table for two with the chair across from her temporarily empty.

Outside, people walked by, minding their own business like typical New Yorkers. Occasionally, a person or two would stop and take a look at the outdoor menu in the glass case by the front door. The restaurant had only been open a couple of months, but it was already capturing all the attention of the food critics and anyone willing to throw obscene amounts of money at a meal that was the size of a chicken nugget.

If her nerves were on edge, she didn't let it show. Layne turned her attention to the half-drunk glass of rosé in front of her that she was idly swirling in light circles. That certainly didn't hurt keeping her anxiety in check, either. It hadn't been her drink of choice, but it contained alcohol, and that was good enough for her. She needed to get through this evening in one piece.

Her neutrally-colored fingertips tucked a loose strand of her hair back behind her ear. A thin silver ring in the design of Celtic knots adorned her pointer finger. It had once belonged to her mother and was thought to have brought good luck. Layne had chosen to braid and twist her hair back into a contained bun at the back of her head for the evening.

She refused to fully dress up for the evening, despising the impracticality of dresses when she was engaged in work matters. As far as she was concerned, Eric was going to be all work in her book. Layne had already worn one dress this year, and one man had made it worth her while. Such high hopes for tonight were nowhere to be found.

Instead, she compromised with a flirty black lace top that left her shoulders fully exposed but covered the length of her arms. Matched with the top was a pair of fitted black pants. Around her waist was a satin sash mimicking a belt knotted at her hip in a bow.

A presence sat down across from her, stealing her attention away from the stretching of the wine legs down the inside of the glass. Eric took his seat with a delighted smile directed at her. It was no surprise he had dressed his finest when Layne suggested they finally take a night out to celebrate their union as business and life partners.

"Apologies, I had to take a business call." He tucked the cell into the inner pocket of his suit jacket.

Even in the dim lighting of the dining room, his frigid blue eyes stood out against everything else about him that was dark and brooding. His raven hair, his fully black ensemble, and probably his black heart, too. One of these days, she'd have to confirm that assumption.

"I thought maybe you were going to make a run for it," she grinned at him.

Eric shook his head. "From you? Wouldn't dream of it. Running towards you? Now, that's something else, little harpy."

When the waiter approached, Eric ordered himself an Old Fashioned with the unusual twist of a lemon peel instead of the more traditional orange peel. The hairs on the back of her neck briefly stood on end, and the scar on her heart ached. That was exactly how her dad always drank his Old Fashioneds, his signature drink. Something deep down told her that it was no coincidence that Eric had chosen it.

Layne swallowed down another mouthful of wine along with her feelings.

His hand reached across the table and took hold of hers. "I can't tell you how much I was looking forward to tonight. I know there have been a few bumps along the way, but I'm confident we can smooth things out." His thumb caressed over the tops of her knuckles reassuringly.

She offered him a light smile and then nodded to the waiter, who returned with Eric's drink and offered another pour of wine. "So, just what is your plan once Liam gathers the last pieces of information you requested?"

He sat back in his seat after releasing her hand. "I don't want to talk business tonight; I'd rather talk about us."

That sounded awfully personal, and she hated mixing her private life with business. Though, in Eric's case, he was shoring up to be a bit of both, wasn't he?

She lightly pulled in a deeper breath into her lungs before slowly exhaling. "Alright. Then, what did you want to talk about?"

A victorious smile appeared on his smug face. "You. I know all about the fiery Layne O'Reilly on paper, but I'm more curious about what's underneath the surface."

"What you see is what you get," she assured him as she sat back in her seat. "But, if you've got time on your hands, I'd be more than happy to share a few stories that may not have been told to you."

Eric couldn't pass up the offer as his lips made contact with the whiskey-heavy cocktail in his glass.

Some stories may have been slightly embellished for his listening pleasure, but Layne shared some of her biggest wins in the business and a few of her early mistakes. It kept the conversation rolling throughout dinner.

"What about you? I've been talking about myself all evening. I think it's only fair." She folded her arms across the edge of the table as she leaned forward, prepared to sit there and listen to him do a little sharing of his own. The emeralds of her eyes peeked down at the time on her watch discreetly to take note of the time. It was nearly a quarter to nine, and she would have preferred to stretch this time here with him out just a little longer.

He polished off the rest of his beverage, sliding the empty glass away from him. "Now, that is something I'd be happy to do, but I think it requires a little more privacy." Eric stood and came over to her side, offering his hand for her to take.

Scooting her chair back, Layne reluctantly took his hand and stood. Once she was on her feet, he released her hand and slid his arm around her lower back. Pulling her in closer to his side, he whispered in her ear, "Did you think I wouldn't know what you're doing?"

There came back the bit of paranoia that had been quieted by the wine. She tilted her head curiously as she looked at him. "And what am I doing?" Better to appear ignorant and unknowing than to reveal one's secrets unknowingly.

His lips found their way onto her cherry-glossed lips and coaxed a kiss from them. "Let's talk about it in the car on the way back home." Eric gave a nod to the restaurant's manager on duty, having previously arranged the bill to be taken care of.

Outside, waiting for them moments later, was a black SUV. Eric let her into the back seat first and joined her a moment later after saying something to the driver that she had been unable to hear.

Layne automatically crossed one leg over the other as she settled in. After the vehicle pulled away, Eric's hand patted her thigh. "I think you underestimate how well I can read you, Layne."

She doubted that very much. "What makes you say that?"

The warmth of his hand should have been welcomed in this freezing weather, but instead, the cold settled into her bones. His gaze seemed to analyze every movement she made. "You can tell me all your stories about your successes and your failures, but you still don't want to acknowledge one very important thing about yourself."

"That I don't like cryptic talk?" She didn't try to hide the disdain in her voice.

He chuckled, removed his hand from her leg, and settled it on the side of her face. "I scare you. You're not intimidated by me, but you do harbor fear inside of you when it comes to this—to us. You're worried that you're going to let yourself enjoy the life you are destined to have. You got a taste of it the night of the concert, and now you are doing your best to close yourself off."

She saw the street signs indicating they were approaching the corner lot where his residence was located. Layne looked back into Eric's eyes and gave him a playful smirk. "Maybe you'd get the girl from that night if you asked nicely."

"One thing I will share with you is I don't ask nicely." To prove his point, he crushed her lips under the weight of his mouth as he consumed the taste of her. Layne pulled herself up against him, letting him take his share for the time being, knowing their destination wasn't too far. His hands began to wander down over her body, and right as his tongue pushed past her lips, the car came to a stop inside the multi-car garage of his home.

He pulled away from her reluctantly. "I have more fun for us inside."

The way the word 'fun' rolled off his lips made her think that his idea of fun was quite different from hers.

A few moments later, they were inside the vaguely familiar home she had last seen the night of his party. As they made it up to the third floor, where all the numerous bedrooms were, Layne questioned how much house one man needed.

As if reading her thoughts, Eric spoke up. "I know that the house is exceptionally bigger than I need, but I couldn't resist all the possibilities of how, one day, each of these rooms would have a specific purpose."

Layne nodded before Eric stopped at the entrance to one of the many closed doors in the hall. His hand dropped to the brass handle and gently swung the door open to the dark room. "This one is my favorite." He gestured for her to step inside before he reached in to flip the lights on so she could take it all in for herself.

What she saw was not the master bedroom she had expected to see. No, the master bedroom would have been very much welcomed. Eric came behind her, his hands on her hips and breath on the back of her neck. "It gets me excited every time I come in here. Consider it part of my wedding gift to you."

It was rare for Layne to find herself in a state of shock, but what was waiting there for them had managed to leave her brain unable to reconcile what was happening.

CHAPTER TWENTY-TWO

The lights illuminated the room, exposing its dark secrets. Along the walls were all the tools of the trade of a sadist's dream torture chamber. Various sharp-edged weapons, blunt objects, bindings and restraints, pliers, thumbscrews, choke pears, stun batons, and some items that she couldn't fathom their use. The tiled floor even had a few drains installed for easy cleaning.

Despite the violent decor along the walls, it almost looked like he put enough effort into dressing it up with fancy blackout curtains, several framed pieces of artwork, and elegant light fixtures. Her brain tried to comprehend to what extent this man was so sick that he went from wanting to devour her to proudly showing off this macabre part of his life.

When she looked in the center of the room, her lungs stopped after a short gasp as she held her breath. A man with his back to her was on his knees, hands restrained behind his back and chained to the floor with his head hanging down. A black hood was over his head, keeping the man and his identity in the dark.

She pressed her teeth into her tongue in an attempt to control her facial reactions despite an overwhelming sense of dread washing over her.

"Well? Why don't you go take a look at what I got you?" Eric's voice startled her as he moved up directly behind her. His hand pressed lightly against her lower back to urge her to approach the man.

Swallowing down the saliva pooling in her mouth along with her greatest fears of who she should expect to see underneath that hood, she slowly approached. Her beige heels quietly tapped against the floor with each step.

Her eyes glanced down at the hands bound behind the man's back, and she slowly released the breath she had been terrified to let go of. There was not a single tattoo to be seen on his hands or fingers.

Layne stopped in front of the man, glancing up to see Eric waiting patiently for the big reveal. Looking down at the poor soul before her, she reached down and slowly lifted the hood from his head.

The man squinted at the light with weary eyes that had fresh bruises and swelling around them.

"Andrew?" Layne questioned as she saw her former income source on his knees before her. The very same Andrew Corelli that had been poached by Russ Spencer. She hadn't been able to hide her surprise from her face, and it prompted a wide grin beaming with pride from Eric.

"Since things are official now, I wanted to make it clear to everybody that disloyalty will not be tolerated. Andrew, here, has made very poor choices and now will be suffering the consequences." Eric gestured to the various wall decor at her disposal.

She dropped the black hood onto the floor and stepped away from the man who was now looking at her with eyes pleading for mercy and forgiveness. Layne walked back over to Eric, keeping her voice low to spare Andrew from overhearing. "Eric, this wasn't needed." It sure as hell wasn't wanted either.

The back of his finger stroked across her cheek. "This is just the beginning. After seeing the way you asserted yourself at the Brass Mirror, it is only fitting that we can consider this a little foreplay before we proceed with our evening." His finger trailed down over her skin beyond her jaw and dragged over the bare skin of her shoulder, skimming past the scar on her left shoulder and down her arm.

To further reiterate his point, his lips brushed against her ear as he whispered to her. "I'm getting hard just thinking about watching you work. Don't insult me by not accepting this gift I have given to you."

Her eyes closed to try and force her mind into a disconnected frame where she could get through this. Joey's words echoed in her mind as a reminder.

"Do you even know what type of monster Eric Ellis is?"

She recounted all the things she knew that Andrew was tied up in. The way he watched little girls with too keen of an eye and too evil of a hand. She reminded herself that the world would be better off without him. Andrew was owed a world of pain and suffering. Eric wasn't wrong in pointing out that disloyalty couldn't be tolerated if her family's reputation were to be restored. All of these things could easily justify what needed to be done.

When she opened her eyes, she felt nothing but a dissociative numbness as she nodded at Eric. "This was very thoughtful, thank you."

She gave him a gentle kiss of appreciation before she stepped away to review her options on how to punish and execute the pervert on his knees before her. He didn't deserve a quick death, but she didn't want to have highlight reels of his torture on repeat in her head for the next year.

Layne opted for one aggressively serrated blade with one hand and a rusty hammer with the other. This was going to get messy, and she wished she had known to dress for a little torture with her fancy evening out.

As for Andrew, his eyes reflected the rising panic inside of him when she approached with both objects in her grasp. "Layne, please, I'm sorry." Here came the begging for his life, the part that she cared for the least and the reason why she kept torture short and sweet just to avoid listening to it.

She squatted down and leaned in to whisper to him. "Andrew, there is nothing more I would love to do than to shove one or both of these up your ass, knowing what you like to do in your free time. However, I'm going to need you to man up and be fucking grateful that it's me you're dealing with and not him." Her eyes flicked to Eric, who was watching with a smirk, tugging at his mouth in anticipation of what was to come.

Then, it was down to business. Using the hammer, she inflicted blows to fracture his ribs one at a time. The only reprieve she gave him was when she slid the razorlike edge of the blade across his body, leaving one shallow cut after another on his body. The forked nail-puller part of the hammer was used to dig into his open wounds every so often. Andrew's howls of pain echoed in her ears while he begged for death.

When her eyes tore away from the bloody, broken mess before her, she saw Eric enjoying the show. No, he wasn't just enjoying the show, he was *enjoying* the violence. He stood there with his pants undone and his stiff cock in his hand. Slow and long strokes over himself at the sight of her inflicting pain on Andrew. Fuck, she was going to need to stock up on more ways to mentally escape her nightmares after this.

Not breaking eye contact with Eric, she tossed the hammer to the side, leaving her with just the jagged and blood-stained knife at the ready. Her hand grabbed the back of the whimpering man's neck to steady his writhing body. She plunged the blade into his chest, giving it an extra twist to make sure she thoroughly ripped into his heart.

Eric moaned out, seeing how Layne put an abrupt stop to the man's suffering. "Mmm, that's my bad little harpy."

She let go of the knife along with Andrew and pushed down the urge to re-experience her dinner that briefly threatened to make a second showing. There may have been one less predator in the world, but the one left watching her wasn't going to make her rest any easier at night.

She walked over to Eric, glancing down at the blood on her hands and then up at him. "Where can I go clean up?"

He released his hold on his still throbbing dick. "Don't bother." Eric grabbed her by the arms and pinned her against the wall as his mouth latched onto her like a rabid dog. The unexpected advance left her struggling against him before she succumbed and grabbed onto his sides to keep him close.

His hands roughly grabbed at every part of her in a lust-filled frenzy. His erection jabbed at her lower stomach. Layne returned the rough play as her nails dug into his chest. She shoved his jacket from his upper body, balling it up before pitching it to the side, leaving it a little lighter in weight before she did so. While his affections smothered over her, the weight she removed from his jacket dropped down into the pocket of her pants.

Eric breathed into her ear with a dark growl on the cusp of his words, "I'm going to show you exactly how you should be fucked." His hand yanked on the fabric belt of her pants, the shape of the bow falling flat as it came undone.

Layne internally cringed while her thoughts continued to strategize her escape from this hellhole and the monster standing before her.

A nervous voice interrupted the beginning of what Eric likely wanted to be a thorough ravishing of her, and Layne couldn't have been more thankful for the reprieve. "Um, sorry, boss. We have a situation."

A barrel-chested man stood at the doorway of the torture chamber. He looked to be too skittish and meek for his size, indicating he had a healthy dose of fear for Eric's demeanor.

Eric tensed up as he snarled. "Later."

Layne slid away from between him and the wall, causing a flash of annoyance in Eric's eyes.

The nervous employee spoke again. "There might have been an intrusion downstairs earlier this evening."

The news didn't settle well with Eric as he shoved himself back into his pants and buttoned them back up in frustration. He walked over to the man, and they stepped outside out of earshot for a few minutes. It allowed Layne to take a breath or three while she retied her belt, giving it an extra-strong tug while knotting it back into the bow.

When Eric returned a few minutes later, he appeared a little more composed. "I'm sorry, but we will need to continue our celebration another night." His hands came to her face and drew her in for a brief kiss as an apology. It was an apology she was more than happy to accept.

A dark smirk appeared on his mouth. "I look forward to sharing the rest of my gifts with you. But, until then, I will have my driver take you back home for the night while I handle things here."

"I completely understand." She tried not to give too eager of a smile that she was going to be getting the hell out of this room of horrors.

Now, being such a true gentleman, Eric walked her out to the car, waiting to take her away. "See you soon, Layne."

CHAPTER TWENTY-THREE

Back home, she turned the shower faucet on to begin warming up the water in her bathroom. Layne felt a layer of grit all over herself that needed to be washed away. Perhaps there was a little bit of her soul that also required some cleansing, too.

While she waited for the steam to begin filling the room, she peeled away her clothes, dropping each article to the floor. A quiet sigh of relief escaped from her lips as she pulled her elastic tie from her tresses, relieving the tension of her hair on her scalp. Her fingers ran through the locks of her hair a few times to allow herself to ease into a more relaxed mood after the toll the evening had taken on her.

Her hand pulled open the glass door to the shower as she stepped inside, immediately feeling the heat of the streams of water pelt against her skin. The temperature was almost unbearably hot, just the way she liked it. The shower door lightly clinked as it came to a close behind her.

Layne tilted her head back underneath the water from the showerhead, letting her hair soak up all the moisture until it was fully saturated. As the water ran down over her body, she already began to feel more at ease. She closed her eyes and just stood there under the waterfall coming from above, relishing in the moment.

There was a small swirl of cool air that breezed through the bathroom briefly. She opened up her eyes and tilted her head forward at the unexpected air movement. Her hand pressed against the foggy glass wall as her ears strained to hear any unusual sounds.

Clink. Clink. Swish. Zip.

The sound of a belt being unlatched and pulled from its loops followed by a zipper sliding down. Her breathing sped up. Her eyes darted around at her surroundings; she was caged in here like an animal. There was nowhere to go, and her only weapons were hair products and soaps, a shitty razor that she forgot to replace last week, a vibrating rose for the days when she needed a little relief, and a purple loofah.

Given the options, she opted for the razor with the anti-nick guards on it. Silently, she cursed herself, wondering why she was even bothering.

She wished that if someone was going to attack her, it wasn't while she was naked in the shower. It takes a special kind of asshat to take this approach to violence. At least they could have the decency to wait until she was clothed and attempting to eat a balanced meal.

A pair of large hands grabbed onto the top of the shower's glass wall. Her eyes darted north to see the tips of the fingers curling over the top. Swallowing hard, she swiped her hand across the steamy glass to get a better view of the outline of whoever was standing right outside her shower.

Joey smirked as he stood there completely nude. All of his muscles stretched out on display from the lean lines of his arms, down over the front of his inked chest, the cuts of his abs, and right down to the main event.

It didn't matter how many times she had seen this man without his clothes on; it took her breath away every damn time. Layne stood there dumbfounded to the point she dropped the razor. The shallow movement of water at her feet carried it down to the drain, where it halted.

He dropped his arms down and opened up the door to invite himself into the shower with her. "Did you think after watching you with that asshole all night that I wasn't going to want to get a piece of you afterward?"

The white tiles of the wall were suddenly at her back, and she didn't even recall backing up. Her eyes had been so distracted by his raging hard-on that her head wasn't thinking clearly. "Are you admitting to stalking me?"

The water began to cascade over Joey's body, drenching every part of him before he stepped up to her. His hands latched onto her hips, squeezing them firmly while he pressed her back to the wall so she had nowhere to go. His face gave a sexy devil's grin as he leaned down and trailed his mouth over the side of her neck. "I'll admit to stalking when you admit to eye-fucking me every chance you get."

Layne's mouth curved into a sassy smile. "Are you sure you're not just imagining things?" Her hand slid across the front of his body until it moved over his shoulder to run up along the back of his neck. Her slender fingers grasped onto it to encourage his mouth to continue its path.

His length pressed up against her lower stomach as he leaned into her. Joey's hand ran up from her hip onto her breast, roughly kneading it with his palm as he began to stake his claim on her. His teeth lightly grazed over the spot where her neck met her shoulder. "The only thing I'm imagining right now is how tight your pussy is going to clench around my dick." His words rumbled into a growl as he emphasized who was going to be the man reaping the pleasures of her body tonight.

The thought alone had her thighs pressing together as the excited sensation was intensely building between them. "A little presumptuous, aren't you?" Her fingers slid through the hair on the back of his head, grasping a handful of it in her hand.

"Hm." That was all he said before he eased up off her for a moment. Joey leaned over and grabbed something off one of the built-in shelves. "We'll see."

He grabbed her arm and spun her around so the front of her body was pressed up against the slick tiles of the shower wall. Her hands had nothing to grasp onto on the flat surface. Layne started to push back, but Joey's hand tangled up in her hair, keeping her right where he wanted.

A familiar sound echoed behind her. The vibrations of the rose from her adult toy collection were humming at a low frequency. His hand reached around in front of her and down between her legs. "How confident are you feelin' now that I was being presumptuous?" He tilted her head back to look at him so he could watch her face.

Before she could respond, he connected the toy with her sensitive clit that had already been aching with need. Her body jolted with the onset of immediate pleasure that shot through her.

Layne gasped out. The sweet sound of her moan filled the small space of her shower. Joey didn't ease up on assaulting her body with the silicone toy against her bud. Her legs could have given out right then and there. "Mmm, that's not playing fair."

He pressed his chest along the back of her body, his cock nestled right up against her ass. She pushed her hips back into him, drawing out a moan of approval from him. "Playing fair is for nice guys. We both know what type of guy I am."

Vibrations continued to hum viciously against her clit, quickly bringing a tremble throughout her body. Layne writhed and squirmed between two immovable objects: the wall and Joey.

"I love the way you squirm against me," his gravelly voice purred into her ear. His hand pressed the toy against her harder, sending wave after wave of intense pleasure straight up into her core. The swollen head of his member dragged down along the crease of her ass until he was positioned right at the opening of her pussy.

Layne's hands furiously began slipping against the slick

tiles as the divine sensations began to overwhelm her. "Oh, God!"

Seeing that she was barely hanging onto her sanity, Joey sank himself deep into her in one smooth motion. His eyes locked on her face as she instantly became undone for him.

Her release erupted in a magnificent display of pleasure that took her hostage. Her primal screams were unleashed as her body immediately took him in and tightened around him.

Loudly, he groaned at the pressure of her body. "Fuck, Layney. You're going to be the death of me."

Joey damn near lost it the way her walls squeezed and spasmed around him. Typically, he was a pinnacle of self-control. Tonight was different. Having seen the way Eric was pawing at her tonight, Joey needed to have her. He needed to feel her. He needed to know that she was all his.

Her legs could barely feel themselves after she came with such force. So, when Joey made his sudden movements, she was hardly in a spot to protest.

The toy was removed from her body and tossed to the side with a clang against the floor as it rolled over to the corner. He released her hair and grabbed her by the hips. Before she knew it, he pulled her away from the wall and had her completely bent over with her one hand planted on the shower floor and the other braced against the wall.

Hard, firm thrusts began railing into her body. His cock claimed her precious cunt for his own pleasure tonight. Joey's hands dug into her hips as their bodies smacked together. "That's it. Take *my* dick like a good girl." His movements were harsh as he slammed his length into her. The tip of him continued to pound away at that delightful spot deep inside of her.

Layne's world began spinning as she cursed out between her heavy pants. "Joey! I can't take… You're gonna make me…." Her climax wracked her entire being, nearly causing her to collapse as it shook throughout every fiber of her body.

Even with her orgasm strangling his cock, Joey didn't ease up as he rammed into her. He needed to feel her body taking him, even at its limits. His hands latched onto her body so tightly it was likely to leave bruising on her fair skin.

The water continued to rain down on them both, washing away the sweat and sins of their bodies. Layne gasped for air as the aftermath of her release was stretched out while he continued to own her body and the pleasures of it.

He withdrew from her and pulled her up straight. Joey turned her face to him, drunk with lust. Roughly, his mouth claimed her lips, forcing them open to allow his tongue entry. The kiss was short-lived when he pulled back and urged her down onto her knees. "Now, I'm gonna fuck that mouth, beautiful."

It was a perfect view from his angle, seeing her now below him with those full green eyes gazing up. Joey's hands buried themselves in her wet locks of hair, grabbing onto her head and drawing her forward.

Layne parted her lips and opened up her mouth for him. As Joey guided himself into her mouth, the sensation of her velvety tongue dragging along the underside of his dick caused him to quiver in a moment of bliss.

Joey's cock twitched in excitement as she took every inch he pushed into her. He drew back only to immediately push forward into her mouth, this time deeper. The tip of his cock pressed at the back of her throat. He repeated the motion until it formed a rhythm. His hands held her head exactly where he needed it.

The movement of his hips picked up as he glided in and out of the depths of her mouth. Layne hummed against his flesh, instigating a deep growl from him.

"Fuck, I'm not gonna last much… mmm, longer." His thrusts became less smooth. The moment he took another look at Layne's eyes, peering up at him under her wet eyelashes and the streams of water running down her face, he lost control of his release.

He shoved her mouth onto him as his thick cock pushed past her gag reflex that pulsed against him. Ropes of his hot seed burst out of him and down her throat as he roared out in ecstasy. Joey removed one hand from Layne as he leaned forward, gasping for oxygen while he braced the hand against the wall behind her.

With each pulse of his dick still buried inside her mouth, he gave a quieter moan and eventually a whimper followed by a satisfied sigh.

Slowly, he pulled back and assisted her back up onto her feet. Joey laid light kisses on her swollen lips that were plastered with a euphoric smile. Layne returned each one of his kisses in reassurance that she only wanted him.

Her hand came up to rest on the side of his face while

he slid his around her waist to hold her close. A strong feeling inside of her wanted to bubble up to the surface as she stared into the affectionately warm brown eyes she had come to rely on to make her feel safe. Layne's lips slightly parted to say something, but the words never made it off of her tongue.

CHAPTER TWENTY-FOUR

"I wish you had stayed home. I don't like the idea of you tagging along for this." Joey kept his voice low as they stood there waiting inside the small cafe.

Layne grinned and shook her head. "Since when do I ever listen to what you want?"

"Well," his hand slid up along her spine and began to possessively take hold of the back of her neck.

After her cheeks began to feel warm with a slight flush, she interrupted his response. "Don't answer that."

Joey smirked at her, leaving his hand gently massaging the tiny muscles on the back of her neck a few times before dropping his hand back down to his side.

The young barista at the *Every Day I'm Grindin'* coffee shop in Greenwich Village looked like she barely was in her twenties. She looked at Joey with wide eyes that damn near had hearts popping out of them. "Can I get you anything else?" She extended her arm out to hand him the coffee he ordered.

Layne reached over and gently took the coffee from the girl's hand. "He's fine." Not bothering to toss a smile at the girl. Helping herself to the piping hot beverage, she walked with Joey out of the cafe.

Joey chuckled as he looked over at Layne. "You weren't getting jealous, were you?"

Layne scoffed at how ridiculous that sounded. "Of a girl that looked like she should be the spokesperson for Squeaky Clean magazine? Please." She walked with him toward their destination, an unassuming brownstone at the end of the block that had a "FOR RENT" sign in the front window with an invalid telephone number listed on it.

She caught the amusement in Joey's face when he took her elbow with a gentle hand and paused her in her path. He leaned in and gave her the type of kiss that was slow but did powerful things low inside of her body. When he pulled back, she had almost forgotten all about the googly-eyed barista.

He smiled at her. "You're cute when you're jealous and don't want me to know it."

She wrinkled up her nose at him. "You're a pain in my ass."

His hand lightly patted said ass. "Maybe later if you ask me nicely for it."

She shot him a look that was an attempt to be irritated with him, but he made it difficult when he gave her a wink that promised dirty things. Layne finished off the coffee before dropping it into an empty trash can next to the front steps of the house in front of them.

Joey jogged up the front steps of the rental and knocked on the door. Layne followed, letting him take the lead since these were his people, not hers. A raspy and cranky male voice came over the intercom to the left of the door. "What do you want?"

Joey grinned. "Open up, jackass." He placed his hand on the doorknob, waiting for access inside.

With suspicion in his voice, the unknown guy's voice replied. "Who's the broad?"

Layne straightened and stepped forward to give the man an earful, but Joey put a hand out to get her to back down. "She's good. Stop fuckin' around and let us in."

There was a grunt on the other end of the line before the door audibly unlocked, and Joey opened the door and went in ahead of her.

When she got inside, she closed the door behind her and took a look around. It appeared to be a vacant home that hadn't yet been rented out. There was no furniture, no personal touches, and the wooden floors could use a good cleaning from the dust and dirt gradually collecting on them.

Joey waved for her to keep up as he went to the door that led down into the basement. Once they descended a level underneath the house, the air became musty from lack of air circulation, and the lights remained dim. There was only the glow of an excessive number of computer moni-tors displaying lines of code on the wall above an oversized desk that sat two men with several keyboards in front of them.

The man to the right had scraggly grey hair that hung down to his shoulders. He had to be approaching sixty if he wasn't already there. When he turned, he huffed at the sight of Layne and then looked over at Joey. "Do you have it?"

Joey reached deep into his pocket, pulled out the thumb drive, and tossed it over to the gruff old man, who caught it in his hand and began to get to work extracting the data from it.

The man to the left had short and spiky brown hair and a set of wire-framed glasses over his eyes. He was considerably younger looking; Layne would have been surprised if he was even of legal drinking age.

When he turned around and saw Layne, he made a sound akin to a schoolboy giggle. His pale face turned a dark shade of red as he fumbled to get out of his chair. "Oh, um, hi. I'm Brandon, but my codename is Cowboy." The poor guy was barely able to avoid tripping over his feet as he approached Layne, extending a hand out to her.

"Cowboy? Somebody ought to save a horse. I'm Layne." She shook his hand with a smirk, teasing the poor kid who seemed like he had never spoken to a girl before in his life.

While the innuendo went over Brandon's head, leaving him looking confused, Joey caught onto it and rolled his eyes at her. She flashed a cheeky smile right back at him.

Brandon nervously chuckled while standing there staring at her and fidgeting in his spot. "Uh, do you have it? The phone?"

Layne pulled out Eric's phone from her jacket pocket and handed it over to him. She was more than happy to be relieved of it after what she had to endure to get it the other night in the makeshift torture chamber. "I powered it down as soon as I could after I got my hands on it."

Brandon took the phone and smiled crookedly at her before he shuffled back to his seat and began working some sort of techie magic on it. While the data may have been on the drive Joey had taken during his break-in to the Ellis residence while she and Eric had been at dinner, it was something on Eric's phone that was able to provide access to it.

Layne didn't pretend to even understand the level of nerdiness required to get the data Joey had been hired to acquire. She preferred a more brute-force approach of pulling information out of people.

The cranky old man looked over at Brandon. "You good?" When he got the nod from the youngin', they both began to type commands on their respective keyboards. After a few minutes, the monitors lit up and began processing data.

Layne leaned over and whispered to Joey. "What are we looking for?"

Before he could respond, images popped up on a few screens, driver's licenses on another, lists of names and addresses, receipts, videos, and other large amounts of information.

Something caught Layne's eye, and she abruptly spoke up. "Wait! Stop! Go back one." She stepped up to the desk and pointed to a monitor that had flickered with an image that had captured her attention.

Brandon clicked a few things, and when the image came up, she blinked. She stood there staring at the image with her brows furrowing together while she tried to process what was staring right back at her.

Joey came up behind her to take a look at what had her giving funny looks. "Is that…?"

"Andrew Correlli," she confirmed for Joey. Her eyes read the text accompanying the image, seeing the file path indicating he was in a folder dedicated to employee bios. Continuing to soak in the data, it appeared that he had started working for Eric almost two years ago, long before Eric moved to the city. It noted that he was in charge of a territory covering all of Staten Island but doing what it didn't say.

She shook her head. "This doesn't make any sense. If Correlli was working for Eric, why would he want him dead?"

"I-I think I found something," Brandon spoke up while he filtered down to some information on the central monitor.

An audio clip file appeared, and when it began to play, it was obvious it was a conversation between Andrew and Eric.

"How many times have I told you not to sample the product?" Eric's voice seethed with anger.

Andrew responded like a nervous wreck under Eric's threatening tone. "S-sorry. I just thought that it needed a quality check. To make sure it is up to standards, ya know?"

"Your goddamn job isn't to quality check. It's to make sure the packages move safely from point A to point B so they can be cleared to be distributed across the state line!" Eric's voice thundered back in response. "If you ever fuck up this bad again, I will make sure that you get the ending you deserve. Am I clear?"

"Absolutely. Very clear."

"Good. Now, make sure that you go make good on our arrangement and go make friends with Russell for me."

The clip ended. Layne grimaced while grinding her teeth as she bowed her head down. Her hands clutched the edge of the desk so tight it began to turn her knuckles white as the realization hit her.

"He played me." She spoke through her clenched jaw. "Fuck!" Layne pushed away from the desk only to run right into Joey's chest. His hands steadied her by her arms and made sure not to release her, even when she pulled against his grip.

Joey didn't allow her to squirm away from him. "Hey, hey. Hold up." He looked past her at the two men still running an analysis on all the data. "See what else is on there that's useful; I will be right back."

After she felt Joey's hands release her, she pushed past him and quickly went right back upstairs. He was quick on her heels, though, and once she was upstairs, she spun around to face him.

"He's been playing me like a goddamn fiddle! I knew he had motives to strengthen his power in the city, but God knows what else he's been doing to make sure that Liam and I were desperate!" She placed a hand on her forehead, struggling to keep up with the storm of scenarios crashing into her brain. If he coordinated Andrew getting in with Russ Spencer, the potential for other puppetry was limitless.

"Layney, calm down." Joey's voice tried to ease her down from her escalating temper.

She glared at him as he told her the one thing that most certainly was not going to bring her temper down a notch. "Don't tell me to calm the fuck down!"

When he reached out to hold onto her shoulders, she swiped his arms away. "I'm going to kill him, Joey. I don't care. I will hunt his ass down, make him suffer in his freakish torture room, and he can get off on his own demise on his way down to hell."

Joey's eyes settled on her, and he waited until she was finished. "Are you done?" When she didn't interrupt him, he continued to talk. "He will get what's coming to him, don't worry about that. There's enough data there that my client is going to want him wiped from the playing board. After a little more due diligence on the details of what he's peddling and how far he's peddling it, then this can be handled."

She tried to ease her anger down with a deep breath and think a little more rationally while Joey laid out what would hopefully be the next steps.

After making sure that she wasn't going to go off on him like an Irish car bomb, he wrapped his large arms around her and drew her in close. He kissed the top of her head reassuringly. "We will handle Eric *together* when the time comes. Until then, we keep the status quo. Okay?"

Layne desperately wanted to argue with Joey, but having him hold her so close managed to ease the flare of her irritability. She sighed quietly as the tension in her body melted away one breath at a time.

"I hate you right now," she murmured against his chest as her arms wrapped around his waist.

"Only because you know I'm right." A cocky smile appeared on his mouth.

After Joey was confident that Layne wasn't going to go on a mission to immediately hunt Eric down, he went back to the basement to wrap up discussions with his associates. It turned out that they hit a snag in the encryption of data that would take some time to bypass.

There was enough time for her to soak in everything he had said to her. When he came back upstairs, ready to leave, she stopped him. "Did you mean what you said?"

He lifted a brow at her. "Which part?"

"That we would handle this together. The way things went down with Franzetti—" Her words were interrupted by his finger pressing against her lips.

Joey's eyes met hers to make his intentions very clear. "You're stuck with me, Layney. Hell or high water. I just need you to be on the same page. And, until you are," his hands moved to embrace her face, "I'm going to slay any demons standing in your way to get you there."

Words were pretty things. Layne wondered if they would hold the course of time or if he would end up another chapter that abruptly closed in her life.

CHAPTER TWENTY-FIVE

Now that Layne knew how much Eric had taken up the role of puppet master in her life, she struggled to play her part now that the veil had been lifted from her eyes. Regardless, she pushed through her feelings, knowing there would be inevitable retribution if only she played the game intelligently.

Joey had been keeping his distance while working diligently with his tech-savvy associates to uncover how far Eric's web stretched and exactly what secrets it held. He didn't want Layne's involvement in this to get any deeper or last any longer than necessary.

As a way to refocus her energy on something other than violence and sex, she found a healthier form of escape in running through Central Park. There was something cathartic about her feet against the ground, the brisk winter air against her face and in her lungs, and her muscles being pushed to move faster for longer.

She was three-and-a-half miles into the run and finally

getting into a groove of things. Layne had her earbuds in, listening to *Let the Sparks Fly* by Thousand Foot Krutch to keep up her pace. With frigid winter temperatures in full swing, she was thankful she had decided to toss on ivory gloves to keep her fingers warm and a matching knit hat on her head before she had left the house.

As she began to feel a surge of energy to keep gunning for her planned five miles, the sound of an incoming call dulled the upbeat music inside her ears. She groaned as she slowed down to answer the call through her earbuds. She panted as she tried to gradually ease her legs down to a walk.

"Hello?" Her voice sounded as out of breath as she felt.

Eric greeted her on the other end warmly. "Little harpy, I've been trying to get a hold of you. It seems you have been quite busy."

She winced at the stupidity of not screening her call before answering. Layne stepped off to the side of the path as she kept walking so her muscles didn't seize up on her. "I've had a lot going on."

"Oh? You'll have to tell me all about it. I will come meet up with you, and we can catch up."

Layne suppressed a groan as she placed a hand on her hip. "I'm actually in the middle of a run. Now's not a great time."

His voice during the start of the call had sounded cordial, but now there was something darker lurking underneath the words. "I wasn't asking whether or not it was a good time for you. Would you prefer I send my men to pick you up instead?"

She shook her head as she glanced around the section of Central Park she was in. It wasn't the most populated section, but she could quickly remedy that. "No, that's okay. I'm in Central Park; I can meet you near the first-mile marker."

His tone was quick to switch back to that lighter tone he had started the call with. "That sounds better. I will be there in fifteen minutes."

The call ended, and all the inner peace and calm she had begun to achieve on this run was quickly dissipating.

It only took her ten minutes to sprint back to the mile marker she had told Eric to meet her at. When she arrived, he was just walking up to it a solid five minutes early.

She pulled her earbuds from her ears and tucked them into the pockets of her leggings. Her face was still flushed from the mixture of physical exertion and the burn of icy wind hitting it during her workout. The warmth of her labored exhales was visible as it hit the freezing air.

Eric gave her a light smile as he looked her over. He had on a navy winter coat with a pair of dark leather gloves to fend off the cold.

When he leaned in to greet her with a kiss, she leaned away from him. "I'm all sweaty from my run."

His eyes narrowed but seemed to brush it off. "I wanted to talk about expectations that I may not have made clear enough, Layne. Let's walk." Eric's hand didn't make it a suggestion as he linked his arm with hers and began to escort them both down the path toward the more scenic and wooded area of the park.

Layne walked with him, already calculating the odds of

various things he wanted to talk with her about. Had he known she had taken his phone? Was he upset that Liam was still struggling to get access to the last of the primary bank accounts?

"What type of expectations did you want to talk about? Aside from a few minor items, I feel like this arrangement has been going fairly smoothly." She tried to keep things in a positive light and not immediately jump to doom and gloom.

Eric reached into his pocket and pulled out a turquoise jewelry box. "I realized that I may have been unfair in expecting you to take us seriously when I haven't held up all of my end of the bargain. If I want you to act like my wife, I should at least act like your husband." He drew back the top of the box to reveal a diamond ring nestled inside.

The surprise on Layne's face was authentic, if nothing else. This was one time she didn't have to pretend around him. Taking a look at the piece of jewelry before her, it definitely wouldn't have been the ring Layne would have chosen. It was a ring designed for show and status.

The ring held its own brand of beauty with its thick gold band with a large round diamond in the center and smaller diamonds inset around the entire band. While some woman somewhere would have been over the moon to be offered the ring, it couldn't have been further from Layne's tastes.

He stood there, letting her take in the sight of what he was offering to her. "I want everyone to see this ring on your finger and know that you're mine. When you see it on your finger when you wake up in the morning, let it be a reminder of all my promises to you."

After removing the ring from its box, he reached down for her hand. Not waiting for any type of response from her, he slid her glove off of her hand so he could slide the ring onto her finger. "There."

The ring felt heavy and cold on her hand. It felt more like a set of shackles than a romantic promise. Layne finally gathered some coherent thoughts together as she looked up at Eric. "This… This was not what I was expecting today."

Eric took her chin in his hand and pulled her into his kiss as though it was going to elevate the moment into something more meaningful. Afterward, he smiled at her. "Now that we have that taken care of, I wanted to let you know I have the movers coming in two weeks to pack up your things and move you into my house."

"What?" She blinked as her brain did a hard shift.

As with everything he said or did, it came off as non-negotiable. "I've done my part and given you more than sufficient time. Now, you need to show me you're willing to do yours."

Layne reminded herself that she needed to bide her time. She wanted nothing more than to strangle the life out of the man standing there before her. Patience was not at the top of her list of things she was great with, but she was stuck having to do her best.

While Eric seemingly was holding off the figurative underworld hyenas from attacking the remains of her family's business, it was at a cost. After learning how he had manipulated the entire Russ Spencer and Andrew Correlli situation, she didn't trust that anything he said or did was as it was being presented to her.

They continued their stroll around the park. Layne put her warm glove back on her hand, at least covering up the eyesore on her ring finger. Though, she could still feel the odd sensation of it shifting around on her hand.

Later on that evening, she was sitting in the driver's seat of her car with Rebecca in the passenger seat after picking her up.

"Holy Christ, woman!" Rebecca exclaimed as she stared at Layne's hand and the massive rock now adorning it.

Layne grimaced. "I know."

Her friend grabbed her hand to take a closer look at the ring on it. "I don't even want to know how much this is worth." Then, her face shifted into one of concern as she let go of Layne's hand.

Immediately, Layne was already ahead of her and was quick to speak up. "It's temporary and complicated. It's all for business purposes. I just didn't want you to be caught off guard."

"Too late for that!" Rebecca gave a small shove to Layne's shoulder of minor annoyance.

Layne released a breath of relief, now getting this heavy secret off her chest to the person who had been in her life since childhood and always treated her like blood.

"To make matters more complicated," Layne winced as she was about to drop another bomb on her bestie, "there's something else."

Rebecca's mouth dropped open. "Are you pregnant?"

"No!" Layne immediately responded, almost having a minor panic attack at the thought of how that would turn this entire situation into an even bigger shitshow. "Remember the guy? *The* guy?"

"Oh, you mean the one that did you dirty? That one? The one I would like to smack for what he put you through?" Rebecca huffed, recalling how much she wanted to lay into the man who managed to put Layne in such a dark spot. She hadn't gotten all the specifics, but as the best friend, it had been her duty to be pissed off on Layne's behalf.

"Well…" Layne struggled to fully come out and say it. Thankfully, she didn't need to when Rebecca made the leap that Joey was back in the picture.

Rebecca's eyes widened. "Girl!"

Layne gave a slightly apologetic smile. "I know, I know. It's different this time. I don't know how to explain it. Things are just… I don't know. It's different. Like, it's beyond not being able to breathe around him. All I want to do is breathe him in. God, he just has this ability to make me feel like I'm the only person that exists in his world."

Rebecca nodded as she listened, a smirk easing onto her face.

Layne picked up on the expression Rebecca had that said she had some thoughts on all of this. "What??"

"I'm not going to say it." She grinned as she picked her water bottle up from the cupholder and took a sip.

Staring at Rebecca, Layne picked up a random crumpled-up receipt from her last fill at the gas station and tossed it at her. "Tell me!"

Smugly, Rebecca sat there, knowing something that Layne wasn't even aware of. "No, I'm not going to say it because you're going to get all freaked out and spooked. I'm not going to be held responsible for that."

Layne sighed and shook her head. "You're lucky that I would be unable to function without you around. Otherwise, I would drop your ass off at Penn Station and ship you down to Baltimore to go visit your mom."

Rebecca laughed. "You wouldn't last a week."

"I know, that's why you're still here. You're the one piece of sanity and normalcy in my life." Layne smiled, knowing that without Rebecca, she likely would have taken an even darker path in her life.

CHAPTER TWENTY-SIX

There was still a week before Eric had stated he was sending movers over her direction to pack all her shit up and move it. Layne had been doing her best not to stress over it while Joey was pushing his team to work as fast as they could.

With the knowledge that Eric was manipulating the entire criminal ecosystem to fit his agenda, Layne needed to start planning on how to get it back under her control. What did that mean? Late nights figuring out which contacts were trustworthy, financial planning, and stressing over all the strategizing to avoid her family business becoming defunct.

By the time the evening rolled around, Layne was exhausted. While she sat on the couch, nearly dozing off with the television in the background, the doorbell chimed.

Layne lifted her head and stirred groggily. Another ring of the doorbell echoed throughout her home. Her hand rubbed across her face, trying to shake off the excess fatigue.

"I'm coming." She muttered out to the emptiness of her home.

Shoving herself off the sofa, she shuffled to the front door and took a peep outside to see who was there at—she glanced at her watch on her wrist—nearly eleven-thirty at night. When she saw the familiar face of Eric, she shook her head. Did nobody call anymore?

Layne pulled open the door as her hand brushed some hair away from her face. "Hey, I didn't expect you here this late at night. What are you doing here?"

Eric pushed his way inside without a word.

She shut the door behind him while the expression on her face turned sour. "Nice to see you, too." Something was off about his demeanor.

Eric reached into his pocket and pulled out his new phone. He opened it up and pulled up security footage from her house's camera system. She leaned in to take a look at one video in particular that he was pulling up.

Layne didn't recognize the angle of the camera as she never had a camera posted on that side of her house. She glanced at Eric in confusion. "What am I supposed to be looking at here?"

"Give it a second." He responded dryly.

As a body appeared on the screen, that's when she knew they had fucked up. The only thing on that side of the house was an egress window that led into her cellar. She forgot that it even existed because she never went down there unless she had to dig around for holiday decorations.

The silver lining was that she now knew how Joey had been getting in and out of her house. The big-ass dark thundercloud, who was Eric, unfortunately, had evidence of it.

"It looks like a visitor to me." She attempted to keep both her face and her tone neutral to avoid giving too much away.

After the video ended, Eric put the phone away and turned to face her, not having an ounce of pleasantness on his face. "I was concerned that there was a safety issue after seeing this, and I went back, and to my surprise, I found this wasn't the only incident."

"What do you want me to say, Eric? Did you think I was going to ditch my security detail the second we made this official? We run drills to make sure we both are on top of our game in the event someone does try to make a go at me." Damn, that sounded like some of the better bullshit she had come up with on the fly in a while. She was impressed with herself for it, especially given how tired she had been before his arrival. Her eyes stared directly at him, hoping to make him feel stupid for even questioning her.

As good as it was, it didn't settle with Eric as well as she had hoped. "I have been more than reasonable with you. I have been fending off all the vultures of the city from swooping down and feeding off of what's left of your pathetic empire. I've been doing my part in our agreement, and what have you done to repay me for it?"

She could see Eric's jaw twitching and his nostrils flaring. He turned his back to her while clenching his fists at his side.

Before she could attempt a response to his question, he

spun around to face her, his hand going flying. Layne may have been half asleep, but thank God her muscle memory kicked in, and her arm shot up to defend against a direct blow.

Eric didn't wait for her to counter, he grabbed her by the forearm and propelled her toward the stairs. Layne stumbled, and her hands caught herself on a step several up on the staircase.

When she turned, she felt his body knock into her, the edge of the steps painfully pounding into her back on impact. His hands wrapped around her throat, squeezing with a force that could rival a boa constrictor.

Layne's initial cough and gasp were immediately cut off as her airway was closed off. Staring up into Eric's face, his eyes were wide and lit up with the psychosis of an entire mental ward. He pulled her by her neck upward, only to slam her back down onto those unforgiving wooden stairs that had her brain rattling inside her skull.

Her hands scratched at his hand, pulling at individual fingers and straining to get even a brief moment of air while her face began to pale from the lack of oxygen.

Eric's words were vile and bitter as he spit them out at her. "You thought you could hide it from me?! The way you look at each other? It all makes fucking sense as to why you were reluctant to whore yourself out to me!"

Layne used a foot against the wall that bordered the staircase to push off to rotate them both while she shoved his back into the iron-clad stair spindles. It was enough to loosen his grasp.

She gasped for air but didn't wait long to recover.

Pushing off the stairs with her feet, she jetted up the steps toward the second floor. Her feet pounded against the floor as she flung herself around the ninety-degree angle at the top of the mid-floor landing before dashing up the rest of the way to the second floor.

His words shouted behind her. "Little harpy! Come back!"

He had to be out of his damn mind if he thought she was going to go anywhere near him. She reached her bedroom and slid down onto her knees toward her bed, where she reached underneath to where she had a partial arsenal stored. Her hands grabbed frantically for the first available weapon of choice.

She drew forth a semi-automatic pistol and flicked the safety off. When she pulled back the slide to load the chamber, she didn't hesitate to aim it at the doorway as Eric came charging in. Her finger pressed against the trigger.

Click.

Her eyes glanced down and noticed the bullet jam from the top view of the chamber. *Fuck.* She popped up onto her feet, not having time to mess around with the mechanical failure. She spun the pistol around in her hand and swung the grip at him.

Eric caught her forearm while his other hand twisted her wrist painfully until she couldn't hold onto the firearm any longer. It fell to the floor with a clunk. "That's not being a good little bird, now is it?"

Layne winced at the painful angle of her wrist, but it didn't diminish the hatred raging behind her eyes. "I will never be your bird to keep in a cage." She gave a front kick towards his gut.

While his grasp on her wrist was released, it was only in exchange for capturing her foot's attack. Eric pushed back on her leg, changing her momentum against her to knock her off balance as she fell back, smashing into the area where her mattress met her nightstand.

Her arm knocked her lamp onto the ground with a shatter of porcelain while her other arm tried to brace her fall as her hand grasped at the down-filled comforter. The engagement ring he had forced on her had also been on top of the nightstand and was also knocked off onto the floor.

The anger in Eric's glare at her was reaching an all-time boil. "Did you think I wouldn't know? You could have had the best life has to offer with me." He loomed over her while she was cornered there. "It's a shame because I was looking forward to showing everyone how I could own and tame the wild Layne O'Reilly."

His hands reached down, grabbed Layne by her shirt, and yanked her up onto her feet. Eric pulled her in so she was face-to-face with him.

With ragged breaths, Layne didn't shy away from looking him in the eye. "Go fuck yourself. I was never going to be yours."

His fist slammed into her temple. Layne dropped to the floor as the impact sent her mind for a brief mental vacation riddled with darkness.

When her consciousness slowly came back to her, she lay there on the floor as her eyes squinted. A splitting headache loomed over her brain, and an unparalleled grogginess suffocated her thoughts. Layne groaned and placed her hands on the floor to push herself up. It felt like it took the effort of a thousand lifetimes.

When she lifted her hands, they stopped midway up to her face. That's when she noticed the cold rounds of metal handcuffs latched around her wrists. Her mind fought to recognize why they were there.

As her wits became about her, she tugged on the chain connecting each wrist to feel it did not give her much leeway. Between the joints of the cuffs was a length of a metal chain that connected directly to the underside of the bed frame in front of her.

The ringing in her ears was deafening. Glancing around, it seemed that she was alone, but the roaring in her ears wasn't easing up, it was only getting worse.

She coughed as she managed to shift onto her knees with her hands linked together. Her eyes burned each time she blinked. Her nostrils flared with each breath, taking in an overwhelming odor of burning wood.

Soon, she recognized the source of the ringing in her ears. It wasn't inside of her head; it was inside of her home. The smoke detectors were all sounding off. Their high-pitched sounds sliced through the air.

Layne looked over to her wide-open bedroom door. The sight had a panic rising inside her chest. The billowing smoke and visible flames at the end of the hallway were eating away at her home.

It was all like a vicious monster slowly creeping towards her bedroom, ready to consume her. Frantically, she pulled at her hands, and the connected chain prevented her from getting very far from her bed. Each pull was harder than the one before it. Layne grunted with each yank, feeling the pinch of metal biting into her skin.

She used her body weight to lean back and her foot against the edge of the bed to try and overcome the strength of steel. Continually, she glanced over at the open doorway to notice her time was running short as the smoke continued to edge towards her room.

She ferally screamed out in frustration. Tears leaked from her eyes as she choked on a sob. Layne couldn't let this be how her story ended. "God, please, just this once," she begged for the pity of her maker.

The fear and adrenaline left her uncontrollably shaking as the situation felt insurmountable. She leaned forward, pressed her head against her mattress, and shut her eyes tightly. The sheets soaked up her tears. "Please…"

She sank back to sit on her ankles. Her eyes hurt from dryness in the air, licking away her emotions. Feeling lost, she stared at the metal bracelets around her wrists, which were now painfully raw from all her frantic struggles.

A sensation came over her in that moment of hopelessness. One final renewed effort filled her. Layne laid herself on the floor and took a look under her bed to see where the chain connected. Her one shot at a miracle presented itself to her. There may not have been hope in breaking steel, but a long shot presented itself.

Her eyes caught sight of the box underneath her bed that stored all her kinky toys. What were the chances that the keys from one set of cuffs were likely to open another? Using her legs, she maneuvered the box of goodies closer to her until she could use her hands to open up the lid and begin digging for what she hoped was still in there.

Her fingertips finally tracked down the key. It belonged to a set of Smith & Wesson cuffs, and looking at the etching on the ones around her wrists, she frowned. It was another brand, Peerless. "Fuck."

Not having any other bright ideas, she tried the key in the assembly anyway. When the most beautiful clicking sound was heard, and she felt the loops loosen on her, she could have sat there and cried if she had enough time to do so, but she didn't.

She removed the restraints quickly and dropped them to the floor. She wasn't going to be burning in hell today, as luck would have it.

The panic tugged at her chest as the overwhelming surroundings became more urgent. The burning smell. The smoke alarms. The heat. Pushing through the fear, she ran over to her bedroom window. Sliding the window pane up, she popped the screen out and watched it gracefully flutter to the ground two stories below.

No part of her was willing to burn to death in her own home. She put one leg through the open window and straddled the frame as she peered outside, looking at the best options to get down in one piece.

Strategically, she lowered herself out of the window. Her hands grasped the ledge as her muscles strained under her weight to control her descent. Her legs dangled beneath her as her feet stretched to touch the motorized sun awning casing just below.

Layne was now thanking her lucky stars that Rebecca

had talked her into getting one installed to stretch out over a portion of the back patio for the hot summer days when there was no shade to be found elsewhere in her backyard.

It wasn't a graceful descent after that point, but the rolled-up awning cover helped buffer her fall. She rolled against the ground, scraping her arms up in the process against the cement. It was better than going down in a fiery blaze.

She backed up to take a look at her house, seeing the extent of how much the fire had already spread. The luck of the Irish had been on her side. Layne had been fortunate to get out when she did.

While she stood in her backyard staring, the flames reflected in her eyes as her home and everything inside began to be burned into ash.

CHAPTER TWENTY-SEVEN

All that she had worked for had been in that house. She sat there across the street on the edge of the sidewalk and stared at the burning ruins. The FDNY had arrived and was slowly working the house fire under control with hoses from several trucks.

The smell of the fire hung heavily on the air, her clothes and even her hair as a reminder of the events that had just transpired.

That bastard had robbed her of everything that those walls held. Layne shut her eyes. It wasn't just the material belongings that were lost to the blaze; it was all the intangible memories that went with it.

"I'm not a good guy, and you're not a good girl."

Joey's voice echoed in her mind from the day he first set foot inside that house.

"No, watch! This is the part where he drops the entire plate of food on his date!"

Trashy television girl nights with Rebecca alongside tacos and margaritas.

"It's yours, Layne. You've earned it."

The way her father dropped the keys into the palm of her hand the day he bought the house for all the hard work she had done for the family business.

All of it was on its way to being nothing but charred wood and ash now.

"Layne?" Liam's voice prompted her to open her eyes. He half jogged over to her. "What the hell happened?"

Her fingertips quickly swept away a rogue tear from underneath her eye. "What are you doing here?"

"The company handling the fire alarm system had my number on file." He looked over at the extent of the ongoing damage to the property. "Fuck."

"Yeah." She had the same damn sentiment.

He stood there silently, staring at the destruction with Layne while she sat there doing the same. There was nothing but the sound of the fire roaring and the water pouring from the hoses trying to contain it. Emergency lights from all the firetrucks continued to reflect off the windows of all the surrounding houses and parked cars on the street. Nearby nosey neighbors peeked out from their houses to watch.

The sound of tires squealing against the pavement could be heard at the end of the street. It was followed by a set of headlights as a car rounded the corner and sped up to the other end of the street, where all the emergency vehicles were parked.

The black car quickly pulled off to the side as close to

the fire engines as it could get. The lights went dark, and a car door was shut as a voice yelled out. "Layne! LAYNE!"

Immediately, she pushed away from the ground to get up onto her feet after hearing Joey's emotionally charged voice. When her eyes caught sight of him, he was trying to push past three firefighters toward the blaze that had been lit with the intention to consume her.

"Joey!" She took off running towards him. "Joey!"

Hearing her call his name, he shoved off the hands of the first responders, trying to keep him from charging into her house. Joey stopped struggling with the men standing between him and her house when he heard the sweetest voice call his name again from the other direction. When he caught sight of her, he immediately sprinted toward her.

When they met in the middle of the street, she threw herself up against him. Her arms wrapped around his neck, and her face burrowed into his shoulder.

He caught her as she flung herself at him, his arms lifted and held her tightly as he pressed his face into her hair. He didn't care that she smelled like singed daisies from the smoke and ash. He only cared that he would still have more days to wake up next to her intoxicating scent that reminded him of summer rain on a hill full of daisies.

Layne wrapped her legs around his waist, refusing to let go of him. No matter how closely she held herself against him, it wasn't close enough. Her body shuddered as the floodgates behind her eyes burst open. His shirt soaked up the tears from her eyes and muffled the sounds of her sobs. Her hands clawed at the shirt on his back, scrunching it up in her hands as she held herself to him.

Joey protectively placed a hand on the back of her head as he hushed into her ear. "I've got you. It's okay, Layney."

She choked on her own words as she tried to explain everything that had happened. "I-it was Eric. He saw you on the cameras, and... and he was furious. I tried, but—"

He stopped her right there, holding her tightly in the safety of his arms. "Shh. I'm here; nothing is going to happen to you."

After what felt like the longest release of emotional turmoil, she lifted her face to look at him. The tears had left their red marks down her cheeks. Visible was the bruise and slight swelling at her temple where she had taken the hit that had rendered her unconscious.

He immediately gave her several kisses of reassurance, not just on her lips but across her face to replace the salty tears. Joey was careful to kiss even more tenderly around the visible injuries.

Layne used one hand to hold onto the back of his neck as her other came up to brush away the strands of hair from her face. The raw abrasions from the cuffs were still fresh on her skin and stung with each flex of her hands.

She sniffled, trying to recover from the emotions that were still taking their toll on her after the evening's events. "How did you know to come here?"

Joey pressed his forehead against hers, his hands still protectively holding her to him. "I heard it over the police scanner. I recognized the address and..." His voice trailed off, unable to finish what horrible thoughts had entered his mind.

Realizing that he had run straight for the inferno taking

over her home, she frowned at him. "You ran towards the house. That was stupid; you wouldn't have even made it to the stairs."

He looked her directly in the eyes and shook his head. "Layne, I love you. I would have let the flames take me straight to hell to pay for all my sins before giving up on you."

Her lower lip trembled as she released a few fresh tears from her eyes. Her lips kissed him several times from hearing him speak those words to her.

A sarcastic voice interrupted what should have been a sweet and tender moment. "Yeah, right." Liam chimed in, overhearing the private conversation. Her brother always had spectacular timing to decide to open his mouth and subject everyone to his assholery.

Joey's eyes lost their warmth as he looked over at Liam. Gently, he set Layne down on her feet. He stepped up to Liam, looming several inches taller than the younger O'Reilly. "Do you have something to say?" The sharp edge of his tone indicated that Liam was walking on very thin ice.

Liam scoffed and didn't back away. "I do. You're full of crap. If Layne didn't have her head all fucked up by your inability to stay out of her pants, our family wouldn't be in this mess! You don't give two shits about her."

He forcefully shoved Joey to add emphasis to his words. The second Liam put his hands on Joey, it set off an immediate reaction. Joey grabbed Liam's shirt and pushed him back roughly into a parked car. There was no hesitation as Joey's fist crashed into Liam's jaw.

"You're a fuckin' shitbag!" Joey's words yelled back at him.

From there, Liam began throwing punches back, and the two of them began wrestling with one another. Layne stayed out of the way and watched, knowing Liam could use a little tough love from someone other than her for once.

Joey landed a few more body shots on Liam, who wasn't anywhere near the same weight class by comparison. It was all too easy for Joey to keep the upper hand while they both wrangled with one another.

Finally, after several minutes of jabs and hooks exchanged, Joey landed one last hit across Liam's face, sending him to the ground. Liam landed on the ground and rolled onto his side while groaning from the ass-kicking Joey had just handed him.

Breathing heavily, Joey wiped his mouth with the back of his hand, noticing a small smear of blood from one of the few half-ass hits Liam did manage to land. "I swear to God, if you ever disrespect your sister and all she's done to fix your fuck-ups again, I will not hesitate to make sure to break your jaw so bad it will have to be wired shut for months."

Layne walked up to Joey, placing a hand gently on his flexed bicep, still tense from the scuffle. "Let's just go. I can't be here anymore." She gestured to the fire, still contrasting against the night sky as it consumed what was once her home. The exhaustion of everything she had been through was evident in her voice.

There was still an intensity in Joey's stare at the spoiled

brat writhing on the ground. Finally, he noticed Layne's hand tugging at his arm, and he nodded in agreement. Joey wrapped his hand around hers, intertwining their fingers as he led her back to the Challenger he had arrived in.

Once they were both inside the car, Layne latched her seatbelt and then looked over at him. "Did you mean what you said?"

He raised a brow at her. "The next time he opens his mouth, Layne, I am not holding back. Someone needs to make him learn that there are bigger fish out there that don't give a fuck."

"No, that's not what I was talking about." Her emerald hues looked at him with the weight of all the evening's emotions in them.

Realizing what she was questioning, he turned in the driver's seat, and his hand reached over to take hold of her face. The warmth of his palm against her skin made her want to melt into his touch.

"Every damn word of it, and I never plan to let you forget it, either. You are everything that makes me want to continue breathing. I love you, Layney." Joey leaned over and made sure she felt every ounce of his words as he pulled her into a tender kiss.

CHAPTER TWENTY-EIGHT

"You're a real stubborn pain in my ass, you know that?" Joey sighed as he watched Layne shove another box into the corner of O'Reilly Manor's master bedroom.

She smoothed back a piece of hair from her face. "There's more space here than your place. No one is forcing you to move in here with me." Layne stated it matter-of-factly.

Joey wrapped his arms around her waist and drew her against him with a smirk. "Did you think that I was going to let you out of my sight?"

Layne pushed herself up onto her tiptoes to lightly kiss him. "No, and that's why I knew I'd get away with doing things my way." She smirked right back at him. Her hand patted his solid chest before she slid out of his arms.

Thankfully, she had some extra belongings in her old bedroom there in the house she grew up in. She had never moved them into the now-condemned property that had been her home for the last several years. Not to mention, between Joey and Rebecca, they both made sure that she had everything else she needed.

His eyes watched as Layne moved about the room, adjusting things to the way she wanted. Her ponytail swayed back and forth with each step. The way her hips moved just begged for his hands to grab them. When she bent over to grab another box off the floor, his cock stiffened at the sight of her magnificent ass that needed his hand, leaving red marks on it.

Joey was two steps away from acting on his desires when his phone began to ring in his pocket. He grumbled quietly as he answered it. "Yeah?"

After lifting the box off the ground, Layne turned at the sound of Joey speaking to see him taking a call. She prayed it was the call they had been waiting on. The call would reveal all of Eric's secrets and the green light for Joey to proceed with the hit.

Her eyes watched every shift in his movements as he listened to the person on the other end of the phone. One hand came up to rub over his forehead, the tattoos on his fingers flexing with each movement.

"What do you mean there's been a small issue?" The tension in Joey's voice indicated that whatever he was hearing on the other end of the line wasn't what he had hoped to hear. "I'm not going to wait for-fucking-ever. Figure it out, or else I'm making my move whether the client wants me to or not."

The call ended, and Joey forced his phone back into his pocket as he finally looked over at Layne with conflict and frustration in his eyes. "There were some issues with the integrity of the data. They're rerunning a few things, but the client is now getting gun-shy."

She put the box back down on the floor and walked over to him with a frown. This wasn't the news either of them wanted to hear about Eric. "Look, Eric's not going anywhere right now. He's in too deep, especially trying to sort through all of my business contacts he took over. I doubt he's going to take that big of a financial hit just to up and take off."

Layne rubbed her hands along his sides, hoping to ease his stress some.

He shook his head. "I'm sure by now he knows there were no casualties in the fire, thanks to the damn paper. Eric isn't going to just shrug this off and forget that you still exist, and he isn't getting a hefty life insurance payout."

"I know, but I've got you here with me. Do you think Eric is good enough to take both of us on? I'd like to see what army he would have to send." She tried to put Joey's concerns to rest, that waiting just a little longer wouldn't be the end of the world.

Seeing that Joey still wasn't feeling at ease, she grabbed his hand and tugged. "C'mon, I have something to show you that should make you feel a little bit better."

Joey's brow lifted curiously but didn't hesitate in allowing Layne to lead him out of the master bedroom. They both walked down the hall until Layne led him downstairs. Eventually, she stopped at a closed door with a giddy smile on her face. "Are you ready?"

She swung open the door, and the motion triggered the lights to pop on, revealing what was in the room. The lights illuminated the room to unveil several black leather movie theater seats across from a large screen in an entertainment room designed for residential use. Fiber optic star ceiling tiles lined the ceiling, and theater-style wall sconces added to the atmosphere.

Layne pulled him inside with her so he could see the entirety of all the room had to offer. "This has always been my favorite room in the house. There are reclining seats, a professional-grade sound system, a snack station, and you can watch just about anything in here."

She wasn't exaggerating either. The room even contained a smaller version of a popcorn machine that you could find at the actual movie theaters.

He had never had the chance to fully explore O'Reilly Manor while Layne's dad was still alive, but he was pleasantly surprised to see that this room existed. Ever the typical guy, Joey imagined all the sports games he could watch in here.

Layne stopped and turned to him. "Oh, and my favorite part about this room?" Her eyes twinkled in mischievous delight as she was about to share some big secret. She leaned in and whispered to him. "It's fully soundproof. You can make me scream as loud as you want in here."

She grinned while pressing her teeth into her bottom lip as her eyes looked up into his while all the dirty thoughts in her mind ran rampant.

Joey immediately forgot about the disappointing phone call as Layne shared that little fact with him. His hand took her by the back of her neck while his other hand dropped down to grab a handful of her ass. His gravelly voice dropped into a possessive growl. "I'm going to need to test that out."

Excitement tugged somewhere deep inside of her between her thighs as she recognized the feral look in his eyes that he gave when he had her in his sights. He released her ass and began walking her back until she was against the black wall. Leaning forward, he rested his forearm against the wall as his mouth barely drifted over the side of her neck. "But first, you're going to do something for me."

Playfully, she bantered back. "Oh, am I?"

"Mmhmm. You're going to be a good girl for me." His hand wrapped around her throat, applying momentary pressure before releasing and running his hand down the center of her body. His fingers stopped at the top of the leggings she had on.

"That is unless you don't want to feel me here." His hand slid down a little further over her pants and pressed his fingers against the apex of her legs. With his fingers finding her weak spot, she quietly gasped out at the aching need flaring up.

"Or maybe, even here." His hand slid further back between her legs until his fingers pushed against the hole of her ass. "The way you've been shaking your fuckin' ass at me all damn day makes me think it needs to be taken."

Layne's body squirmed under his touch as her need for him escalated. Very quickly, she realized she would agree to do anything this man wanted her to do if he would just take her as he pleased. Her hips pressed against his touch as her hands pulled on his tee. "Joey, I need you to stop teasing me."

Slowly, he dragged his fingers back along her crease until his hand moved away from her entirely. "Uh-uh. You're not the one calling the shots right now."

She groaned as a sense of electricity in her body was lost the second he severed contact with her body.

"Strip." That was all he commanded of her before stepping back to give her enough space to comply.

The urge to just rip all of her clothes off in record time was overwhelming, but she knew that Joey couldn't resist a good show. While her shoes were the first to come off, she took her time with everything else. Her fingers lifted the bottom of her shirt and peeled it up away from her body, exposing one inch of flesh at a time.

After the black and gold lace bra underneath was revealed, she pulled the shirt up over her head and dropped it to the floor. She trailed her fingers down over her body before turning her back to him. Layne's hands reached back to find the hook of her bra, unclasping it with one smooth movement. She looked back at him over her shoulder to see that he had taken a seat in one of the theater-style chairs.

Her eyes met his as she smiled seductively. Her fingers slowly dragged the straps of her bra down over each shoulder. The bra joined her shirt on the floor. Keeping her back to him, she hooked her thumbs on the waist of her leggings and shimmied her hips a little extra for his viewing pleasure.

It must have been just the right move because she heard

him groan in delight as he sat there behind her, his hand resting on the bulge pushing against the fly of his jeans.

Layne tugged the stretchy material down over the swell of her ass, bending over as she did so. It became quickly clear she was still being his good girl and abiding by his no underwear rule.

"Fuck, Layney…" His voice sounded out of breath.

She remained bent over for a few extra seconds so he could get a good look at her body before she stepped out of her pants. Layne straightened back up and walked over to him, inviting herself to straddle his lap on her knees.

"Was that what you wanted from me?" Her hands ran over the tops of his broad shoulders and up his neck until her fingers got lost in his hair. Her exposed tits and their stiff peaks were right in front of his face.

He rubbed his hands over the bare skin of her legs up over her hips before they grabbed her at her waist. "I want everything from you. You're too goddamn perfect not to indulge in everything your body has to offer." Joey latched his mouth onto her nipple, sucking hungrily on it. His tongue circled the stiffness while tasting her.

Her hands tightened their grasp on his dirty blonde locks of hair as she held his head up against her. She moaned out as his teeth nipped and prompted a pleasurable pain while the harsh scruff around his mouth brushed against her skin's softness.

Joey moved his mouth over to her other breast, being sure to give it an equal amount of attention. This time, however, he moved a hand between her legs and plunged two fingers deep inside of her.

Her body's dripping arousal made for easy entry and smooth movements as he began pumping his digits into her. She tilted her head back as a moan was drawn out of her. Her chest rose and fell with each sensation he thrust onto her body.

He took his mouth off of her to admire the sight of how her face moved as she felt the pleasure he was giving her. "Such a good girl getting all nice and wet for me, Layney. I bet your pussy is begging for me to give it a nice hard fuck, isn't it?" He circled his thumb over her clit, causing her hips to buck against his touch as she cried out.

She could barely put coherent thoughts together while his fingers continued to dive deeper into her. "Yes! Yes! I need you."

He pulled his fingers from her with a smile. His hand grabbed her jaw and pulled her face down to his so he could get a taste of her mouth. Overwhelmed with desire, it felt like he had consumed her soul with the kiss.

When he breathlessly broke the seal of their lips, he nodded behind her. "Go get on your hands and knees for me. I want to admire your sweet ass while you take all of my cock."

Layne complied, getting herself down on the floor as he asked like a lioness in heat. She heard the sound of his clothes hitting the floor, and soon the strength of his hands pulled on her hips to yank her back so she could feel his dick against her opening while he kneeled behind her.

Her body ached to feel him inside of her, prompting her to push back against him to get what she wanted. "Make me scream for you. Please."

"Oh, that's not going to be a problem." He smirked as he sank the hard thickness of his length into her. Once he was fully inside her, with her cheeks up against him, he groaned at the depths of her tightness that wrapped around him.

She yelled out in relief as he finally gave her what her body was craving from him. Joey drew back and rolled his hips back in again as he moved in and out of her pussy. Each stroke of him deep inside of her brought her closer to release.

Joey slammed himself harder into her as he felt her body tensing up in anticipation of her climax. "That's it, Layney, I want you to tell me who this tight cunt belongs to when you come."

With her hands holding herself up on the floor, she felt the shaking in her limbs as he continued to ram into her. She clawed at the carpet underneath her, and her body felt an explosion deep in her core as she screamed out. Her cries were drawn out as she clenched down onto him. "You do, Joey! You do! God! Yes!"

He growled as he felt the wet warmth of her cover his cock. "That's right. And that's not the only thing I'm going to own."

Joey pulled out of her, his fingers briefly diving back inside of her body, prompting another squeal from Layne. He ran the slickness of his fingers between her ass, working one inside the tight hole. His finger pushed and stretched her using her own cum to make the entry easier.

Her heavy pants from her orgasm were slowing, and now a new sensation was pressing inside of her. Before she could give it more thought, Joey's cock filled her soaked pussy once more, making sure he was well-coated by her body's wetness.

His finger was removed from her ass before he pulled his dick from her. Then, he lined himself up with the hole he hadn't yet taken.

She glanced back at him breathlessly as she felt the rounded head of his cock line up again, this time at a much tighter entrance. "Joey, you're not going to be able to fit."

He devilishly smirked at her. "Oh, don't worry, I will fit just fine. Now be a good girl, and let me finally fuck this ass."

She swallowed down a little bit of her apprehension before letting her trust in him take over. Layne nodded to give him the go-ahead.

With her body's natural lube still covering his cock he began to inch himself into her. Joey moaned out at the immediate tightness enveloping him, being sure to refrain from going too quickly to start.

Layne gasped lightly at the initial discomfort as her body had to stretch to accommodate him. The full sensation of him pushing into her backdoor for the first time had her hands trying to grasp at the carpet. With each push forward that he made into her, he allowed her to adjust before continuing.

"That's it, Layney. You're doing so well taking each inch of my cock in your sweet ass." He groaned as he pushed into her further, nearly to the hilt. "Mm, you feel so fucking good and so goddamn tight." His voice was strained from the way her body had to stretch around him.

After the full length of his member was seated inside of her, he sighed at the sensation. Layne moaned at the fullness he was providing her, finding it brought on a whole new and different level of pleasure.

"Joey, God, you feel even bigger when you're in my ass." She pushed her hips back against him, letting herself find enjoyment in having him take her body this way.

He pulled himself back until just the tip of his cock remained inside of her and pushed back into her, this time with one smooth movement. A feral moan escaped past her lips as she felt him fill her back up. Her hand reached down between her legs, and her fingers rubbed over her throbbing clit that was aching for attention.

Joey's hands tightly locked onto her hips as he began with slow thrusts before picking up the pace. The sound of their bodies slapping together filled the room. He grunted each time he shoved his dick into her, and she groaned at the way her body felt perfectly designed for him.

Layne's fingers worked over her small bundle of nerves, quickly working up to another orgasm as he fucked her ass as though he owned it, and own it, he did. Her body came to the familiar ledge of glorious release. Panting hard, she opened her mouth to tell him she was going to come, and instead, all that came out was another scream of ecstasy.

As Layne's climax tore through her, Joey whimpered while clinging to the last bit of control he had. "Fuck!" Following her over the same cliff of satisfaction, he cursed as he fully shoved himself deep inside her tight hole, and his seed shot forth violently inside of her ass.

Moments later, they were both a hot mess on the floor; Joey still buried inside her while his chest was pressed up against her back. His mouth kissed the crook of her neck while his warm breaths melted against her skin. His hand caressed over the side of her body lovingly.

Layne lay there with him, feeling a sense of satisfaction that had gone beyond anything she knew possible. She knew that he was her everything, and yet she still couldn't bring herself past the other edge of fear to say those three words to him.

CHAPTER TWENTY-NINE

Despite the fact that they were waiting impatiently for word back on the data to be reevaluated by Joey's associates, Layne couldn't complain too much. It allowed the two of them to enjoy spending time together.

Earlier in the day, they had each gotten a workout in, with Joey helping Layne refine some of her skills that would be useful against someone significantly larger than her - which was most people she encountered. After their training session, they had another type of workout. The type without any clothes.

Layne heard a knock at the door, prompting her to go answer while she was on her way to the kitchen to grab another round of drinks for both her and Joey. When she looked out the side window, nobody was to be seen standing out front. She opened up the door, and there was a bouquet of black magic roses wrapped in black and burgundy floral paper.

What should have been a welcomed delivery for most other women, Layne's face fell at the sight of them. She leaned over and picked them up, bringing them back into the house. Setting the unexpected gift on a side table, she plucked out the card from the center.

Her fingers opened up the black envelope and pulled out the crimson card. Flipping it open, something fell out onto the floor. The black ink was sprawled across the inside in neatly written words.

You fucked around. Now, you're going to have to play my game with my rules. – Eric

When Layne bent over to pick up the fallen contents from the floor, she saw it was a piece of hard plastic. Turning it over in her hand, she immediately noticed the face on the driver's license. Rebecca. Her heart couldn't have sunk faster if it had been tied to a twenty-ton anchor.

"No…" The words were hardly above a whisper.

"Who was at the door?" Joey asked from the sofa in the living room while the television had a replay of the NHL Winter Classic on.

She dropped everything onto the floor and pulled her phone out, immediately placing a call to Rebecca's number. Layne ran into the office she had been sharing with Liam, pulled out her gun, and checked to see that it was loaded as she waited for her best friend to answer. After it rang several times, it went to voicemail.

"Damnit!" She tried calling again as she tucked her pistol in the back of her pants as she left her office and nearly ran Joey over now that he was coming to check on her.

The concern in his eyes was heavy as he saw the frenzied look on her face. "Layne, what's going on?"

Ring, ring, ri—

The call was answered, and she was quick to blurt out her friend's name with panicked hope. "Rebecca?!"

A sinister and all too familiar voice spoke on the other end of the line. "This is Rebecca's answering service; she is currently unavailable right now."

"Eric, you motherfucker! I swear to God, if you have so much as looked at her wrong, I will put a bullet in each of your fuckin' eyes, then I will rip out each of your pathetic little balls and shove them into your eye sockets." Her body was shaking from the anger filling her up.

"My, my. There's no need for violence, little harpy. I just wanted to get to know your friend a little better. She means so much to you; it only seemed right that I make an effort to see how strong of a friendship you truly have." Eric's tone taunted Layne, and it was working.

Pinning the phone between her shoulder and her ear, Layne went to the coat closet and began digging through the various clips and rounds available in their stock. "Put her on the phone." Layne gritted her teeth, picturing all the ways that she was going to make Eric suffer the second she laid eyes on him.

Overhearing enough of the conversation, Joey gathered a bag and began filling it with his own selection of supplies. He grabbed his mask, shoving it into his pocket for now.

Eric chuckled darkly. "Only if you ask politely."

She took the phone back into her hand, squeezing it until her knuckles were white with tension. The temptation to just toss it down on the ground out of frustration was overwhelming. Yet, that wouldn't get her very far. Layne put the phone back up to her ear and fought through every insult she wanted to unleash on him.

Not hearing anything, Eric prompted her again. "I'm waiting."

"*Please*, put Rebecca on the phone." Her words weren't pleasant, indicating she was struggling with his request.

A dark chuckle could be heard in response to her ask, "I'm not sure that was nice enough. I know you can do better than that."

She shut her eyes to find a part of her deep down inside that she could summon enough of what he wanted to hear. "Eric, I would really appreciate it if you could be so kind as to let me speak with Rebecca. Please."

There was a pause on the other end before Rebecca's voice, riddled with fear and panic, spoke up. "Layne! Layne, please help!"

Simultaneously, there was relief her bestie was alive and heartbreak that this nightmare was actually transpiring. Layne took the small window of opportunity to speak quickly. "Listen to me, Rebecca. I am not going to let anything happen to you, I promise. Just hang in there, please. I will get you out of there as soon as I can. He's not going to—"

It was unclear how much Rebecca heard as Eric responded with a cruel and mocking tone. "You have such a habit of making promises. Are you sure you can keep that one?"

Impatiently, she snapped at him. "Just tell me what you're looking for."

"I thought you knew by now. I want you, my little harpy. All to myself." Eric made it sound damn obvious and simple.

"You let her go unharmed, and you'll have me." As Layne spoke those words, Joey's attention was caught as he looked over at her and shook his head. He had a warning in his eyes.

Eric made a half-assed attempt to sound apologetic. "It's not going to be that easy, I'm afraid."

"Then, make it that easy. I'm not going to play games with you." So many thoughts ran through Layne's mind. Mostly, they involved torture and death if Rebecca shed even a single tear because of this psycho.

"But you are if you would like your friend to remain unscathed. Meet me at Smitty Fitness Center in an hour. Leave your side piece at home. I know he's already standing there, ready to fight your battle for you, but that is not the game we are going to play." The health club formerly known as Smitty's was shut down earlier this week thanks to some repeated health code violations. That meant it was left to be a dark and deserted playground.

Without hesitation, she responded. "It's a deal."

The phone beeped as the call ended. Layne pocketed the phone and gathered the remainder of the arsenal she intended to bring.

"What did he say?" Joey finished stocking up the bag full of bloodthirsty goodies.

"Does it matter? He has Rebecca. He has the one person in my life who hasn't signed up for any of this." She walked up to Joey and looked up at him, her hand reached up and lightly rubbed the side of his face over the stubble on his cheek with an apology in her eyes.

"Layne." A subtle warning hung on the way he said her name, not even trying to sugarcoat it.

She pulled his face down to hers as her lips captured his. Her tongue soaked up the taste of his mouth. Layne wanted to be able to remember this moment with him in case she never got the chance to experience it again.

Joey grabbed her shoulders and pulled her back. "Whatever you're thinking, you're not. You know as well as I do that he's going to be playing by his own set of fucked up rules. He's just trying to lure you into a trap."

"I know." She gave a sad smile as her emerald pools memorized every feature of his face. A quiver tugged at her chin, and tears were pricking at her eyes. "I love you." Her voice cracked as her heart got caught in her throat. "So much. More than I thought I could ever love anybody. You have always had my heart, and there isn't anything in this world that can change that."

Hearing her say those three powerful words for the first time provided just enough of a split moment where he was caught off guard that Layne could make her move. The electric crackle was the only thing that gave it away when she pressed the taser into his ribs.

Immediately, he flinched before his body seized up as it

soaked the electrical shock and dropped to the ground harder than a bag of bricks. He yelled out, cursing as his muscles locked up during the time the metal probes were in contact with his body.

"I'm so sorry, Joey." Genuine remorse hung on her words, but she knew that this was the only way that she could buy herself enough time to go take care of business without him compromising her ability to focus on what needed to be done.

Layne dropped the taser into the bag of goodies Joey had assembled and stepped around him before he was able to recover. She left him lying there on the floor as she left to save the person who had always been there to support her in her life.

CHAPTER THIRTY

The fluorescent sign above the building was no longer lit up, but you could still make out the bubbly outline of a bodybuilder next to the dark blue words "Smitty Fitness Center." Layne stared up at the sign with her bag of fun slung across her body.

She had done a quick change of clothes in her car in the designated flat lot across the street into an all-black ensemble. If Eric wanted to play his games, she was going to play hers.

Her hand reached into her pocket and pulled out a small piece of black cloth. She slid it over her face, covering the lower half. A familiar emblem was stamped across the front of the fabric, one mimicking Joey's skull-faced mask. The only difference was that this one had orange and green ribbon criss-crossed across the teeth, imitating stitches keeping the mouth shut.

Layne walked around to the side of the building, finding the side entrance already propped open with a dumbbell for her. Undoubtedly, it was Eric's invitation. Well, here went nothing.

She pulled out her favorite baby Glock and stepped foot in the darkness of the abandoned building. The only thing lighting her way was the dim red glow of the EXIT signs.

Quietly, she stepped one foot in front of the other as she kept her hands on her gun in a two-handed grip. Her green orbs darted to the right, then to the left as she looked for anything or anyone that might jump out at her.

As she walked further into the establishment, she felt something underneath her boot. It didn't crunch. No, it was something much softer that gave away under her weight. If she hadn't been on high alert, she wasn't sure she would have noticed it otherwise.

Layne knelt and placed her fingers on the floor where she had just stepped. Locating the object, she picked up the bulb and realized it was the head of a now partially squished rose. The silky texture of the petals between her fingers gave it away as she examined the shape of it.

Eric was being a fuckin' dramatic bastard.

Dropping the floral prop back down to the floor, she stood back up and returned her hand to her weapon as she continued to advance through what appeared to be the cardio section with all of its machines lined up in neat rows.

Her ears perked up as she heard the sound of classical music playing lightly over the gym's speakers. He was definitely being a fuckin' dramatic bastard.

Layne wasn't sure what she should be prepared to see or hear, but she did know that she was mentally prepared to do what needed to be done if she was going to get Rebecca out of there alive. Whatever the cost was going to be, she was prepared to pay it in full with interest.

She had only been inside of Smitty's a few times before, and it was a couple of years ago. Her recollection wasn't particularly spectacular with remembering how this joint was laid out. However, she did remember that it housed many of the standard amenities. It had an indoor pool, an extensive weight room, group fitness studios, and a spin room, in addition to all the typical features of locker rooms, saunas, and tanning beds.

Bang!

A gunshot rang out and shattered the illusion that danger wasn't immediately present. Layne immediately dropped to the floor. The sound of the impact was on the other side of the room, indicating that she hadn't been close to being on the receiving end of it this time around. Deciding not to be a sitting duck, she pushed herself back up onto her feet and burst into a full run.

Bang! Bang!

She flinched, her arms automatically raised and shielded her head as her legs propelled her forth as fast as they could. Layne ran into the first room that she came across. Dashing inside, she immediately crouched behind a corner, trying to silently catch her breath. Tightly, she pressed herself up against the wall, her hands readjusting her grip on the pistol.

Eric's voice came over the speaker from the ceiling, interrupting the background music. "What a good little harpy, you did so well at following directions by coming by yourself. Let's play a little game. If one of my men finds you first, you come along quietly. If you find me first, then you and your friend will be allowed to go on your way."

Layne hated games. She hated them even more when it was clear the odds weren't in her favor.

He spoke up one final time. "Welcome to my playtime." The loudspeaker cut off.

She leaned her head back against the wall and steadied her breath. Quickly, she had to strategize on the fly. The darkness was both an asset and a hindrance, and she needed to take the path he didn't anticipate her to take.

In a barely there whisper, she cursed under her breath. "Fuck me." She needed to commit to a decision and do it quickly.

Finally, she made a move and got back up and moved away from the wall, waiting for a bogeyman to lurch out of the shadows at her. The second she stood up, though, the game's rules suddenly changed. Light after light began flickering on throughout the center. The weight room she was in was no exception.

Eric's voice rang throughout the place once more. "Oh, I did forget to mention that I don't like losing." Of course, he didn't. Lunatics rarely did.

Layne needed to move quickly now that it was likely eyes would quickly be on her. As quietly as she was able to manage, she scurried through the weight room to the door on the far side. With its blocky, rectangular symbol adhered to the front, she knew it had to be the men's locker room.

She pushed the door open silently to be greeted with yet another seemingly empty area. Making each turn carefully, she kept her eyes focused to avoid any surprises. When she made it to the back, past the showers, there was a second doorway with the strong scent of chlorine and other pool chemicals floating in the air surrounding it.

Using her body, she pushed open the door slowly to take a peek into the pool area. The coast was clear from the limited angle she had. Continuing to emerge from the locker room, she nudged the door open a little wider with her shoulder.

The pool itself had taken on a swamp-like green color, presumably from the lack of chemicals being used to maintain it after the center shut down. The surface of the water was eerily still and glasslike.

Suddenly, the door was pulled open on her by an unknown man. Instinctually, she straightened up and rammed the rest of herself into the door to give it enough momentum to smash into his face. He shouted out as he released the door and put both hands over where it connected with his face.

Layne aimed and fired off a shot into his stomach. The acoustics in the pool area seemed to amplify the sound of the shot enough that she may as well have used an air horn to announce her location.

The man who was struck in the stomach by her bullet dropped to the tiled floor, and before his cry of pain could continue, she re-aimed the lethal end of her gun at his forehead and silenced him.

With a heavier set of breaths coming from her, she had less than a few seconds before she heard a pounding echo through the pool area from up high. The muffled yells of her name were shouted. When Layne looked up, there was another floor up where offices overlooked the pool. Behind the large glass windows was Rebecca, with her hands bound together in small fists banging against the glass.

Her friend was suddenly pulled back away from the window, and Eric appeared there with a shit-eating grin etched across his face. In his hand was the receiver of a phone, and his voice came over the speakers once more.

"You're not very good at hiding, little harpy. I'm disappointed."

Layne flipped him off with her non-dominant hand, and her eyes set in a hard glare. Then, she saw three men emerging from various points around the pool.

"If I were you, I'd ditch your toys and let my boys bring you up here to have a chat about what to do with your friend. Alternatively, you can do things the hard way, and I will just have to pass the time up here with Rebecca. I've been telling her all about my favorite room in my house while I've been waiting for you." The way he spoke promised terrible things no matter which path she took.

Layne dropped her duffel to the floor with a light thud. She tossed her gun down on top of it carefully.

"Good girl." The words he spoke didn't have anywhere near the same impact on her as when Joey said them to her.

Though he couldn't see it underneath her mask, a small smirk twitched at the corner of her lips, and the glimmer of rebellion reached her eyes. She had him right where she wanted him: feeling confident.

Two of his crew members came up beside her, each grabbing an arm painfully hard. They led her away from the pool area and took her up a set of stairs right outside the humid room that led to the office one level up. The sole asshole that didn't have his hands on her separated from the group and took up the lead ahead of them. Eric must have been worried if he had four of his men ready to take her on, minus the one she left in a bloody puddle outside the locker room door.

When the office door opened, she immediately scanned the interior of the office. Her escorts filed into the room with her, and the door lightly clicked shut after the last of them. Inside, there were two desks, one wall of large floor-to-ceiling windows overlooking the indoor pool, a television mounted on the wall, some filing cabinets, and a sofa.

The sofa is where Rebecca was seated with Eric next to her, his arm draped across her shoulders like they were old buds. Her hands were in her lap, visibly trembling, while the wrists were secured tightly with duct tape. Her blue eyes were red from tears that had been shed.

Her voice shook as she looked over at Layne. "Layne, I'm sorry…"

Layne shook her head at Rebecca. "Don't worry, you're getting out of here." Her eyes darted to Eric, who had an arrogance wrapped around him.

He reached up to Rebecca's face and took a handful as he squeezed her cheeks in his hand. "She's just as cute as a button, isn't she?"

"Drop the theatrics, Eric. You got me here. Release Rebecca, and we can talk things over." Her voice was emotionless despite the rage running rampant inside of her that he dared to lay a finger on her friend.

He laughed outright and dropped his hold from Rebecca's face before standing up from his seat there on the sofa. Eric approached Layne, stopping directly in front of her, and waved off the two guys with their aggressive grasps on her.

"Theatrics, you say? Let's not throw stones here, Layne." His finger reached up to hook on the top of her mask and lightly began to tug it down. Before it got halfway out of position, she abruptly threw a fist at his smug face.

Her knuckles smashed into his cheek before his men were able to react quickly enough to snatch her back. Unfazed by her attack, Eric grinned as his fingers rubbed his face where she made the connection. "There's the little harpy I know and love. You've got so much fight in you."

He stepped up to her as she pulled against the grasp of the two brutes restraining her. The fires of violence lit up in her eyes. Eric's hand yanked the skull mask the remainder of the way down her face. "It will be so much fun breaking your spirit." Then, his fist thrust harshly into her stomach.

The blunt pain caused her to grunt out and double over. Immediately, a wave of nausea rolled through her, causing her to cough and gasp for air simultaneously.

Eric nodded to his two men as they released their hold and dropped her to the floor. Layne placed a hand on her stomach as she winced. Before she could fully recover, Eric's foot connected with her ribs in a kick that sparked another type of pain as Layne cried out and rolled in on herself. Immediately, she knew he had injured one of her ribs from the sharpness of the pain accompanying each breath.

With her hands hidden underneath her body, she covertly located the previously planted mini switchblade inside the waist of her pants. She encased it in her grasp while she was curled up in the fetal position.

Rebecca shot up from her seat. "Stop it, asshole! Leave her alone!"

One of the three hired hands inside the office shoved Rebecca back down onto the sofa to prevent her from interfering. His gruff voice barked instructions at her. "Shut your cockhole, blondie."

Eric knelt and grabbed a handful of Layne's hair to lift her head so he could look at her face. "Let that be a lesson of what happens when you step out of line. It seems that you didn't learn anything after being left to burn. At first, I was furious that you hadn't perished in the fire. I stood to inherit a pretty penny from the insurance policies you signed."

Through clenched teeth, she struggled to breathe through the pain, including the pain that came with every breath she took. Her eyes met his, reflecting the resilience and stubbornness she was born with. Hell, if he was going to be the one to snuff it out. Layne gritted her teeth and managed to push words out of her mouth. "What the fuck do you want, Eric?"

"Oh, you already know what I want." An amusement dangling on his words before he released his hold on her hair.

She swallowed down a little more pain and nausea

and nodded her head. "Okay, I'm all yours. Me and everything that I come with." She propped herself up on one arm while the other hand remained on her stomach. Her eyes met Rebecca's across the room, and then she looked up at Eric. "But she gets out of here unharmed first."

He gave a drawn-out sigh. "Promises, more promises, and all of them fucking lies. That's all I've been getting from you, so how am I supposed to take you at your word now, hm?"

Layne groaned through the pain as she chuckled. Slowly, she pushed herself up onto her feet, wincing but fighting through the pain.

Eric didn't share the same amusement in whatever was going on in Layne's head. "What's so funny?"

"You. You were so desperate to get me here. So desperate that you kidnapped my best friend and went through all of this trouble. I'm the one thing you can't buy, and it pisses you off. You make business deals all the time, yet you can't even close a deal on a real woman." The pain still lingered on her face despite her amusement at the situation.

The flicker of rage on his face as she bruised his ego was paired with an angry snarl, predictably so. She braced herself as he grabbed her by the back of her neck with a painfully tight grip and dragged her over toward the large windows overlooking the pool.

Eric pressed the side of her face up against the glass, her cheek flattening against the smooth surface. The warmth of her breath left a small circle of fog on the glass.

Layne braced herself with one of her hands against the window.

Her eyes caught a small detail down below. The bag of goodies she had left at the poolside when Eric's men grabbed her was nowhere to be seen. She suppressed the smile that wanted to pull at her lips.

"Do you remember when we first met? I made it clear that one day, you'd beg for my soft touch." Eric's mouth roughly sucked on her ear and gave it a hard nip before he hissed into it. "I'm going to be cashing in that bet."

His mouth and the words that came out of it made her stomach twist into more knots. "One request?"

Intrigued, Eric tilted his head some. "Hm?"

"At least look me in the eyes like a damn man. I don't beg for cowards."

He spun her around to face him, slamming her back up against the window. His cold eyes looked to penetrate deep into her soul. "That is one request I will grant because I want to see your face as I take you past your thresholds and into a whole new world of pain. The very same world that I thrive in."

Her eyes met his, and she smiled sweetly at him. "I want to see your face, too." *Click.* The switch of the blade in her hand flicked open and then sank into his upper stomach, getting lodged just underneath his ribs.

The look on his face was everything she had hoped it would be as she kept the knife held deeply embedded into his gut. Her green gemstone eyes didn't look away from him, even when the door was nearly knocked from its hinges as it got kicked in.

CHAPTER THIRTY-ONE

With his skull mask drawn over his face, Joey unleashed a flurry of chaos the second he kicked in the door. Layne shoved Eric to collide with one of the men coming to his aide. The two men fell to the floor together.

With two guns drawn, Joey easily dropped one of the other two with a single shot. However, the smarter one of the bunch was already using Rebecca as a shield. He shuffled, keeping his hold steadfast on Rebecca as his insurance that he wouldn't meet death today.

"Rebecca!" Layne stepped forward but stopped when she noticed the man had a shaky grip on a gun against her friend's side. Joey's eyes never left the most critical target, which was the man threatening the innocent young woman.

Eric remained on the ground groaning as the knife remained stuck in his midsection. However, Layne sensed the movement of the one jackass she had knocked Eric into. He made the unfortunate decision to take a run at Layne.

She hunched down, lowering her center of gravity using the man's height against him as he attempted to tackle her. Using his momentum, she deflected his attack, sending him careening into the cheap metal filing cabinet, where his head collided with the sharp corner before dropping motionlessly to the floor.

The maneuver caused her to wince and curse at the harsh reminder of her injured rib that continued to be a bitch and protest rather loudly inside her body.

When she looked back at the situation with Rebecca, Joey was slowly stepping to the side to make sure he maintained enough space to not spook the man into doing something stupid. As the man edged towards the door, seemingly with his ticket out of there, he smiled, feeling more confident.

The man yelled at Joey and her. "I will shoot the bitch if you follow me! Stay back!" Layne didn't doubt that this man was going to make good on his word. He was so on edge; they were lucky he hadn't already pulled the trigger by accident.

"Just be calm." Layne's words were meant for both Rebecca and the man threatening her wellbeing. She came up next to Joey, her hand sliding to the back of his pants, finding an extra firearm there that she helped herself to.

The man backed out of the open door, roughly jerking Rebecca with him out the door. Layne glanced over at Eric lying on the floor, suffering, and then at Joey. He already read the conflict in her eyes between dealing with Eric and saving her friend.

Joey softly spoke to her. "Go get her. I will take care of things here."

Trusting him to do as he said, Layne bolted for the door leading out of the office. Her feet ran down the steps as fast as they could before she lept over the bottom two. The painful thought of losing someone who was closer than a sister outweighed the physical pain of Layne's injuries getting aggravated by her movements.

She set eyes on the man dragging Rebecca away. Layne raised her gun but then realized she didn't have a clean shot. "Damnit!"

Layne ran after them as they quickly moved alongside the pool. She shouted at them to get the guy's attention. "Hey, asshole!"

He turned, and the tiny window of opportunity opened up as he exposed himself and gave Layne just enough of a space to comfortably fire off a round into his head. The impact caused him to fall back into the pool with a ceremonious splash. Simultaneously, the man's falling body pulled Rebecca off balance, and she also fell into the slimy water.

Knowing damn well that Rebecca didn't have use of her hands and had never learned to swim, Layne dropped the gun and dove in after.

Meanwhile, upstairs in the office, it was just Joey and Eric. Joey had Eric up on his feet in front of him with his bicep wrapped around Eric's throat in a tight hold. Joey's hand twisted Layne's knife deeper into the wound she had made.

Roughly, Joey spoke into his ear. "I have been waiting a very long time to snap your fuckin' neck. There is nothing more that I would like to do right now than feel the breakage of your C2." So many violent thoughts of Eric's demise were filling Joey's head. The way this man had thought he had a claim on Joey's woman had him seeing red.

Eric gasped for air as the hold around his throat made receiving oxygen a struggle.

"What was that? I couldn't hear you." Joey gave the knife another push in a new direction. Joey's arm eased up just enough to hear the yell of pain that pulled a pleased smile across his face. He wished he could spend all day up in that office, finding new ways to spread the pain across Eric's body. Despite his wishes, he wasn't going to risk leaving Layne to fend for herself very long.

Panting from the onslaught of pain wracking his body, Eric's strained words were barely audible. "You're no… better than me."

Joey ripped the knife out of Eric's body. "Maybe not, but Layne is. And, I plan to be the man who sees to it that it stays that way." He heard the gunshot from downstairs, and it served as a reminder that he had better places to be than letting Eric take another breath.

Eric coughed, the blood leaking from the corner of his mouth. "She'll never—"

One bloody hand grabbed the back of Eric's skull while his other grabbed his jaw and cut off Eric's words with one sharp force, fracturing a cervical vertebra. He released Eric's body, letting it fall to the floor lifelessly.

"Fucker."

Joey's client be damned, Eric was never going to leave

here alive if he had anything to do with it. He stepped over the shitbag's corpse. Quickly, he ran downstairs to track down Layne and, hopefully, an unharmed Rebecca.

The previously still water was now showing signs of being recently disturbed, indicated by the ripples on the surface. A tint of red from the blood seeping from the last of Eric's men swirled unnaturally in the already swampy-looking water.

Layne shoved Rebecca up to the surface as her legs burned under the weight of her kicks to get them both back up for air. Her hand reached up and grasped onto the pool ledge to pull herself up with her other arm around Rebecca's waist to get her above water as well. Rebecca gasped as the air finally greeted her lungs.

Joey ran over and immediately hoisted Rebecca up out of the water to sit her on the floor next to him. She coughed and took several deep breaths for air. After seeing she was okay, he turned his attention to Layne.

With a pained sigh of relief, Layne hooked both her arms on the wall and rested her forehead against them while trying to catch her breath from rescuing her bestie from a watery grave. Layne was the only one here who ever needed to have experienced that.

Each gasp for oxygen prompted a sharp jab from her very pissed off rib.

"Come on, you too." He grabbed Layne, lifted her from the water, and set her on her feet. His hands held onto her face as he stared at her with a light smirk. "What is it with you and water?"

With the water dripping down along her face in tiny

rivers, she gave a small laugh followed by a groan as she placed a hand onto her rib. Before Joey could get himself all fussed over it, she shook her head to head him off. "I will be fine."

He pulled his mask down so he could capture her lips with his to help ease some of her pain. It was a small gesture but one he could offer at the moment. When he pulled back, he leaned in and whispered into her ear. "You're going to have a lot of making up to do after that stunt you pulled tasing me earlier." He kissed her temple with a grin.

Rebecca sat up, having recovered enough oxygen to get back to her sassy self. "I hate to break you two up, but I could use a little help here." She raised her bound wrists.

Layne's attention was finally drawn back to Rebecca, helping her onto her feet. "Sorry." A sheepish smile appeared on Layne's face, having nearly gotten lost in Joey's words.

Joey pulled a knife from his pant leg. Taking Rebecca's hands, the tape was quickly severed.

Immediately, Layne tugged Rebecca into a big hug. "I'm so sorry you got pulled into this. It should have never happened."

Rebecca pulled back and looked at Layne with her stern mama bear face. "Stop that. Don't you dare apologize for something a mentally unstable creep did."

Layne's mouth pulled down into a frown, still letting her guilt weigh on her.

"You know what you can apologize for?" Rebecca eyed up her best friend.

Layne raised both of her brows, wondering what else she was going to bring up in the moment.

Rebecca motioned over at Joey. "Not introducing tall, dark, and handsome over here. How the hell can I do my obligatory best friend due diligence if you keep these things to yourself?" She gave a little wink to Layne.

The light tease chased away some of the guilt as she glanced over at Joey. "Rebecca, this is Joey—*the guy*. Joey, Rebecca." Her hand motioned at each of them.

Rebecca scanned Joey with a suspicious eye. "Oh, so you're the one? Hm. Well, just know that the jury is still out on you."

Joey grinned at how much spunk Rebecca had. He shouldn't have been surprised, given anyone lucky enough to have Layne in their life needed to have a bit of a spark.

Before Rebecca could give Joey the third degree, Layne looked at them both. "We should get the hell out of here."

Nobody argued with that plan of action. While they were walking out, Layne looked over at Joey as a question nagged at her. "How did you know where I was?"

He smirked. "I can't give away all my secrets. Although," he reached over to take a look at the soaked mask down around her neck, "it looks like I'm not the only one keeping secrets."

After getting Rebecca back home safely, Layne met Joey back at O'Reilly Manor. She parked her car out front. The Beamer had been the one thing that had been spared from the fire, all thanks to the inability of people to read a damn sign that said not to block the driveway.

Layne turned off the engine and sighed as she leaned back in her seat. It had been a hell of a night. She tried to summon what little energy she had left to get out of the car.

One final sigh, and she opened the car door. That's when she remembered that Rebecca had written down the name of a doctor who could squeeze her in for a quick look at her rib. Layne had insisted that a doctor wasn't necessary, but Rebecca threatened to never make her famous berry oatmeal bake for her again if she didn't agree.

She opened up her console and saw the note sitting right on top. However, something else caught her eye. Layne had completely forgotten that she had left the blue envelope she had found in her dad's paperwork in her car. She reached in and pulled it out to take inside with her.

Joey was already waiting for her when she walked in the door, though she still had her eyes focused on the envelope in her hands with her name written across it. She opened it up and unfolded the papers inside. Her eyes looked over the contents with the expectation that it would be nothing important.

When Joey saw her jaw drop and her expression go wide-eyed, he walked over to her side to see what she was looking at. "What is it?" His eyes scanned over what she was staring at on the first page before he muttered. "Holy shit."

CHAPTER THIRTY-TWO

To Layne's surprise, it had taken much longer for the NYPD to be alerted that there were decomposing bodies inside Smitty's Fitness Center. Apparently, no one had been checking on the abandoned property on any sort of regular interval.

There was a pitiful investigation done by the police. After the realization that Eric Ellis had been a major player in the underground sex trafficking world thanks to an anonymous tip from someone by the name of Cowboy, there was little public outrage to look into what transpired inside the gym that night. It was assumed that the dangerous criminals of the world took out the trash living in their own backyard. They weren't entirely wrong.

Layne had been more than happy to celebrate her status as Eric's not-so-grieving widow. Particularly since it turned out that the insurance policies and his assets went to her by default. She bet he had never expected that one. Needless to say, finances were looking up for the O'Reilly organization.

As for the documents left for Layne by her father? Layne and Joey decided to keep that to themselves for now. There was no sense in rocking the boat…yet.

Several months had passed, and on this particular night, Joey stepped inside O'Reilly Manor at nearly three in the morning. He shrugged his jacket off and hung it up in the coat closet right near the front entrance.

In what should have been a minor job that night, it had taken longer than expected. The house was expectedly cast into pitch darkness, indicating that Layne was already in bed fast asleep.

Quietly, he made his way upstairs and to the master bedroom. Pushing the door open, it only gave the slightest of creaks while swinging on its hinges. He walked over to the bed they had been sharing nearly every night for the past couple of months.

His hands reached behind him, grabbed the back of his shirt, and pulled it up over his head, exposing the muscled physique underneath that was home to all the tattoos he had. Joey walked over to her side of the king-sized bed to check on her before he planned to hop in the shower to get cleaned up.

As he reached out to feel for Layne, his hand felt nothing but the cold sheets. His hand patted the mattress, finding no one was there in the bed. Sighing, he hoped she hadn't fallen asleep in the office again. He had carried her upstairs to bed on several occasions as a result of her spending hours diving into figuring out damage control of the failing criminal empire bearing the O'Reilly name.

Joey headed back downstairs to check the office. A

glimmer of light was shining from underneath the door. When he walked inside, he was surprised not to find her asleep on the desk with her head on top of the keyboard.

As he approached the desk, a small but powerful body rammed into his back, knocking him forward unexpectedly. Slender arms wrapped around his throat, and bare legs around his waist. Fortunately, he was easily able to upright himself. The arms around his neck squeezed threateningly, and a sultry and demanding voice whispered into his ear.

"It's just you and me now, handsome. I'm only going to ask my questions once, and you're going to be a good boy and answer them."

He inhaled the familiar scent of daisies after a rainstorm. His hands grasped onto Layne's legs, wrapped around him as he smirked. "Is that right?"

"Mmhmm." She responded as her hand spread out and ran over several of the tattoos covering the front of his chest. "Where were you tonight?"

He tensed at the question before he walked over to the desk with her still clinging to his back like a little monkey. "I told you I had a job to wrap up."

She slid down off of him, placing her feet firmly on the floor. Layne's hands spun him around to face her. "That's not what I heard."

Joey looked down at the sight before him, his eyes lighting up in excitement at what he saw. Layne stood there wearing a pair of black panties with a matching bralette. Her long locks of chestnut hair hung down freely in loose waves around her shoulders. However, it was the dark and twisted mask stretched across her face with the green and orange threads crisscrossed over the skull teeth that sealed the deal on his cock quickly jumping to full attention in his pants.

"Doing a little stalking of your own?" He lifted a brow at her curiously.

Layne nudged him back until he voluntarily sat on the edge of the desk. Her hands grabbed his knees and pushed his legs apart so she could stand between them. "I believe I asked you a question. Are you making me ask twice?"

A grin stretched across his face in amusement at being on the receiving end of inquiries that were typically his. "No, I wouldn't want to do that." His hand reached out and tugged that black mask down over her face to expose her full and currently pouty lips. "You want to know where I was?" His thumb traced over her bottom lip slowly.

She gave a small nod in response.

He moved his hand up to slide over the side of her face until his fingers wrapped around the back of her neck while his thumb stroked over her cheek softly. "Seeing someone about a deal I made."

That answer didn't quite satisfy her if the look in her eyes was any indication.

He pulled her head in closer as his lips met with hers. Joey's mouth lovingly claimed her mouth slowly and sensually to ease whatever unfounded concerns she had. When he relinquished his sweet hold on her and drew back, he presented her with what was in his other hand. In the center of his palm was a small black box made of satin.

Layne went still as she saw what was in his hand. Her eyes stared at the closed box for a few seconds and then darted back up to look at his face, seeing his eyes set on her.

"I have never wanted anyone the way that I want you. Since the night I first saw you sitting inside McGregor's, I was immediately hooked. There are days you drive me fuckin' insane, but those are the days where I want to be your everything the most. I don't care what battles we have to face, but we will be the storm that everyone should prepare for. I love you, and I would die a thousand painful deaths for you."

He pulled open the box, revealing an eye-catching, thin platinum band with a sparkling oval diamond at the center, surrounded by a black rhodium-plated collar with black diamonds. A small emerald to match her eyes was set at both the top and the bottom of the diamond in the middle. "Will you marry me?"

Layne stood there, not even looking at the uniquely gorgeous ring but looking at his face in shock.

"Don't make me ask twice, Layney." He did his best to mask the slight uptick of anxiousness in his voice.

Her bottom lip trembled slightly, followed by a large smile as she threw herself up against him. Layne's lips crashed onto his as she devoured the taste of his mouth. Her response came out between several kisses. "Yes!" *Kiss*. "I love you." *Kiss*. "Yes."

A wave of relief washed over him as he welcomed her onslaught of affection and returned it with his own. His tongue slid its way into her mouth as he savored all of her taste. After several moments of their lips wrangling together, Joey pulled back with a smile. "Let's get this ring on you before another guy thinks he can take a shot at what's mine."

After removing the ring from the box, he lifted her hand to slide the small piece of metal onto her finger. "There, a perfect fit."

Layne smirked playfully at him. "Much like something else." Her hands dropped to the belt on his pants. Her fingers unlatched his belt and yanked. It slid from the belt loops with the tail whipping around until it was freed. She dropped it down to the floor.

That's when Joey possessively wrapped an arm around her waist as he got up off the desk. With a single arm around her, he lifted her and turned to have her take his place on top of the desk where he had just been seated. His hand took hold of her chin while grazing her lips with his mouth as he spoke in the low and husky tone that always set her insides on fire. "Be a good girl and spread those legs for me."

Her breath caught in her throat as he gave that demand. Layne's lips parted slightly as she did as she was told. "I need you." The words barely came out above a whisper.

Joey shoved his dark cargo pants down, taking his boxer briefs with them. Unleashed was his large, hard cock, ready to go. His smirk was full of dark desires and promises. "You're going to get me." He stepped up to her while his hand gripped and twisted the bralette in his fist. "Every damn day."

Before her gasp could fully be released from her mouth, he pulled her forward by the flimsy lace containing her breasts. A searing kiss locked onto her, and his hands pawed at her chest, sliding the straps of the bralette over her shoulders and the remainder of it to her waist.

Layne feverishly returned his kisses, imagining their life together. In a rush of anticipation and excitement, she shoved the lace undergarments off her body. Her mask was pulled off from around her neck and tossed to the ground.

He lowered himself to capture one of her feet in his hands and began sowing a garden of kisses leading up the length of her leg. Layne leaned back on her hands while sitting there on the desk as his mouth worked its way closer to her core.

When his mouth finally made it to the top of her leg, he licked a long line along her inner thigh. She whimpered as he edged closer to where she needed him. Layne needed to feel his mouth consuming her arousal like it was the damn fountain of life.

The strength of Joey's hands pushed her thighs even wider as he licked his lips. "You better hold on tight, Layney. I'm going to fill myself up on the taste of you."

That was all the warning she got before he was burying his face against her pussy. Layne immediately surrendered to the pleasure he brought her. Her hands knocked several items off the desk as her body reacted to his mouth.

His mouth brought her over the edge into sexual bliss several times before he pulled her off the desk. Layne's head was delightfully clouded with pleasure as she smiled at him. "Somebody has an appetite tonight."

Joey gave her a smirk. "Only for you." He carried her over to a chair, where he took a seat with her in his lap.

With his cock teasing at the opening of her sex, Layne

leaned in and kissed her way over the shadow of facial hair along his jaw until she reached his ear. "You should hold on; you're not the only one who is going to get their fill tonight." She lowered her body down onto him. Her hands held onto the sides of his body, one of her hands covering up the 'Chaos Addict' script tattooed along his ribs.

His hands landed on her waist as he groaned in approval of the way her pussy took him in. He looked into her eyes, getting lost in them as she began to move her hips to ride his cock.

The two of them tangled themselves up in carnal pursuits there in the office until the sun began to filter in through the windows, and they ended up together on the floor. Both of their bodies were covered with a mix of sweat and arousal.

Joey lay there with his arms wrapped around her, staring up at her face as she lay on top of his chest. "You'll always be mine, forever."

Layne stared down into the face of the one man who had gotten past the walls surrounding her heart; she smiled happily. "You'll always have me, forever."

W hen Layne walked into Cassidy's Cave, the upbeat music was pulsing throughout the entire strip club. The place was packed with primarily male patrons looking to get their dicks hard by watching a bunch of girls remove one article of clothing at a time while flashing smiles of fake interest.

In the dimly lit space, several small stages cluttered the floor; the main stage was at the back, and two birdcage-style platforms hung from the ceiling. Glitter was every-where. It looked like there had been a reverse harem of unicorns that had all jacked off all over the joint.

Joey was at her back, scanning the room for any sign of Liam. His hand rested on the small of her back to confirm his presence there with her after not getting past the doorman nearly as easily as Layne had with a flash of her pretty smile.

It didn't take long to pinpoint Liam's location. He was making a spectacle of himself over at a VIP table surrounded by no less than four women who were employees of this establishment, evidenced by their lack of clothing. Easily, Liam had probably dropped a head-spinning amount of money on this night out.

Liam stood up with his shot glass in the air and yelled. "Shots on me!"

Layne groaned. "For fucks sake." She didn't want to deal with this, but she was going to have to. If not her, who else?

Joey leaned down and spoke into her ear. "Can I just take him out back and give him a dose of reality?"

She tried not to let the smile fully tug at the corners of her mouth at the thought. As tempting as the offer was, she knew that this was going to require more finesse and less brute force. After shaking her head to decline Joey's request, she walked through the crowd, avoiding men tripping over themselves to get a better view of their visual entertainment.

Her brother leaned over and wrapped an arm around one of the girls, planting an aggressive kiss on the side of her face before whispering something into her ear.

Layne had been told by one of her associates that he had been here since they opened up six hours ago. Based on his noticeable level of intoxication and disheveled appearance, she fully believed it. His shirt was half untucked from the waist of his pants, and the top few buttons were left undone enough to bare his pale chest in front of all his monetarily compensated admirers.

When Layne got to the table, she began picking off one girl at a time while Joey stood back and didn't get in her way like the smart man he was. He leaned against the wall with his arms crossed in front of his chest while he casually observed. Joey still wished Layne had let him knock some sense into her brother. The night was still young, though, so perhaps there was still a chance.

Liam was too busy guiding one of the dancer's hands onto the crotch of his pants when he finally noticed Layne physically moving one of his admirers from the table to make a path closer to him.

"Well, look who it is! Come to join me in the celebration?" He lifted a half-empty bottle of vodka that was easily worth a grand.

"Li, you've done enough celebrating for the entire club. Let's go." She motioned with her hand for him to stand up.

"Don't be such a stuck-up bitch. Our business is on the way to being back on fuckin' top!" He tugged the girl to his right, closer to his side. "Right, baby?" His drunken stupor caused him to forget that Layne was standing right there trying to have a conversation with him as he began to make out with the girl hanging onto his arm.

The only thing that would make this situation worse is if Kristill were here to curse him out and cause an even bigger scene. Thank God for small favors from the universe that she wasn't here.

Layne's hand grabbed the girl's arm and pulled her up to her feet. "Here, take this." She shoved a hundred-dollar bill into her hand and shooed her away.

Predictably, Liam had an angry outburst like the manchild he was. "What is your goddamn problem, Layne?!"

Tiredly, she sighed. "I'm not doing this here with you, Liam. Let's go outside and deal with this."

"You're not the damn boss of this family." Liam snorted at the ridiculous thought of it.

It was clear this was going to be a battle. Layne attempted to soften her tone. "That's what we need to talk about."

He shook his head, not seeing that there was anything to discuss.

She was losing the little patience she had for his bull-shit. "Liam, get the fuck up. *Now*."

"What the fuck ever." He pulled his wallet out and dumped a wad of cash on the table amongst the various shot glasses and empty bottles.

Layne looked over at Joey. "Watch him while I close things out here and make sure he doesn't do anything stupid." The last thing she needed was ill will towards the O'Reilly name now that a new era was on the horizon.

She looked at Liam and gave him a stern look. "Stay here, keep your mouth shut, and your hands to yourself, or so help me, Li, I will call every club in the five boroughs and have them blacklist you for life."

She turned and walked away to go to the bar to speak with the owner to make sure she smoothed things over for any troubles Liam may have gotten himself into. Layne pulled out a credit card to cover any of the miscellaneous charges and idly tapped it against the bar top while she waited.

"You were looking for the owner?" The steamy and smooth voice came from behind her. When she turned, she was met with a man who looked to be in his early thirties, far younger than she would have expected for a strip club owner. Not to mention, he had these light brown eyes that were like freshly melted milk chocolate that could lure you in with as much of a wink.

Layne lifted an eyebrow, not hiding her surprise that this guy wasn't who she was expecting. Most strip club owners she had met were sleazy and creepy old men. No, not this one. He was dressed semi-casually, with a white dress shirt with the sleeves rolled up to his elbows, exposing the cords of his muscular forearms, and a pair of lightly distressed jeans. It was hard to tell with the lighting and the gel in his hair, but he looked to be an ashy shade of blond.

He extended a hand out to her, the top of his hand was inked up with tattooed letters that spelled out 'WRATH' across the tops of his knuckles. "Name's Gage."

She gave a light smile as she took his hand and gave it a quick shake. "Layne. Look, my jackass brother had a table over there," she motioned in the direction of the table that his back was to, "and I don't know what type of trouble he's caused tonight, so I just wanted to make sure I clear everything out."

Without even turning to look at the table she refer-enced, he responded quickly. "It's taken care of." He grinned at her.

Tilting her head in confusion at him, he continued. "He's lucky to have a sister that cares enough to help him out. Loyal siblings are a rarity. Besides, it means I got the pleasure of meeting you." A charming smile spread across his face.

She grinned and shook her head at how thick he was laying it on her. "Thanks, but I don't like owing favors." Favors were very dangerous things.

Gage leaned over and whispered to her. "I won't tell if you won't."

That's when Joey came up to Layne's side. "Liam is in the parking lot puking his brains out. So help me, if he pukes in my car, I'm going to make him lick it all up." The irritation was weighing in hard on his voice.

Joey glanced over at the man Layne had been speaking with and went as still as the dead. Tension locking in across his body. His cocoa-brown eyes swiftly shifted as he hardened his gaze.

A large smile came over Gage's face, accompanied by a chuckle of amusement. "Look who it is. After all these years and all the places, I didn't expect to run into my big brother tonight."

Stay Tuned for *Incoming Layne Shift*

ABOUT THE AUTHOR

Sadie Winchester is a romance author residing in the Pine Barrens of New Jersey with her husband, her son, and their two cats (Thor & Loki). She began her love for writing in high school, drafting stories on a popular internet platform.

The dream of writing and publishing a full-length novel first manifested a couple of years after she married the love of her life. However, it took a back burner as she focused on other adventures and goals. Finally, after becoming a mother and finding a way to rediscover herself, she was inspired by another new author to commit to this long-term dream.

When Sadie is not writing up her stories or getting lost in books, she is spending time with her family. She enjoys working out, cooking, visiting microbreweries, and binge-watching *Supernatural*.

You can connect with Sadie in the following ways:
SadieWinchester.com or Linktr.ee/SadieWinchester

Photography Credit: Pryceless Moments Photography

amazon.com/author/sadiewinchester
facebook.com/sadiewinchesterauthor
goodreads.com/sadiewinchester
instagram.com/sadiewinchesterauthor
tiktok.com/@sadiewinchesterofficial
bookbub.com/profile/sadie-winchester

ACKNOWLEDGMENTS

To My Alpha Readers, Amanda and Nicole: Thank you for dealing with my crazy! I'm sorry for all the mini-cliffs I pitch you off of (not really though). Without both of you cheering me on, I'm not sure where I would be in this crazy journey. All your support, encouragement, and feedback is invaluable. I love you both!

To All My Readers: Wow, your ability to accept my stories with open arms has been absolutely incredible. You all continue to inspire me to keep writing all the words. Without you, Layne & Joey's story would continue to be locked up inside my head for no one else to enjoy. Thank you all so very much!